Penguin Books
The Mordida Man

Ross Thomas was born in Oklahoma City in 1926.
He graduated from the University of Oklahoma and
served with the American Division in the Philippines.
He has been a reporter, an editor and public relations
director for numerous organizations. He lives in
California.

An outstanding suspense novelist, Ross Thomas is
widely accepted as one of the best living writers of
thrillers. He also writes under the pseudonym of Oliver
Bleeck. He has written twelve books under his own
name, including *The Cold War Swap* (1966), which won
the Edgar Award from the Mystery Writers of
America, *The Seersucker Whipsaw* (1967), *The Singapore
Wink* (1968), *The Fools in Town Are on Our Side* (1970),
If You Can't Be Good (1973), *Chinaman's Chance* (1978)
and *The Eighth Dwarf* (1979).

Ross Thomas

The Mordida Man

Penguin Books

Penguin Books Ltd, Harmondsworth, Middlesex, England
Penguin Books, 625 Madison Avenue, New York, New York 10022, U.S.A.
Penguin Books Australia Ltd, Ringwood, Victoria, Australia
Penguin Books Canada Ltd, 2801 John Street, Markham, Ontario, Canada L3R 1B4
Penguin Books (N.Z.) Ltd, 182-190 Wairau Road, Auckland 10, New Zealand

First published in the U.S.A. by Simon & Schuster 1981
Published in Penguin Books 1983

Made and printed in Great Britain by
Cox & Wyman Ltd, Reading
Set in Baskerville

1

It was an almost perfect disguise. To begin with, he had lost all that weight, at least twenty-five pounds, and the cleverly concealed lifts in the heels of his stodgy plain-toed black shoes had raised his height by nearly two inches and subtly altered his walk. The beard helped, too, of course; probably because it was so neatly trimmed.

Not long before, no more than three months back, he had been more or less clean-shaven and of medium height and rather dumpy, if not quite fat. Now he was a bit under six feet and trim, indeed almost slender. His clothes were different, too. Gone were the jeans and the Army surplus field jacket and the black turtleneck—an outfit that once had been virtually his trademark. Now he wore a blue pinstripe—not too old, but not too new either—and a crisp white shirt and even a neat bow tie that he had learned to knot himself. In his left hand he carried a worn leather briefcase that seemed to be an old and shabby friend— another nicely calculated touch of respectability that also helped.

The only thing that even hinted at concealment were the glasses. Their lenses—plain, but tinted a deep amber—made it difficult to see his eyes with their strange rain-gray giveaway color. But the glasses' carefully selected frames were of a clear unadorned plastic that suggested practicability and necessity rather than concealment.

Much thought had also gone into his dark hair, which once had been a long, oily mess. Now it was short and neatly trimmed, both back and sides. Like his beard, it was sprinkled with gray. The gray was natural. It was also new and had crept into both his hair and beard during the past three months.

When he came out of the Maida Vale tube station and turned right up Elgin Avenue, the woman in the taxi across the street clutched the large purse tightly to her chest, sucked in some air, coughed once, and said, "That's he. That's Felix."

The man sitting next to her said, "You're sure?"

"That is he," the woman insisted and wrapped her thin arms even more tightly around the purse, which was made of black leather with a silver clasp.

"It sure as hell doesn't look like him," the man said. He had an American accent of some kind.

"It is he, you fool."

The American nodded dubiously, lowered the taxi window, and tossed a crumpled red pack of Pall Mall cigarettes onto the pavement. Across the street, a smallish middle-aged man who wore a brown three-piece suit and an old child's mischievous face noted the pack's fall, turned quickly away from the newsstand, and fell in behind the man identified as Felix. The smallish man walked with short mincing steps and carried a tightly furled black umbrella that he swung up and rested lightly on his right shoulder.

In the taxi, the American leaned over, opened the door nearest the curb, and said, "Out."

The woman had to cough first. They were deep, hacking explosions, four or five of them, which racked her body and pinkened her face. The American ignored them, just as he ignored her when she stumbled across his long legs as she dragged herself out of the taxi, still coughing. Once outside, she squeezed the

6

purse even more tightly to her chest. It seemed to ease the coughing—possibly because it contained a comforting balm in the form of twenty thousand dollars in twenty- and fifty-dollar bills, which is what the American had paid her to lead him to Felix. The woman, her lips now tightly compressed, as if determined to cough no more ever, hurried away from the taxi without looking back.

The smallish man with the umbrella was now only five or six steps behind Felix. He picked up the pace with a neat little skip and closed the distance between them to no more than three feet. He swung the umbrella down in an arc that ended when its tip was less than an inch from Felix's back—high up and dead centered between the shoulder blades.

The smallish man pressed the button in the umbrella's handle. The button released the steel spring that shot the chromium-tipped plastic dart containing a hundred milligrams of a stepped-up fast-acting tranquilizer called Doxxeram through Felix's coat and shirt and deep into his back. Doxxeram had been used only once on humans during a controlled experiment in a hospital for the criminally insane in upper Michigan. Although remarkably fast-acting when injected intramuscularly, its side effects had been labeled "unwarranted," the experiment had been stamped "inconclusive," and the drug had been withdrawn.

When the Doxxeram went into Felix, he stopped abruptly. His left hand went behind him and up, clawing for the dart. His hand found part of it, the plastic part—empty now—that had contained the drug. He wrenched it loose, stared at it briefly, dropped it, and smashed it with the heel of his shoe. The chromium tip, slightly barbed, remained in place. Felix quickly shifted the old briefcase to his left hand, clapped his right hand up and around his neck, and tried to reach the chromium tip over his left shoulder. But his arm wasn't long enough for that. Almost no one's is.

Felix turned then, spinning really, and fumbled at the clasp of his old briefcase. By now the smallish man, his umbrella back on his shoulder, was already well past him and heading for the corner with his quick-step sissy's walk. A middle-aged woman stared at Felix curiously for a brief moment, but then looked away and hurried on.

Felix groped around inside the briefcase until his hand closed over the butt of the short-barreled .38 Smith & Wesson revolver. While groping for the pistol, he tried to identify his assailant—the one he would have to shoot. He decided that there were four possible candidates, all of them extremely improbable.

Two of them were a couple of fortyish women shoppers with string bags—possibly sisters. The third was the jockey-sized news vendor who was now engrossed in counting his change. The fourth was an elderly man of more than seventy who stood leaning on his cane as he stared thoughtfully into the butcher's window at a row of fat capons. The old man seemed to be debating whether he could really afford one.

Felix felt the first slight effect of the drug just after the small-ish man with the umbrella turned the corner and disappeared. Felix's shoulders sagged involuntarily, and his knees began to tremble—although both may have been caused by the relief that flooded through him when he realized that the drug wasn't a poison.

Tranquilizer, he thought. Somebody's shot you full of tran-quilizer. Yet the drug didn't seem very strong, and he wondered if they had used enough. Perhaps they had made a mistake and he wouldn't need the pistol after all. He removed his hand from inside the briefcase and crossed, not quite dreamily, over to the door of the greengrocer, where he turned, yawned, and started rubbing the spot between his shoulder blades against the door-jamb. He only succeeded in driving the barbed chromium tip in even more deeply as he rubbed away unhurriedly, almost lan-guorously, as though trying to rid himself of some old familiar itch.

It would still take minutes for the drug to work, and across the street the American waited patiently in the taxi, his eyes flicking from his watch to Felix and back again. In the greengrocer's doorway, Felix kept rubbing away and trying to decide whether to head for the underground entrance. But perhaps that's where they wanted him to go. A fast train. A quick shove. Felix decided to think about it some more.

At last, the American looked up from his watch, leaned forward, and said to the driver, "Let's do it."

The taxi made a U-turn and pulled up at the curb less than three yards from where Felix stood yawning and rubbing the dart into his back. When Felix saw the taxi pull up, he knew why it was there and that he should do something about it—providing it didn't require too much effort. He thought almost idly of the pistol again, but then he noticed that his vision was beginning to blur. Reality seemed to be edging away. He decided it would probably be better if he simply started walking. Not too fast, of course. No need to attract attention. Just up to the corner, slowly, very slowly, because he was tired, and then right.

He took a step away from the greengrocer's doorway and then another. But he could no longer control his legs. They began to wobble and his feet were beginning to refuse all commands. Still he managed another step, then yet another, but after that he sank slowly to his knees.

The American got out of the taxi and approached him cautiously. A few people turned to stare. With his eyes fixed on the American, Felix again started groping around inside his briefcase. The American reached down and took it away from him. Felix watched indifferently as the American tucked the briefcase away under an arm.

They stared at each other for several moments, and Felix found himself wondering about the American's increasingly wavery outline. Perhaps it was the light—the dusk. But there could be no dusk at noon. Reality took another few quick steps away from Felix. Then, from what seemed to be a long way off, he heard the American say in awful border Spanish, "Vamos, amigo."

Felix closed his eyes, licked his lips, and thought about asking where; but it was simply too much effort. At least it wouldn't be Israel. At least it wouldn't be the Jews. He wondered vaguely how the Americans had got onto the informer—and how much she had been paid. But all that could be sorted out later after he had rested. Perhaps even a nap. It would be so pleasant to curl up right there on the walk. He had almost decided to do exactly that when the smallish man in the three-piece brown suit reappeared. The smallish man no longer carried his umbrella.

"May I give you a hand with your friend?" the smallish man said in a sweet British voice that matched his mincing walk.

The American nodded. "I'd be much obliged."

Together they each got an arm around Felix and lifted him to his feet.

"Likes his nip now and then, does he, poor dear?" the smallish man said.

"Now and then."

The smallish man opened the taxi's rear door and they tumbled Felix into the back seat.

"Thanks a million," the American said as he climbed into the taxi.

"Don't mention it," the smallish man said. He watched the taxi pull away, and when it was gone he turned toward the butcher shop. He had almost decided on a plump capon for his supper; but if the lamb chops looked particularly good, he might even treat himself to a pair of those.

2

There were four of them in the dank cellar of the old boarded-up house in the short street in Hammersmith. Two men and two women. The houses on either side were also boarded up and vacant, waiting for the wrecker who was now three weeks past due. The cellar smelled of dead cat.

One of the women had been stripped almost naked and bound with yellow insulation wire to a heavy dining-room chair. Her name was Maria Luisa de la Cova, and she was a thirty-four-year-old Venezuelan. She was also the coughing woman who had sold the man called Felix to the American for twenty thousand dollars in twenty- and fifty-dollar bills.

The money was now stacked neatly on a water-ringed oak dining-room table that matched the chair. The table had only three legs. A substitute fourth leg had been fashioned out of two Cutty Sark whisky crates. Next to the stacked money was the large black leather purse with the silver clasp. The purse had been turned inside out and its lining ripped away. There was no electricity. Light came from six pink candles stuck into beer bottles.

One of the men, a pallid, almost lashless blond with a slab body and a flat solemn face, lit a cigarette with a disposable lighter. He was called Frank by the others, although his real name was Bernt Diringshoffen and he had been born thirty-two years ago in Hamburg. After lighting the cigarette, he puffed on it inexpertly, not inhaling, obviously a non-smoker.

The de la Cova woman watched him. Her eyes were pink and her face was tear-streaked, but she was no longer crying. There were angry red burns on the left side of her neck and on her small breasts. Four burns in all.

"Tell us," Diringshoffen said and blew on the coal of the cigarette.

"I've already told you," the de la Cova woman said and began to cough harshly. Diringshoffen waited patiently until the coughing at last had ended. "Tell us again," he said pleasantly.

She began speaking in a rapid monotone so low and indistinct that the others had to bend forward to hear.

"He said his name was Arnold. I don't know if that was his real name or not. I don't even know if it was his surname or his given name. I don't care. I just called him Arnold, if I ever called him anything. We met several times, maybe four, maybe five. Twice in Soho, at least twice there, and again in Islington in a cafe he knew. Maybe three times there. In Islington. Maybe just two. I can't remember."

"Did he say he was CIA?" the other woman asked. The other woman also spoke English, but with an almost crippling French accent. Her name was Françoise Leget, and she had been born twenty-nine years ago in Algiers. She had large black eyes that she blinked rapidly and a thin stylish body, and many thought her to be quite pretty.

The de la Cova woman seemed to find Françoise Leget's question stupid. She sighed wearily and said, "I've already explained that."

The second of the two men was older than the rest, nearly thirty-eight. He was also Japanese. The others called him Nelson, although his real name was Ko Yoshikawa. His English had a hard American edge to it.

"Please explain it again," he said. "We would appreciate it very much."

The de la Cova woman sighed. "He didn't say anything like that—that he was CIA. He didn't have to. He just sat down at my table that day in Soho and said he knew all about me—that I was thirty-two and sick and needed money for the baby and that Felix was going to dump me anyhow." She looked at the Japanese. "That part was true, wasn't it—about Felix?"

Ko frowned and said, "What did you tell him about us?"

"Nothing. He wasn't interested in any of you. He seemed to know all about you—about all of us. But the only one he wanted was Felix."

"And you gave him Felix," Françoise Leget said.

"I gave him Felix. The baby was sick. I was sick. I'm still sick." As if to prove it, she started coughing again.

After the coughing finally stopped, Diringshoffen said, "When did it happen—exactly?"

"At noon," she said. "At exactly noon today. I called Felix this morning and told him I'd heard something bad—you know, something I couldn't say over the phone. We arranged to meet at the Lord Elgin pub in Maida Vale at noon. I was in a taxi with the American—with Arnold. I don't think it was a real taxi. When Felix came out of the tube station, I pointed him out. The American wanted to know if I was sure. I said yes, I was sure. He had already given me the money. He made me get out of the taxi. I don't know what happened to Felix."

She looked up at the Japanese and in a soft plaintive voice said, "Won't you please kill me now?"

At first, Ko didn't reply. It was almost as if he hadn't heard her request because his thoughts were in some distant, more interesting place. But after a moment he nodded in an abstracted way at the German, who dropped the cigarette, ground it out, picked up a length of yellow insulation wire, and stepped behind the bound woman.

The Japanese looked at Maria Luisa de la Cova then. "Well,

13

yes, of course," he said almost apologetically. "We'll attend to that right away."

It was Ko himself who made the call to the Embassy of the Libyan Arab Republic. He made it from a pay phone in the lobby of the Cunard Hotel. The call was taken by Faraj Abedsaid, who was listed on the Embassy roster as Attaché (Cultural Section), a position that left him with considerable free time.

After identifying himself as Mr. Leafgreen, Ko said, "Call me at this number," and read off the number of the pay phone, carefully transposing its last two digits as a routine precautionary measure.

Twelve minutes later the phone in the Cunard lobby rang. After Ko answered with a toneless "Yes," Abedsaid said, "Well?" and Ko said, "The Americans have Felix."

There was a brief silence until Abedsaid whispered, "Well, shit." Abedsaid was thirty-eight and one of the first Libyans to earn a degree in petroleum engineering from the University of Oklahoma. Or for that matter, from any university.

Ko spoke quickly, outlining what he felt were the facts. When he was done, there was another silence until Abedsaid sighed and said, "The Colonel's gonna be madder'n a shot bobcat with a toothache." During his four-year stay in Oklahoma, Abedsaid had carefully acquired a large collection of aphorisms, metaphors, and similes peculiarly indigenous to the American southwest. He delighted in peppering his conversation with them, especially in London, where it seemed to offend almost everyone.

"How soon can you get word to him?" Ko asked.

"Within the hour."

"We've decided it would be best if we went back to Rome."

"All of you?"

"Yes, all three of us."

"Do you need anything—money?"

"No, there's sufficient money," Ko said, thinking of the twenty thousand dollars in twenty- and fifty-dollar bills.

14

"I can let them know in Rome that you're coming."

"Yes, that would help."

"The Colonel is . . . well, he's not going to like this at all."

"No," Ko said. "I don't suppose he will."

"He and Felix were close. Extremely close."

"I know. Have you any idea of what he might do?"

"The Colonel?" Abedsaid paused as though to consider the question. "Something weird, probably," he said and hung up.

The Boeing 727 was painted a light cream color and bore no markings other than the minimum required by international air regulations. It was five miles high and 213 miles west of Ireland when the fifty-nine-year-old doctor shuffled into the customized lounge section and slumped down into an armchair across from the man who sometimes called himself Arnold.

"Well, sir, he's gone," the doctor said with a heavy sigh that wafted whisky fumes into the other man's face.

"What do you mean, gone?"

"Like I said, gone. Dead. He died. You want the technical explanation or you want it in laymanese?"

Arnold sprang up out of his chair and bent down low over the doctor, who shrank back from the large hands that fluttered around erratically as though in search of something to grab—or choke. Arnold's eyes bulged and his curiously rubbery face flushed a dark, dangerous red as his mouth began to stretch itself into odd shapes. The nut's going to scream, the doctor thought.

"He's not dead," Arnold said after his mouth finally had twisted itself into a set smile, which the doctor regarded as more than a trifle mad.

The doctor shook his head wisely. "How much of that junk did you guys pump into him?"

Arnold wiped hard at the bottom half of his face, as though to erase all evidence of shock and surprise. "How much? Just what you told us, Dr. Lush. That's how much. One hundred milli-grams."

15

The doctor frowned, struggling to appear thoughtful, even judicious. "Well, he should've been able to handle that much—providing you guys didn't make some damn fool mistake—or he had some kind of respiratory problem. Or heart condition. Or something." He brightened. "Anyway, the autopsy will tell."

"No," Arnold said, smiling again, although not quite so madly.

"No what?"

"He's not dead."

"Oh, yeah, he's dead all right," the doctor said comfortably, confident of his diagnosis. "He's dead because of all that dope you pumped into him. It probably made him so nice and relaxed he just forgot to breathe. But like I said, the autopsy will tell."

"No," Arnold said.

"No what this time?"

"No autopsy."

The doctor frowned, as if trying to remember some half-forgotten instructions. At last he seemed to recall them. "Well, if there's not gonna be any autopsy, then I gotta do the other thing."

"How long will that take?"

The doctor frowned again. "A couple of minutes. Maybe three."

"Do it then," Arnold said.

When the doctor was finished, it took only four minutes for the 727 to drop to six thousand feet. Its rear door, a device at one time much favored by parachuting skyjackers, was lowered. A moment later the body of the man called Felix fell a little more than a mile into the sea.

3

The real estate agent in Lisbon hadn't told Chubb Dunjee, the ex-Congressman, about the steps. But even if she had, he probably would have rented the house in Sintra anyway, since it was relatively cheap, and the sixty-eight steps that led down to the road provided a bit of exercise and didn't at all bother his visitors, because there weren't any. Or hardly any.

The agent rather grandly had described the house as a villa, but Dunjee always thought of it as a five-room bungalow with an uncanny, somehow depressing resemblance to the red-tile-roof kind found all over his native Southern California. The house was owned by an elderly English widow who suddenly, at seventy-two, had decided to visit her late husband's native Brazil. The widow was said to be particularly curious about what really lay up the Orinoco.

The house with the sixty-eight steps had been rented cheaply to Dunjee on the condition that he keep on its housekeeper-cook, plus the gardener who took exquisite care of the widow's nearly one acre of periwinkles, roses, geraniums, camellias, wild lavender, and a couple of other varieties, one pink, the other yellow, that Dunjee (no flower fancier) couldn't identify but always referred to as the pansies.

During his seventeen-month stay in Sintra, which eventually he came to regard as a kind of exile, or perhaps even banishment, Dunjee had taught himself some four hundred words of Portuguese. This was enough to praise the cook's plain fare, chat with the gardener about the weather, and thank the mailman for climbing the sixty-eight steps to deliver the two-to-three-day-old copy of the *International Herald Tribune*—virtually the only mail Dunjee ever received.

Occasionally, when the weather was fine, he and the mailman would sit outside under the lemon trees near the steps' iron gate and drink a glass or two of wine in comfortable silence. On each of the two Christmases he spent in Sintra, Dunjee had given the mailman a fine Chaves ham from Tràs-os-Montes.

It was four days after the man called Felix fell a mile into the sea that Dunjee had his first real visitor in almost eleven months. He came unannounced at noon by taxi. Noon was a time when Dunjee liked to sit outside under the lemon trees and work the crossword puzzle in the *Herald Tribune*. Before Portugal, Dunjee had never worked crossword puzzles. He now regarded them as a faintly ridiculous vice which held for him some slight danger of addiction.

The visitor down in the road was Paul Grimes. He got out of the taxi, paid off the driver, and turned to give the sixty-eight steps a bleak assessment. When he started up the steps, Dunjee rose, tried to think of the Portuguese word for guest, and headed for the kitchen to tell the cook he was having one.

By the time Grimes reached the top of the steps he was breathing heavily, almost panting. He paused to lean against the brick retaining wall that was covered with morning glory vines. The housekeeper-cook, plump, curious, and a trifle flustered, stood near the wooden garden chairs with a tray that held glasses and two cold bottles of beer.

Grimes, sweating now, but not panting nearly so much, stared at Dunjee for several moments, then smiled and said, "Why Portugal?"

"The label on a sardine can," Dunjee said. "I used to study it sometimes when I was poor. You remember when I was poor."

Grimes nodded thoughtfully, still smiling.

"You want a beer?" Dunjee said.

"God, yes."

They managed to avoid shaking hands—Dunjee by gesturing toward the garden chairs; Grimes by mopping his brow with a handkerchief as he moved over and lowered himself down with a sigh. When the housekeeper-cook served him his beer, he thanked her formally, even graciously, in Spanish, because he knew no Portuguese, but seemed to feel that Spanish would at least be closer than English. The housekeeper-cook smiled gravely and left to find the gardener so she could gossip with him about the visitor.

After producing a cigarette, Grimes lit it, drank half of the beer in his glass, filled it up again, looked around carefully as if really interested in what he saw, and said, "Nice place."

"Quiet."

"What do you do all day?"

Dunjee thought about it first. "I read a lot, run a few miles, do the shopping, hit a few bars, brood a little."

Again Grimes nodded. This time it was an appreciative nod that seemed to compliment Dunjee on some rigorous but productive schedule. After another swallow of beer he got to the point. "How's the money holding out?"

"There's enough."

"Well."

"Well, what?"

Grimes moved his heavy shoulders in a slight, almost indifferent shrug. "Well, I just thought you might like to make some."

Dunjee smiled. He had a curiously lazy, curiously warm smile, very white, that usually managed to charm most people. He had always found it a convenient, almost painless way to say no. Much of the smile was still in place when he said, "I don't do that any more."

"What?"

"Whatever it is you want me to do."

Dunjee discovered it was a pleasure to watch Grimes shift topics. He did it smoothly, effortlessly—in a manner that made old brand names pop into Dunjee's head: Fluid Drive, Hydramatic, Powerglide.

"You know what I've been trying to remember?" Grimes said. "I've been trying to remember how long it's been since we've seen each other. Twelve years?"

"Thirteen," Dunjee said. "Almost fourteen. Chicago, 'sixty-eight."

Grimes nodded, as if suddenly remembering. "That mess. You ever hear from her?"

"Nan?"

"Our Nan." Grimes said the name almost reverently. Nan was Dunjee's ex-wife.

"They say she married a grain broker and lives in St. Paul," Dunjee said. "She's also supposed to be very active in Little League baseball. Coaching. They say."

"Jesus. Our Nan."

The housekeeper-cook reappeared with two more bottles of beer and again Grimes thanked her in Spanish. When she had gone he smiled wryly. "I was just trying to think—of what she kept calling you up there in the Hilton right after you told her there was no way you were going out in the streets and get your head bashed in for the movement. Sort of a pet name."

"Crypto-fascist," Dunjee said.

"Our Nan," said Grimes, nodding and smiling now, as if at some fond memory. "Right after that was when she took off with the Weathermen, wasn't it?"

Dunjee shook his head. "That was the next year—'sixty-nine."

"How long did that last?"

"Six months. Until she turned thirty—and ran out of money."

"And that wrecked it for you, didn't it? Even in your district. Hell, you must've had more dopers and crazies and old retired

Jewish socialists and ex-Trotskyites than any place in the state, except maybe Berkeley."

Dunjee shrugged. "Even they couldn't swallow the Weathermen thing. I got beat over the head with it."

"But you had the one term."

"That's right. I had the one term."

Grimes shook his head sadly. "Our Nan," he said, reproach in his voice this time. "If it hadn't been for her, you'd probably still be there. You had it all going for you then—ex-Special Forces captain, medals down to here, good anti-war plank, and almost the youngest member of Congress with a real fine pinko district. Shoot, Chubb, you'd still've been *planted* there if it hadn't been for her. Our Nan."

"I *was* the youngest member of Congress," Dunjee said, disliking himself for making the point. "At least when I was elected I was."

"Yeah, I guess so." There was a silence until Grimes said, "You know what I'm doing now?"

Dunjee examined him carefully for several moments. "Probably what you've always done—cleaning up after other people's messes."

Grimes chuckled. It was a fat man's low, bubbling chuckle with a trace of wheeze in it. When Dunjee had first known him in school, more than twenty years before at UCLA, Grimes had borne an almost ominous resemblance to Victor Mature, a noted actor. Grimes had always blamed the resemblance for keeping him out of elective politics, since he was totally convinced that nobody would ever dream of voting for Victor Mature for anything.

Now forty-three, possibly forty-four, Grimes no longer bore any resemblance to Victor Mature—except perhaps for that hawklike nose. Over the years, Grimes's face had grown round and plump and pink and smooth, his jaw wreathed by two thick soft rolls of fat. What was left of his hair was parted very low down on the left side, almost to the ear, and combed up and over. But it didn't really help much. He still looked bald. About all that saved Grimes from looking like a jolly fat man were that beak of a nose and those cold, wet, silvery eyes. The eyes gleamed with something, Dunjee decided, possibly amusement, but certainly not jollity.

Grimes was still chuckling his practiced fat man's chuckle when he said, "How'd you like to make a bunch of money?"

"I don't need any money."

Again, there was reproach in Grimes's smile and tone; gentle reproach. "You've got 4,136 dollars and change in that Lisbon bank. It'll last another two months—three if you scrimp."

It was at least thirty seconds before Dunjee replied. "How much is a bunch of money nowadays?"

"Say one hundred thousand—plus expenses."

Dunjee nodded. It was a nod indicating mild interest, but nothing else. It was all Grimes needed.

"We sort of lost touch after the election. The 1970 election. But I—"

Dunjee interrupted. "I lost touch with a lot of people. Ex-freshman Congressmen carry a certain pariahlike atmosphere around with them. Or maybe it's a smell. The smell of defeat and shock. Somebody should come up with a soap."

"As I was saying, we lost touch, but I kept track. You bounced back. You went into oil."

"A cream puff," Dunjee said. "All you had to do was stick a straw down and out it would gush. Well, I raised the money, all tax-shelter stuff. Five thousand here, ten there. And we stuck the straw down and out it gushed. Salt water. A million barrels a day—or something like that. Hell, I don't remember."

Grimes made a sympathetic clucking noise and started lighting another cigarette. Staring at the match flame before moving it to the end of his cigarette, he said, "Then there was that stint with the UN."

"Stint," Dunjee said in a faintly mocking tone. "Yes, my stint with the UN. Forty-two thousand a year tax free, a lot of travel,

22

and useful and productive dialogue with the leaders of the world's lesser-developed countries. It was just like talking to Nan."

"Our Nan. Well, when you left the UN I lost track for a couple of years."

Dunjee stared at Grimes again, then smiled and said, "You didn't lose track. For two years I drove a cab. I drove a cab in Miami and Houston and Denver and Seattle and San Francisco and Great Falls and New Orleans. A good week, I'd make a hundred and fifty bucks. Then one day I decided I didn't want to become a human interest story. You see them all the time. I think there was one in the *Herald Trib* the other day. Something like 'Ex-Boy Governor Now Chicago Hackie,' or some such crap. And it's all about how this guy who was governor of Michigan or West Virginia at twenty-seven or so, until he found out about booze and broads, is fifty now and driving a cab and he's never been happier because of this deep insight he's gained not only into himself but into humanity in general."

Grimes nodded several times as if he too had read the same stories. "So you went to Mexico."

"I went to Mexico."

"The Mordida Man. You got your name in the papers after all."

Dunjee shrugged. "And they got out of jail."

"How many did you"—Grimes paused to select his word—"negotiate out?"

"Sixty-two."

"Bribes and blackmail."

"They got out of jail. I was good at it. My background helped —Congress, the UN. And being a cab driver. You gain a lot of wonderful insight into human nature by being a cab driver."

"They say you made a lot of money in Mexico."

"Who's they?"

"The IRS."

Dunjee smiled. "I'm having a slight problem with them."

"Not so slight. They're talking about extradition."

"I've got a lawyer on it."

"I talked to him. He's worried. The deductions you put down: 251,817 bucks for business expenses. The IRS has decided those were bribes. Bribes aren't legitimate business expenses." Grimes yawned. "Of course, I could fix all that."

There was another long silence until Dunjee said, "You'll stay for lunch?"

"What're you having?"

"I don't know what we're having. I'll go see." He rose and headed for the house, a tall man, two inches or so over six feet, perhaps more. Grimes noticed that there was still that quick, springy lift to Dunjee's heels as they came up off the grass. He thought that at forty-one (or was it forty-two?) Dunjee still looked fit enough to pass for a professional athlete with at least a season of play left in him. Or perhaps only part of a season.

The revised estimate made Grimes feel somewhat better. So did the gray in Dunjee's medium long dark-brown hair. That was new. But the gray and those fresh deep lines were about the only physical changes that Grimes could detect. Dunjee's hazel-green eyes were still more clever than wise, and his features were still rescued from being too regular, almost handsome, by that cheekbone, the left one, that poked up almost three-quarters of an inch higher than the right. From a certain angle the skewed cheekbone made Dunjee look just a bit cockeyed.

Grimes was finishing the last of his beer when Dunjee returned. "Fish," he said. "We're having fish."

"Good," Grimes said. "I can eat fish."

Dunjee sank back down into the low garden chair. "You say you can fix the IRS people."

"I can fix them."

"Who's your client?"

Grimes shook his head.

Dunjee stared at him for a moment and then nodded impatiently. "All right. If you tell me, I'm in. Committed. Who's your client?"

"The White House," Grimes said, savoring the name in spite of himself.

Dunjee scratched the back of his left hand, noticed a hangnail, and decided to bite it. "The White House, huh?" he said between bites. "That could mean the head gardener or the pool man or some twenty-eight-year-old Yalie savant over there in the West Wing basement or—"

Grimes interrupted. "The President."

Dunjee sighed. "Well, hell, Paul. I guess you'd better tell me about it."

4

According to Paul Grimes, there were several reasons why Bristol "Bingo" McKay had not gone to Disneyland with the others, the foremost being that he had always considered the place to be just a trifle dumb. Besides, he had already visited it once before, under protest, nearly fifteen years before. But the real reason he had not gone this time was simply because once you passed through its gates there was no liquor to be had, and the terrible prospect of again encountering Mickey Mouse cold sober was something that Bingo McKay would gladly perjure himself to avoid.

So he had lied his way out of it and filled the early afternoon with twenty-six long-distance telephone calls, three drinks, a light lunch, and five laps around the Marriott Hotel pool. At 4 P.M., which was 7 P.M. on the east coast, he had made his regular five-minute call to his kid brother in Washington. Bingo McKay's kid brother was President of the United States.

As always, they talked politics, domestic politics primarily, which was Bingo McKay's special preserve; and, as always, the President listened carefully to his brother's trenchant, totally unvarnished report, whose more troublesome blips would be reflected in the national polls ten days later.

But by then the President, with his brother's canny guidance, would have worked the legerdemain necessary to correct whatever political imbalances might exist. It was one of the reasons why Jerome McKay, at thirty-nine was often called the most totally political animal to occupy the White House since Franklin Delano Roosevelt, whom the President, try as he might, couldn't quite remember.

Now barely nine months in office, the new McKay administration had failed utterly to work any of the economic miracles it more or less had promised. Inflation was nudging an estimated 19 percent; the monthly balance of payments deficit was steady at around $2.6 billion; unemployment had shot up to almost 10 percent; the Gross National Product growth rate had somehow got stuck at just about zero, and gasoline, although rationed, cost $2.26 per gallon on the east coast and $2.31 in the west. The average wait at a filling station had been timed by NBC News at twenty-seven minutes and twenty-eight seconds, although an hour was not in the least uncommon.

All this was particularly embarrassing for the McKay administration, because it had run on oil—or rather against it. The McKay brothers' strategy had been really quite simple—criminally so, many said later. Jerome McKay had ignored his political opponents and had run instead against OPEC and the giant oil companies—and the Russians.

The future President had an uncommon grasp of the oil and natural gas industry because Bingo McKay had steered him into the business at twenty-two, turning him into a multimillionaire by the time he was twenty-eight. At thirty, Jerome McKay had been elected to the U.S. House of Representatives from Oklahoma's Fifth Congressional District, serving with some distinction, or at least with considerable national attention, for two terms until he relinquished his seat to run successfully for Governor of his native state.

Bingo McKay was fifty-one when he had lugged the huge map of the United States into his kid brother's office in the Governor's mansion on Northeast 23rd Street in Oklahoma City and propped it up on an easel. "What the hell's that for?" the Governor, then only thirty-seven, had asked.

"Basic political geography, lesson number one. How'd you like to be elected President?"

"Very much."

"Lemme tell you how we're gonna do it."

They did it by paying extremely close attention to elementary politics and by running single-mindedly against OPEC and what Jerome McKay branded the oilogopoly—and the Russians. McKay vigorously damned the oil companies' greed and avarice with unassailable facts and figures, thus confirming the darkest suspicions of 69.2 percent of the American voting public, who had long been hankering for just such a readily identifiable scapegoat.

McKay offered apparently practical, eminently sensible solutions and presented himself as an expert on the oil business, which he certainly was, and also as a repentant sinner who had made his fortune by following the same villainous practices he now condemned. His campaign autobiography, which he wrote himself in three weeks, was called *Plunder!* and it stayed on the New York *Times* best-seller list for thirty-seven weeks and then did even better in paperback.

The McKay brothers' strategy was both excellent theater and sound politics. Jerome McKay whipped his rivals in nearly a third of the primaries, secured his party's nomination on the fourteenth ballot at three o'clock in the morning, and went on to win the national election with 48.3 percent of the popular vote and an electoral vote margin of two. A little less than a year later he found himself caught up in a delicate, even desperate, gamble for oil.

It had started with a whisper in the delegates' lounge at the United Nations. Then a hint was dropped into the ear of the American Ambassador in Rome. There was nothing firm, of course, said the hinter, but it was just possible that the Libyan

Arab Republic, a country rich in both oil and truculence, just might (*might* now, you must remember) be willing to increase its production of oil and earmark it for the United States—a firm guarantee, of course—in exchange for the right to purchase some of the latest in American technological gadgetry, including just a few items that might be described as extremely sophisticated weaponry.

Jerome McKay decided to nibble at the tempting bait and sent some murmurings and whisperings of his own to Tripoli by way of Lagos, Nigeria. The American signal in due course reached the ears of the leader of the new military regime in Libya, Colonel Youssef Mourabet, a jumped-up Army major who had come to power after the unexpected death six months before from a heart attack of the still young, often choleric Colonel Muammar Qaddafi. The heart attack, it was rumored widely, had been brought on by a fit of apoplectic rage.

So an unofficial twelve-man delegation headed by Libya's new Minister of Defense, Major Ali Arifi, had been dispatched to the United States on an informal exploratory window-shopping expedition. And since it was all totally and determinedly unofficial, the President had slipped his brother in as tour guide, thus separating the administration nicely from any official recognition of the junket, but pleasing the Libyans enormously because Bingo McKay, although burdened with no government post, was usually regarded to be either the third or fourth most powerful man in Washington. Many even said second.

The junket had gone nowhere near Washington, of course. Instead, it had started in Houston, where the much maligned oil companies, anxious now to scramble back into the administration's grace and favor, had laid on a lavish reception. After Texas, it was straight out to Southern California for a demonstration of the new F-18a fighter, which the Libyans were known to covet, even lust after, feeling that the new plane would give far more pause to their increasingly jingoistic Egyptian neighbor than did their current fleet of aging Soviet MiG 25s.

The fighter demonstrations were scheduled for the next day at Vandenberg Air Force Base, and after that there was to be a quick side trip up to Northern California, to San Jose—or Silicon Gulch—where the latest in electronic wizardry would be wheeled out for inspection—and possible barter.

But first there had to be the de rigueur visit to Disneyland, which Bingo McKay had lied his way out of and turned over to his twenty-eight-year-old assistant, Dr. Eleanor Rhodes, whom he had hired fresh out of Johns Hopkins with the promise that "I can't guarantee you anything except money and the fact that you're gonna be close to the nut-cuttin', if that's the kinda stuff you're interested in."

Since her doctoral dissertation had been entitled "Parameters of Deception in the Second Nixon Administration," it was, indeed, the kind of stuff Eleanor Rhodes was interested in; and her quick mind and remarkable memory had for five years now helped Bingo nearly double his own political acumen, which was immense.

Then, too, he was probably half in love with her, but he had never done anything about it because (1) she was too young and (2) she couldn't remember World War II and (3) he suspected that she was one of the President's occasional bed partners, which was something Bingo had decided to keep his mouth shut about unless the Guteater brought it up. The Guteater was Dominique McKay, the President's one-quarter Choctaw wife.

It was shortly after 5 P.M. (on the day that the man called Felix fell almost a mile into the sea) when the ten-car Libyan caravan, sprinkled with eighteen Wackenhut security men, returned to the Marriott from Disneyland. Members of the delegation immediately retired to their rooms to rest until dinner at eight, when their hosts would be executives of the McDonnell Douglas and Northrop corporations, joint developers of the new F-18a.

At 6 P.M. the call came from Tripoli. The call was from Libya's new ruler, Colonel Youssef Mourabet. It was taken by his Minis-

30

ter of Defense, Major Ali Arifi. They spoke for nineteen minutes in Maghribi, a Bedouin dialect.

At 6:24 P.M., Ali Arifi summoned Eleanor Rhodes to his suite. He spoke for five minutes without stopping or allowing questions. At 6:33 P.M. Eleanor Rhodes was knocking on Bingo McKay's door.

After Bingo opened the door, he started to say something sardonic about Disneyland, but changed his mind when he saw the grim expression on her face.

"There's a problem," she said once the door was closed.

"How bad?"

"Bad enough. They're going to Vegas tonight—for gambling. You'll notice I didn't say they'd *like* to go. They're going."

"Well, maybe I'd better go try and persuade 'em to change their minds."

She shook her head. "I don't think I'd try, if I were you."

"Like that, huh?"

"Like that. They're leaving at eight." She headed for the telephone. "We're invited, but they're going whether we do or not." She picked up the phone.

"You calling the Wackenhut folks?"

She shook her head again. "They don't want them along. I'm calling Milroy in Vegas." Frank Milroy was the Las Vegas Chief of Police.

"Tell him to make it tight," McKay said. "Tell him I want three on one at least."

Eleanor Rhodes nodded and started dialing. By 6:50 P.M., security arrangements had been completed in Las Vegas, the Northrop–McDonnell Douglas dinner had been canceled, and the nineteen Wackenhut security men had been recalled to form an escort for the Libyans from the Marriott Hotel in Anaheim to Los Angeles International Airport, where the delegation would board its especially equipped Boeing 727 for the short flight to Las Vegas. The 727 had been the personal plane of the late

31

Colonel Qaddafi and was manned by a Libyan crew that had been trained by Pan American.

The Libyans were already in their cars when Bingo McKay and Eleanor Rhodes came out of the hotel and climbed into the last limousine in the procession. Five miles from the airport the caravan picked up a four-man motorcycle escort provided by the Los Angeles Police Department, which led it onto the field. The Libyans got out of their cars and hurried up the ramp into the plane. Last to start up the ramp were Bingo McKay and Eleanor Rhodes.

As they entered the plane, they were greeted by a smiling Ali Arifi. "I'm delighted that you both decided to join us."

"Kind of sudden, wasn't it, Minister?" McKay said.

Arifi shrugged. "Who can tell when luck will beckon?"

Bingo McKay began to suspect that something was wrong, extremely wrong, twenty minutes after the 727 took off from the Los Angeles airport. But it wasn't until ten minutes later that he knew positively that their destination that night would not be Las Vegas. For by then the plane was headed due east, and the lights of Las Vegas could be seen glittering five miles below and two miles back.

The Libyans had all gathered in the forward compartment; leaving McKay and Eleanor Rhodes alone in the lounge. McKay nudged Rhodes and made a sharp pointing movement down. She looked through the window and turned to stare at him. There was no need for questions.

"Reckon I better go see what those suckers have got in mind for us," McKay said as he rose.

She nodded warily. "Yes, maybe you'd better."

McKay made his way to the forward compartment and tried the door. It was locked. He knocked and it was quickly unlocked and opened by Ali Arifi, still wearing a broad smile.

"Come in, Mr. McKay," Arifi said. "We were just talking about you."

McKay went in and heard the door being closed and locked behind him. He didn't turn around to look because a gun was being poked into his back, just above his belt. But it wasn't just the gun that kept Bingo McKay from turning. Of equal interest was the tray that had been pulled down from the back of one of the seats.

It was an ordinary tray, the kind on which meals are served during commercial flights. This one was covered with a clean white cloth. On the cloth was an arrangement of surgical instruments. Standing next to the instruments was the delegation's physician, Dr. Abdulhamid Souri, who held a syringe in one hand. Dr. Souri raised his eyes from the syringe to look at Bingo McKay.

"Well, hell, fellas," McKay said.

Dr. Souri smiled. "It's not going to hurt, Mr. McKay," he said softly. "I promise you that it won't hurt one bit."

5

It had been a curious, roundabout message, perhaps garbled in its transmission, but still urgent enough, even desperate enough, to cause the Nigerian Ambassador, His Excellency Olufemi Dokubo, to rouse himself from a sound sleep in his Washington residence on Woodley Road, summon his principal aide and a driver, and arrive at Dulles International Airport at 4 A.M., shortly before the Libyan 727 touched down for refueling.

The message had been radioed to the control tower at Dulles, where it had been passed on by phone to the night duty man at the Nigerian Embassy on 16th Street Northwest. The night duty man was a twenty-three-year-old Ibo from Enugu and a student of economics at Georgetown University.

The student had been reluctant to call the Ambassador, so he had roused the Ambassador's principal aide instead and read him the message.

"It says, and I wrote it down exactly, 'Imperative you be at Dulles to meet our plane. Estimated time of arrival 0400. Fate of civilization may hang in balance.' It's signed Ali Arifi."

There was a long pause and then the aide said, "Are you positive about that last part—that fate of civilization thing?"

The student giggled, but quickly recovered himself and said gravely, "Yes, sir. I made them repeat it three times."

The aide grumpily thanked the student, hung up, and then sat on the edge of his bed staring at the message he had copied down. All Libyans are mad, he told himself. It was a conclusion he had come to after being heavily involved during the past several months in the conduct of their affairs in the United States, a chore the Nigerian Embassy reluctantly had taken on after the rupture in diplomatic relations between the U.S. and Libya.

Still, the message had been signed by Ali Arifi, and garbled or not, it was apparent that something had gone seriously wrong with the Libyans' junket, which the aide also had had a major hand in arranging. He sighed and picked up the phone again, first glancing at his watch. Two-thirty. The old man is going to be absolutely livid. Reluctantly, the aide began dialing.

With the light, almost non-existent traffic, it had taken them only thirty-three minutes to reach the airport. By the time they arrived, there was another urgent message from the Libyan 727. It was a request for the Ambassador to arrange for refueling and customs and immigration clearance. Ambassador Dokubo had gone about this in his usual skilled, even suave manner, exuding his famous charm, which in the more than twenty-one years since independence, had carried him to near the very top in his country's diplomatic service.

After the refueling was almost completed, and the suspicious customs and immigration people mollified, Ambassador Dokubo was driven out to the 727 by an airport official who continued to complain about the irregularity of the Libyans' proposed departure. Ambassador Dokubo smiled and nodded sympathetically, finally observing that, "Well, one must remember, Mr. Druxhall, that most Libyans are just a bit odd. All that desert, probably." The airport official had nodded his gloomy approval of the Ambassador's assessment.

The ramp was already in place by the time they arrived at the

35

plane. The airport official waited in the car while the Ambassador went up the ramp and into the 727. The lounge section was empty save for the Minister of Defense, Ali Arifi, who rose and nodded slightly, not quite bowing.

"So, Minister," Ambassador Dokubo said, glancing around the empty compartment, "I hope you can enlighten me about what I should do to help save civilization at four o'clock in the morning."

"You found my message melodramatic?"

"A bit."

Arifi waved the Ambassador to one of the lounge chairs. The Ambassador was a large, heavy man of fifty, quite tall, with a globe of a head whose chocolate cheeks were serrated with Yoruba tribal scars. He had a famous white smile, which he now turned on as he sank down into the chair, not taking his eyes off Arifi. He's nervous, the Ambassador thought. No, it's more than nerves. It's fear.

Arifi had lowered his lean rump to the edge of the chair closest to the Ambassador. He leaned forward, his arms resting on bony knees, a slight tic twitching at the corner of his left eye. It was a dark hollowed-out face whose dominating feature was a heavily boned nose that poked itself out and then down toward a wide mouth that was almost lipless, like a fish.

"I must make this one point first," Arifi said, his excellent English bearing heavy Italian overtones and his voice curiously deep for so slight a man. "The request I make of you comes not from me, but from Colonel Mourabet."

"The Colonel is in excellent health, I trust."

"Yes, his health is excellent, praise be to God."

"And his family, they, too, are well?" the Ambassador continued, even at four in the morning the total diplomat.

"They, too, through God's beneficence, enjoy excellent health."

"I am delighted to hear so. Now, how may I be of service to the Colonel?"

"He would be forever in your debt if you were to deliver to President McKay a message and a small package. They must be delivered to the President only. Again, I must emphasize—to the President only."

"A small package, you say," Ambassador Dokubo said, immediately suspecting a bomb. "How small?"

Arifi pulled out a drawer from a built-in cabinet and removed a small Gucci box, approximately three inches square and one inch deep. It was tied with red string and sealed with pink chewing gum. He offered it to the Ambassador almost apologetically. "I regret we had no sealing wax."

Dokubo accepted the box gingerly. "A gift?" he said, knowing it wasn't.

"More a token, I would think."

"In appreciation of your tour."

"The tour was not a success," Arifi said stiffly. "We found it necessary to terminate it."

"I am sorry. I was hoping it would prove successful."

"Perhaps another time."

"Yes, perhaps. But you also mentioned a message."

Arifi nodded and withdrew a stiff buff-colored envelope from his inside breast pocket and handed it over. It also was sealed with a wad of pink chewing gum. The Ambassador sniffed and could smell cinnamon.

"It, too, of course, is confidential," Arifi said, the tic near his left eye now throbbing erratically.

"But of vital importance to—uh—civilization?"

"Colonel Mourabet thinks so," Arifi said in a cold voice. "If I were you, Your Excellency, I would not discount the importance of our request because of its melodramatic nature. Great events often seem melodramatic while happening, but tragic in retrospect."

He's completely mad, the Ambassador thought, staring at Arifi's tic, which now threatened to turn into an uncontrollable twitch.

"I appreciate your confidence in my discretion," the Ambassador murmured and heaved himself up out of the chair.

Arifi rose, too, and laid a cautionary hand on the Ambassador's arm. "One more thing, Your Excellency. We would be exceedingly grateful if you would wait until, say, ten o'clock before calling on the President."

That would give them nearly six hours, the Ambassador thought. At, say, 550 miles per hour, that would put them over— what? Morocco, or perhaps Algeria, if they go that way.

"The President is, as you know, a very busy man," he said. "I am not at all sure when my appointment can be scheduled."

"As long as it's no sooner than ten o'clock."

"I shall do my best."

Arifi smiled. His tic throbbed wildly. "One cannot possibly ask for more."

It was not until 11:45 that morning that Ambassador Dokubo was ushered into the Oval Office. The appointment had been arranged through the urging of the Secretary of State, whom the Ambassador had telephoned at home at 7 A.M. Although Dokubo had been cautiously vague about his reasons for requesting the extraordinary meeting with the President, his reputation for sound common sense and his country's enormous oil reserves had convinced the Secretary that the meeting should take place.

"You can't tell me any more than you've already told me, I take it?" the Secretary had said.

"No, I don't see how I really can, Mr. Secretary, and still keep my word."

"Of course. I understand. Although their tour was unofficial we naturally are deeply disappointed that they canceled the balance of it. Did they give you any inkling as to why they decided to cancel?"

"Only that it was not a success. I believe I'm quoting exactly."

"I've always found this new crop of Libyans to be quite . . . strange," the Secretary had said.

"Quite mad, really."

"Yes. Well, I'll see what I can arrange."

After the telephone conversation, Ambassador Dokubo summoned his principal aide, who came in and stood before the large carved desk on which rested the small Gucci box.

"I don't suppose you have any chewing gum."

"No, sir, I don't."

"Do you think you might hunt up a stick or two?"

"Any particular kind, sir?"

"Do you have any idea about what kind this might be?" Dokubo said, indicating that the aide should examine the box.

The aide picked it up and sniffed the chewing gum. "Dentyne, I'd say, sir. Or close to it."

"See what you can do."

In a few minutes the aide had returned with a package of Dentyne gum that he had obtained from a youth in the Embassy mail room.

"Chew up a couple of sticks," the Ambassador said.

The aide peeled the wrapping off two sticks and popped them into his mouth. While he was chewing, the Ambassador carefully examined the Gucci box. He weighed it in the palm of one hand.

"I don't think it could be a bomb, do you?"

"There are such things as letter bombs," the aide said.

"Well, we shall soon see," the Ambassador said. He peeled away the chewing gum that had been stuck to the box's edges. Then he carefully untied the string. After that, he looked up at his aide and said, "You may leave the room, if you wish."

The aide swallowed. "No, sir, that won't be necessary."

The Ambassador nodded and carefully lifted off the top of the small box.

"Good God!" the aide said.

Ambassador Dokubo's 11:45 A.M. meeting with President McKay had been sandwiched in between a photo opportunity with a band of 4-H prize winners from Valley City, North Dakota, and a meeting between the President and the Director of the FBI, whose west coast special agents had been alerted to start a search for Bingo McKay and Eleanor Rhodes after repeated calls to the Marriott Hotel in Anaheim had failed to locate them.

There was always the chance, of course, that Bingo, a resolute bachelor, could have bedded himself down with a companion or two in the farther reaches of Hollywood or Malibu or the Marina del Rey. But if he had, he normally would have arranged for Eleanor Rhodes to cover for him. But when neither she nor Bingo could be located by the resourceful operators on the White House switchboard, the President, in view of the Libyans' hasty departure, had once again silently goddamned his brother's stubborn refusal to accept Secret Service protection.

He grew even more concerned when the Secretary of State telephoned with the news of the Libyans' strange early-morning meeting with the Nigerian Ambassador. "Have we done anything to piss them off—anything at all?" the President had asked.

The Secretary was careful in his reply. "Nothing that I am aware of, Mr. President."

"That leaves a whole lot of territory unexplored, doesn't it?"

"An immense amount, sir."

"Well, check around and see what you can find out. And I suppose I'd better see Dokubo at—let's make it eleven forty-five. Maybe he'll have something I can pass on to the FBI."

"I'll inform the Ambassador of the time."

"And don't forget to check out what we've done to upset that Libyan bunch—you know, like serving them pork chops for lunch."

"I'll see to it immediately, Mr. President."

When Ambassador Dokubo was ushered into the Oval Office at precisely 11:45, the President was quick to note the Nigerian's grim expression. After they shook hands and exchanged routine pleasantries, the President said, "You've brought me bad news, haven't you?"

Dokubo nodded. "I don't believe it will be good." He picked up his attaché case, put it on his lap, and opened it. He took out the buff envelope first and then the Gucci box and placed them on the President's desk.

"I took the precaution of having my security people examine both of these," he said. "They assure me that they contain no explosives."

The President examined the small box first and looked up. "Chewing gum."

"They apologized for having no sealing wax."

"They say what was in it?"

"A token—according to Ali Arifi."

"He's the Minister of Defense, right?"

"Yes."

"He say what kind of token?"

"No, Mr. President, he didn't."

The President snipped the red string binding the box with a pair of scissors, then peeled away the chewing gum and lifted off the lid. He was a tall man with a tennis pro's rangy body and the careless good looks of a man who for some reason had always assumed that he was ugly and didn't particularly care. In a few years, possibly as many as ten, he would look far more distinguished than he did now, but perhaps not as capable. He had a high, wide forehead and deep-set greenish eyes, an unremarkable nose, a mouth that in repose appeared sardonic, but not when he smiled, and an almost perfect chin, which compensated for the batwing ears that had been handed down to McKay men for generations along with enough thick blondish-gray hair to cover them up.

After the President opened the box, his year-round tan seemed to fade and he said, "Sweet Jesus Christ almighty!" and looked up quickly at Ambassador Dokubo, whose eyes had been recording every nuance of the scene for his half-completed memoirs.

The severed ear rested in the Gucci box on a bed of surgical cotton. It was a large ear, quite drained of blood and no longer pink—indeed, almost white—and the Ambassador's eyes traveled from it to the left ear of the President and matched them up. It's his brother's, he finally decided. Those idiots have cut off the brother's ear.

The Ambassador made a slight clearing noise far down in his

throat and said, "It would appear to be an ear, Mr. President. A human ear."

The President's right hand seemed to move unbidden up to his own right ear, which he touched reassuringly. Not taking his eyes from the box, he picked up the buff envelope and ripped it open. He read its contents at a glance, read them again, more slowly, and then tossed the letter across the desk toward Ambassador Dokubo. The Ambassador wasn't at all sure whether he was intended to read the letter, but when the President spun around in his big chair and stared out the window at the White House south lawn, Dokubo almost snatched up the letter and hungrily read its crabbed writing, trying to burn every word into his memory.

There was no date, and the letter's salutation was a brusque "Mr. President." The body of the letter read:

Your notorious CIA jackals have kidnapped Gustavo Berrio-Brito, the freedom fighter known to the oppressed millions of the world as Felix. We have taken as hostage your brother and his female companion. Unless you immediately release Gustavo Berrio-Brito, we will send your brother back to you piece by piece. Herewith is a token of our determination.

The letter was signed simply but rather grandly with the Libyan ruler's last name, "Mourabet." Underneath in a far different, somewhat shaky Palmer method was written, "These suckers aren't kidding." The postscript was signed "Bingo."

Ambassador Dokubo put the letter carefully back down on the desk as the President slowly turned around in his chair, his expression grim, his face ashen.

"You read it?"

Ambassador Dokubo nodded. "I did, Mr. President."

The President rose. So did the Ambassador. The President looked at the Nigerian thoughtfully for a few moments and then spoke, carefully choosing his words. "I'm not sure yet just what steps we will take, Mr. Ambassador. But it could be that we might call on you to serve in an intermediary role of some kind. Would you agree?"

Dokubo nodded gravely. "My country and I are at your service, Mr. President."

"Thank you. And I'm also sure that I can rely on your complete discretion."

"Complete, Mr. President."

After leaving the Oval Office, Dokubo hurried to his waiting Mercedes. Before the chauffeured car had even reached the south gate, Dokubo, using his attaché case as a desk, was making frantic notes about the morning's meeting, which he had already decided to make the epiphanic chapter in his memoirs.

The President, meanwhile, had again turned away from his desk to stare out at the south lawn. When he turned back, his face was no longer ashen. Instead, it had resumed its normal tan except for the rosy flush that had crept up his neck to his ears. His mouth was stretched into a thin, furious line as he picked up the telephone.

When the secretary answered, his voice was a snarl. "Get me that fucking Coombs out at that fucking CIA."

6

The deceptively slight man with the sleek gray head and the small prim mouth had heard all of the words before many times. Words of the barracks, the barnyard, the oil rig, the pool room, and the saloon. Short, harsh-sounding words mostly, with three consonants and a single vowel. He never used them himself and disapproved of their use by others, on the grounds that they betrayed a lack of imagination. Yet he was neither surprised nor dismayed that the words were coming now in a furious stream from the mouth of the President of the United States.

If anything, the words bored him, even though they were being used to describe his own incompetence and lack of character. So after a short span of listening, he tuned the words out and thought instead about his roses.

The slight man whose roses often won prizes was Thane Coombs, who nine months before, on his fifty-eighth birthday, had been named Director of Central Intelligence. Coombs was also nearly the last of the World War II OSS veterans who once had permeated the Central Intelligence Agency. That he had lasted long enough to be named Director was tribute more to his political skills, which were adroit, than to his intelligence, which, while not quite true brilliance, still left him far cleverer than most.

When after six minutes the President showed no signs of running down, Coombs let his mind drift to an idle examination of the fact that the man sitting behind the Woodrow Wilson desk had been only three years old when a twenty-two-year-old Lieutenant Thane Coombs had parachuted into France near Dijon as a member of a three-man Jedburgh team. But since this was only a notional comparison and really not very interesting, Coombs decided to interrupt the President in mid-word. The word he interrupted was "asshole."

"It wasn't us, Mr. President."

The President completed the word he had begun, but stopped in mid-sentence. He gaped, a mouth-wide-open gape of surprise and disbelief, until he realized what he was doing and clamped his mouth shut into a harsh line of total suspicion.

"Not you?" he said, making it somehow an accusation rather than a question.

"No, sir," Coombs said, choosing his next words with precision. "The Agency had nothing whatsoever to do with the abduction or disappearance of the Venezuelan national Gustavo Berrio-Brito—sometimes known as Felix. Nothing whatsoever."

"The Libyans think you kidnapped him."

"I deeply regret that our still rather flamboyant reputation may have endangered your brother and—"

The President cut him off. "Who?"

"Who kidnapped Felix, you mean?"

That drew a sharp impatient nod from the President.

"I have no idea. None."

"But it wasn't you?" McKay said, still almost hoping that Coombs was lying.

"No, sir. You see, Felix— We may as well call him that, don't you think?"

"Yeah. Sure."

"Well, Felix is, or perhaps now I should say *was*, the leader of

45

a five-man or five-person terrorist group which insists on calling itself Red Anvil Five."

"Always some cute fucking name."

"Yes, I tend to agree. The group consisted of Felix, of course; a Japanese man; a German; a Frenchwoman, and another Venezuelan who was also a woman and also Felix's sometime mistress. Her name was Maria Luisa de la Cova."

"Was?"

Coombs nodded. "She was found dead early this morning in London. In Hammersmith, to be precise. By some children. She had been tied to a chair and garroted. Also tortured. Burned."

"Why?"

"We don't know."

"Can't you guess?"

Coombs hesitated, because he never liked to guess about anything. "It's possible that she may have been the one who betrayed Felix to his abductors, whoever they might be."

"This Anvil Five bunch killed a lot of people, as I recall."

"Seventy-two to be precise," said Coombs, who always strove to be just that. He started ticking the dead bodies off on his left hand. "Fourteen in Manila. Thirty-two in that EL AL plane at Brussels. Sixteen in the Gatwick shootout. Six more in Rome—not counting nine kneecappings there. And those four in Beirut, who were probably Israeli agents, although that was never confirmed."

"And there're just five of them?"

"Only five. And now without Felix and the de la Cova woman there are only three."

"Who finances them?"

"At first they were self-financing. Bank robberies and kidnappings. French banks exclusively, for some reason, and Italian kidnappings. Usually either Rome or Milan. After the Beirut killings, Qaddafi offered them sanctuary in Tripoli. Felix and Qaddafi hit it off immediately, kindred souls, I should imagine, and became extremely close. After that, Anvil Five didn't have to

46

worry about money. When Mourabet came to power after Qaddafi's death, he and Felix developed an equally close relationship. Perhaps even closer. In fact, someone floated a rumor that it was Felix who actually did for Qaddafi but we're confident it was only that, a rumor."

The President studied Coombs coldly for several moments and then seemed to reach a decision. He opened a desk drawer, took out the small Gucci box, and placed it in what seemed to be the exact center of his desk. "I want you to see something," he said and removed the lid.

Coombs looked. "Mercy!" he said, which was as close as he ever permitted himself to an exclamation. "An ear, it would seem."

"My brother's."

"Your brother's," Coombs said in a flat tone which he believed to be full of commiseration.

"They sliced off my brother's ear and sent it by the Nigerian Ambassador to impress me with the seriousness of their intentions. I believe them. I believe that unless Felix is released by whoever's got him, the Libyans will kill both my brother and Miss Rhodes. You say you don't know who has Felix. My question is: Can you find out?"

"We can try, Mr. President."

"Try." Try was obviously not what the President had in mind.

"Yes."

"What's your best guess—the Israelis?"

Coombs let doubt spread over his face. "A possibility, except that if the Israelis had Felix I think the entire world would have heard about it by now. You see, the problem is that the Libyans have made a great many enemies during the past ten or twelve years. When the oil money really started flowing, Qaddafi began messing about in the internal affairs of other countries—the Philippines, Somalia, Northern Ireland, Ethiopia, Afghanistan, Lebanon, Chad, Malta, Uganda for a while, even Iran. He had all that oil money to play with, so some of it went to finance terrorist

47

groups like Anvil Five. Qaddafi even pensioned off a couple of burnt-out cases at a thousand or so a month. So we must assume that whoever abducted Felix must have wanted to strike back at Libya. It's a possible assumption, at least."

It was difficult to tell whether the President had been listening. His gaze was directed at some spot just over Coombs's left shoulder.

Still staring at the spot, he said, "I'm going to have to lie. Through the Nigerian Ambassador I'm going to let the Libyans believe that we really do have Felix. That's my first lie. My second lie will be to the media about my brother's whereabouts. And third, I'm going to have to lie about why the Libyans went home in a snit. None of these lies will stand up for long."

"No," Coombs said. "They won't."

"But I will lie to keep my brother alive and to keep United Parcel from delivering his fingers and toes to me one by one. And while I'm busy lying I want that outfit of yours to do two things."

Coombs nodded carefully.

"First, I want you to find out where they have my brother stashed. If it's a city, I want the exact address and the phone number. I want the map coordinates. If it's a room, I want to know how many windows it's got. If it's a tent, I want the color."

"That may be . . . difficult, Mr. President."

"Difficult or impossible?"

"Difficult," Coombs said at last, seeing no good reason why he should lose his job. "May I ask what you intend to do with the information?"

"No."

"I see."

"Second, I want you to find out who's got Felix and to get him back. I don't care how you do it or how much it costs. You've got carte blanche."

"I'd like that in writing, Mr. President."

"I don't blame you," McKay said. He took out a sheet of White House stationery and started writing. He wrote only one

48

sentence, signed it, read it over, and handed it to Coombs. "That do?"

Coombs read the sentence slowly. "Yes, sir," he said. "That will do nicely."

It was just twenty-four hours after the November election when Bingo McKay had walked into the President-elect's suite on the eighth floor of the Skirvin Tower Hotel in Oklahoma City, looked around, and told everybody to get out—including Dominique, the future First Lady.

The President-elect hadn't questioned his brother's order. Instead, he grinned and asked, "What's up?"

"There's a guy I want you to meet."

"Who?"

"Sit down, kid," Bingo McKay told the President-elect, "and listen real good."

Jerome McKay sat down with a very weak Scotch and water and a fond amused smile. "Jesus, Bingo, you've got that end-of-the-world look on your face again."

"Just listen. One of these days, something might happen. I don't know what or when. But it might be messy and I might not be around."

Jerome McKay had started to say something, but his brother held up a hand. "Just listen. If I'm not around, then you're gonna have to have somebody you can depend on who can fix things—just like I can sometimes fix things. You following me?"

"It's not hard."

"That's why I want you to meet this guy now—get to know him. He can fix things."

"But not for free?"

"No, he charges pretty good."

"Have we used him before?"

"You really want to know?"

Jerome McKay slowly shook his head. "But he's good, you say?"

"He's good."

"What's his name?"

"Paul Grimes."

The second meeting ever between Paul Grimes and President McKay didn't take place in the Oval Office. They met instead in a small denlike room on the third floor of the old Executive Office Building. Between them on the desk, still in its Gucci box, lay the severed ear of Bingo McKay, which the President hadn't yet decided what to do with. Later he would wrap it up in a Baggie and place it in a White House freezer.

The meeting took place forty-four minutes after the President had met with the Director of Central Intelligence. Paul Grimes studied the severed ear for a moment, sighed, read the Libyan letter, read it once again, and looked up at McKay.

"Well, sir, I'd say old Bingo's gone and got himself into just one hell of a fix."

"I want him back," the President said. "I want them both back."

Grimes was silent for several moments. Then he sighed again. "It'll cost."

"Can it be done?"

"I didn't say that. All I said was that it's going to cost."

"How much?"

Grimes shrugged. "A couple of hundred thousand up front right off the bat. More later. Probably a whole hell of a lot more."

The President picked up the phone and Grimes noted with appreciation that it was answered immediately. McKay looked at Grimes. "Where do you want it?"

Grimes thought for a moment. "London," he said. "Barclays."

"Your name?"

Grimes shook his head. "Crosspatch Limited."

Into the phone the President said, "Call Wheeler down in Oke City and tell him to transfer two hundred thousand out of that Doremi contingency account in Liberty National to Cross-patch Limited, Barclays, London."

As the President hung up the phone without saying either thank you or goodbye, Grimes found himself staring again at the still open Gucci box. "They really cut it off, didn't they?"

"They cut it off."

"How much time have I got?"

"Not much. Ten days maybe. No more."

"Not much."

"No."

Once again Grimes sighed. "Well, if I can get hold of this one guy I'm thinking of, I can—"

The President interrupted. "I don't really want to know."

Grimes nodded thoughtfully. "No, sir, it's probably better if you don't."

"I just want them back. Both of them."

Grimes rose abruptly, smoothly, the way some very fat people do. "Well, I'll sure see what I can do, Mr. President."

7

Seven hours after the body of the man called Felix fell a little more than a mile into the sea, the Boeing 727 he had been shoved out of landed rather bumpily on the private potholed runway at the northern tip of the Caribbean island that for 204 years had been a British possession and was now a self-proclaimed Democratic People's Republic.

The island was twenty-seven miles long and a mile wide at its widest point. Down its spine ran a chain of mountains whose highest peak lacked just two feet of being a mile high. On the island lived 28,047 citizens, according to the last census, which had been taken in 1974 by the British just six months prior to independence. The census had neglected to count some four or five thousand citizens who lived up in the mountains where there were no roads.

Most of the island's citizens, nearly twenty thousand of them, lived in the capital of the republic, which was situated on its southern tip. At the northern tip was the old Mecarro coffee plantation consisting of nearly 640 acres. The landing strip was located on the plantation, which the Democratic People's Republic had leased for five years to the American for a million dollars, all of which went into the public coffers, plus another $200,000 in cash, which had gone into the pockets of the Prime Minister, the Minister of the Interior, and the Minister of National Security.

No coffee grew on the old Mecarro plantation. No coffee had ever grown there. A rich Colombian called Mecarro had leased the land in 1936 and built himself a fine house. The next year he had planted coffee. The year after that, 1938, the great hurricane had roared by and wiped out the coffee, miraculously sparing the fine house, which had been taken over by an order of nuns. The last member of the order had died just three years before. The Mecarro plantation had stood vacant until it had been leased by the American, who was immensely rich. He was also wanted by the police of seven countries, which is the principal reason he had come to settle in the island Democratic People's Republic. The republic had no extradition agreements or treaties. None at all. The American had already applied for citizenship.

The sixty-three-year-old pilot and the sixty-five-year-old co-pilot of the 727 helped the man called Arnold carry the doctor off the plane and dump him into the rear of the jeep that was driven by Jack Spiceman, the ex-FBI agent. The doctor was dead drunk.

Arnold climbed into the seat next to Jack Spiceman. When the jeep didn't move, Arnold said, "Let's go."

"What about Felix?" Spiceman said.

Arnold made his right hand go out and then down in a steep plunging motion.

"No shit?" Spiceman said.

"No shit."

Arnold wasn't his real name, of course. His real name was Franklin Keeling, and he once had been a highly valued, highly trained, totally trusted employee of the Central Intelligence Agency. In 1975 he had been fired with rancor after $200,000 in gold disappeared in Angola. Keeling had been entrusted to deliver the gold to a right-wing Angolan revolutionary called João Machado. Nothing was ever heard of Machado or the gold again except for a signed receipt, which Keeling produced in his own defense. The validity of the receipt bitterly divided seven CIA documentation experts. Four thought it was genuine; three insisted it was a fake. Nonetheless, Keeling was fired. Nine months later, after he had spent the $200,000, Keeling went to work for the immensely rich American who now sat across from him in the main drawing room of the old Mecarro mansion and listened to his explanation about why Felix had forgotten how to breathe.

After finishing his explanation, Keeling lit a cigarette and waited to see what the rich American would say. He was fairly confident it would have nothing at all to do with Felix's death. The rich American's mind didn't work that way.

"How's the book coming?" the rich American asked.

To while away his spare hours on the island republic, Keeling sporadically worked on a manuscript which was a steamy, implausible account of his fifteen years with the CIA. Keeling thus far had managed the difficult feat of making the manuscript both dull and libelous.

"Page 218," he said.

"Ransom, I think, don't you?" the rich American said. "Ten million at least."

Constant extrapolation was needed to carry on a conversation with the rich American, whose mind roamed unknown planes. The rich American's name was Leland Timble and at nineteen he had been graduated summa cum laude from Cal Tech into the waiting arms of a Hughes think tank with headquarters in Malibu. Timble had spent five years with the Hughes firm thinking about computers. Then on one warm August afternoon in 1976, using only the touch-tone telephone in his Santa Monica apartment for a terminal, Timble had transferred thirty million dollars from the First National banks in Tulsa, Fort Worth, Omaha, Denver, Memphis, Portland, and Indianapolis to a blind account in Chase Manhattan and from there to numbered accounts in Panama and Nassau. Timble was twenty-four then; now he was twenty-nine.

So brilliantly and logically had the money been stolen that it was three full months before it was even missed. From Panama and Nassau the money was eventually traced to a Luxembourg bank, where it had been quietly withdrawn in cash over a period of two months by employees of an armored car firm who later claimed to have delivered the cash at various dates to (1) a middle-aged Frenchwoman, (2) an elderly Arab, (3) a young Texan, and (4) a nondescript Swede, none of whom could ever be found.

Three years after the embezzlement an anonymous article entitled "How Ma Bell Can Make You Rich" had been received in the mail by *Scientific American*. Although the title was snappy, only one of the learned editors at the magazine could even dimly perceive what the article was trying to explain, so esoteric was its symbolic language and mathematics.

The editors turned the article over to the FBI, who had it translated by a Nobel laureate, who advised them to burn every single copy unless they were willing to watch the national banking system collapse.

The only clue the FBI had was the Rio de Janeiro postmark on the envelope that the article had arrived in. It had taken special agent Jack Spiceman six months to track down Leland Timble in Rio. After a quiet chat lasting no more than fifteen minutes, Spiceman had agreed to go to work for Timble for $300,000 a year. It was Spiceman, in fact, who suggested and negotiated for the sanctuary on the island republic. And it was Spiceman who suggested that Franklin Keeling, the disgraced ex-CIA man, would make a valuable addition to Timble's small entourage.

In a reply now to Timble's suggestion that a ten-million-dollar ransom be considered, Keeling came back with a non sequitur, which was what his conversations with Timble often consisted of.

"The doc's back on the sauce," he said. "Dead drunk."

"I should think the United Nations again, don't you?"

"You still want to use Old Black Joe?" Keeling said.

Old Black Joe was what Keeling called Dr. Joseph Mapangou, Gambia's permanent representative to the United Nations. On an annual retainer of fifty thousand dollars, Dr. Mapangou had proved useful in a number of ways, not the least being his uncanny ability to be first with the latest rumor. It was Dr. Mapangou, in fact, who had come up with the hint that Anvil Five might be found in London.

"How much did it all cost?" Timble asked, taking out a small spiral notebook and a ball-point pen. When it came to money, Timble's air of mild bemusement vanished. His large brown eyes narrowed, even glittered, and his face, at twenty-nine still almost as round and unformed as a child's, seemed to lengthen itself into a sterner, more adult shape.

Keeling was ready with the figures. "It took thirty-four thousand just to get the lead on them."

Timble jotted down the figure.

"Then I jewed Zlatev down to nineteen thousand for the umbrella."

"The Bulgarian," Timble said and made another quick note.

Keeling nodded. "The de la Cova woman was a bargain, twenty thousand."

Timble's small mouth pursed itself into appreciation at the figure as he wrote it down.

"That little fag who used to be with MI 6—he wouldn't budge for less than forty thousand."

Timble frowned, but said nothing, and made another note.

"That East End crowd I told you about came through with the taxi and driver for five thousand, and then I had to spread another twenty thousand around out at Heathrow."

"In all, $138,000," Timble said. "Not bad, although I think you could have sliced just a teeny bit more off the Bulgarian's price for his umbrella."

"I could have rented it," Keeling said, not bothering to put much sarcasm into his tone, because Timble never noticed it anyway.

For a moment Timble's face brightened. But it was only for a moment. "No," he said, "I don't suppose that would have done at all."

"No."

"Still, $138,000 isn't bad. I think the ransom will be ten million. Ten million each, of course, or have I already mentioned that?"

Keeling wiped one of his large hands hard across the bottom of his face. "Leland?"

"Yes."

"Lemme ask you something again?"

"Of course."

"And this time you'll give me a straight answer?"

"Certainly."

"Who are we gonna ransom Felix down there feeding the sharks twice to?"

For a moment, Timble's expression changed. The emotion that flitted across it was one of either rage or despair. Like a child, Timble's face had a limited range of expressions which came and went so quickly it was often difficult to determine his feelings.

"You didn't forget my contingency instructions, did you, Franklin? I would be extremely disappointed if you did. Most operations fail because of a lack of contingency planning. An ability to anticipate the unexpected as well as the unforeseen—"

"Leland," Keeling interrupted.

"Yes."

"I didn't forget."

A look of pure joy came and went from Timble's face in less than a second. It was almost subliminal. If I had blinked, Keeling thought, I would have missed it.

"I knew you wouldn't," Timble said and smiled happily with

his lips closed, showing no teeth. When he smiled like that, he reminded Keeling of those dumb faces that some people draw at the bottom of their letters.

"Leland," Keeling said.

"Yes."

"Lemme ask you again. Who are we going to ransom Felix down there in the ocean twice to?"

"Didn't I just say?"

"No."

"Oh. Well, first to Israel and then to Libya. Or perhaps vice versa."

8

The day after his meeting with Paul Grimes, Chubb Dunjee on a very wet Thursday morning flew into Heathrow from Lisbon aboard an Iberia Airlines DC-8. He went through customs and immigration and then headed for the Pan Am counter, where he used his nearly expired American Express card to charge a first-class one-way ticket to Rome on a flight leaving in two hours.

He had decided to put to a test the easy-money proposition Paul Grimes had made him in Sintra. Over the years, Dunjee had abandoned nearly all faith in easy money.

At a pay phone he dialed the London number that Grimes had urged him to memorize. The phone rang its double rings twice before a woman's voice answered with a carefully noncommittal "Yes."

"This is Dunjee."

"One moment."

There were some clicks and whirrings that Dunjee didn't particularly care for, but then Grimes came on the phone with "Where are you?"

"Heathrow. I'll be in the Pan Am VIP lounge for the next

hour and twenty minutes. If half of what we talked about in Sintra isn't here by then, I'll be elsewhere by evening."

"Well, shit, Chubb."

"It's up to you."

Grimes sighed. "It'll be there," he said and hung up.

Dunjee effortlessly talked his way into the Pan Am VIP lounge, which turned out to be a rather grubby place that offered some worn couches and chairs, a TV set, and free help-yourself booze from a rotating circular rack of upside-down bottles. There were also some bowls of peanuts, potato chips, Ritz crackers, and a large mound of glowing orange cheese spread that somehow looked radioactive and no one had touched. Dunjee glanced around, but could spot no one who looked very important. Not even slightly important. He mixed himself a free whisky and water and settled down to wait.

Sixty-two minutes later the messenger from Grimes arrived. The messenger was a tall woman, either approaching thirty or just past it. Even in the rain she had worn large round dark glasses, but removed them as soon as she entered the lounge. Dunjee was mildly relieved to see her put them away in her purse instead of shoving them up on top of her short blond hair that had been turned dark and damp by the rain.

The woman paused to glance around the lounge. She quickly rejected several other waiting male passengers, settled on Dunjee, studied him briefly, and then made her way toward him. Dunjee liked the way she walked.

When the woman reached Dunjee, she stopped and for several moments stood staring at him calmly, almost quizzically. "He said you were a bit cockeyed," she said. "It's rather nice. I'm Delft Csider. That's spelled with a Cs."

"Delft?"

"My eyes."

Dunjee saw that they were indeed blue, perhaps even delft blue. They went with her pale smooth skin and her high-cheek-boned face that seemed to have more than just a touch of Slav in it. For some reason, he found himself wondering how many languages she spoke.

"You were the one on the phone, right?" Dunjee said as he rose.

"Right."

He indicated the large fat manila envelope that her left hand clutched against her damp oyster-white raincoat. There was no ring on the hand. "That for me?" he said.

She nodded and with her right hand dug deeply into the leather purse that hung from her shoulder. She took out a folded sheet of paper.

"You'll have to sign for it."

"Sign?"

"You know—your name."

Dunjee smiled. "You bet."

He took a ball-point pen from his pocket and without even reading what was on the sheet of paper wrote something on it. Then he handed it back to her.

"Felix Krull," she read. "That's rather funny."

"Not as funny as asking me to sign for it."

She shrugged and handed him the fat manila envelope. "He said I should try."

Dunjee tapped the envelope. "Would you like a drink while I check what's inside?"

"I would, rather."

He nodded toward the free-drink dispenser. "Help yourself."

As Dunjee turned to leave, her hand touched him lightly on the sleeve. "What'll you do if it's not all there?"

"It'll be there."

"Then why check it?"

"Because if I don't now, I may wish that I had later, which would be too late."

"That's a complicated attitude."

"It's a complicated world."

Dunjee left, found a men's room, and inside a stall opened the manila envelope. It contained fifty thousand dollars in rubber-band-bound packets of fifty- and hundred-dollar bills. There was also a note typed on a small square of flimsy paper. The note said, "I'll call you around noon." It was unsigned.

Dunjee crumpled the note and dropped it into the toilet. He then went back into the lounge, mixed himself a second drink, and joined Delft Csider, who sat in a corner, well away from everyone else, leafing through a tattered copy of *Country Life.*

She looked up at him as he sat down. "All there?"

"All there. Anyone else in on this mess?"

"No. Just he and I."

"And you're what?"

"The backup."

"Why you—in particular, I mean?"

"I have the languages, should it come to that."

"How many?"

"Six."

"I'll guess: French, German, Spanish, Italian and"—he paused —"Hungarian."

She acknowledged his guess with a slight nod and an even slighter smile. "You left out one."

"What?"

"Arabic."

"Arabic makes seven, not six."

"I don't count English."

"Are you?"

"What?"

"English?"

"No."

"I couldn't tell."

She didn't seem to care. She finished her drink, rattled the ice in her glass and said, "I have a car if you could use a lift."

"Thanks. I could."

"Where're you staying, the Connaught?"

"Do I look like the Connaught?"

She again examined him briefly. "Almost."

Dunjee canceled his seat on the Rome flight while Delft Csider went to get her car, which turned out to be an elderly Morgan 2 + 2 with a patched top. Dunjee put his suitcase in the rear seat and climbed in beside her.

"Old, but reliable," she said. "The car, I mean."

They made most of the fast bumpy drive along the M4 in silence. The hard rain fell in sheets that leaked through the top and coated the windshield with what seemed to be thick layers of gray gelatin. The Morgan's worn blades scrubbed away earnestly but with little effect. After fifteen minutes, Dunjee said, "You should get some new blades."

"Probably."

"And some new shocks."

"They are new."

Five minutes later she said, "I was just wondering."

"What?"

"What kind of name is Dunjee?"

"I don't know. Scotch, maybe."

"And Chubb?"

"My father was a locksmith. I had an older brother called Yale, but he died."

"I'm sorry."

"Don't be. He was three and I was one."

Dunjee's hotel was the Hilton. After thanking Delft Csider for the lift, he allowed the doorman to fetch his bag from the rear and shield him from the rain with a large black umbrella. Inside, the reservation clerk ran a practiced eye over Dunjee and assigned him to a hundred-and-twenty-two-dollar-a-night room on the sixth floor with a view of Hyde Park. Up in the room, the middle-aged porter, perhaps the last native-born English yeoman still in hotel service, deposited Dunjee's bag on the stand and put the room key on top of the television set. Dunjee took out a twenty-dollar bill, folded it lengthwise, and held it out. The porter pocketed the bill smoothly with thanks and then waited to see what Dunjee expected for his money.

"I might like to do some gambling, but I don't want to wait forty-eight hours. That's the law, isn't it?"

The porter smiled. It was the smile of the practiced conspirator. "These things can be arranged, sir. No trouble at all. If you'll check your box downstairs a bit later this afternoon, you'll find a membership card all made out. And a very nice club it is, too."

"Poker?"

"Seven-card stud, I believe it is, sir."

"Thank you."

"And the best of luck to you, sir."

After the porter had gone, Dunjee unpacked quickly. He then sat down on the bed, took out his address book, looked up a number, and called it. The phone rang nineteen times before Dunjee gave up and looked at his watch. It was sixteen minutes before noon. He rose and settled into a chair by the window with that day's copy of the *Herald Tribune*. He again looked at his watch. His record for the *Tribune* puzzle was fourteen minutes. It was a three-month-old record that Dunjee sometimes despaired of ever breaking. Sixteen minutes later, with three words still to go, the phone rang.

Dunjee answered on the second ring. It was Paul Grimes. "Let's have lunch."

"All right. Where?"

"My place." He gave Dunjee a Kensington address not far from Harrods.

"You're not having fish, are you?"

"No. Why?"

"I'm sick of fish," Dunjee said.

Grimes's place turned out to be a narrow three-story house, painted an almost cream, that faced onto a small green park. The park had a black iron fence around it and a locked gate. Dunjee got out of his taxi and watched a veiled Arab woman unlock the gate and wheel a large perambulator through it into the park.

Dunjee went up the six iron steps and rang the bell. He tried to appear surprised when Grimes himself opened the door.

"No butler?" Dunjee said as he went in. "I was kind of hoping there'd be a butler."

"I don't live here," Grimes said. "I can't afford to live here any more."

Dunjee looked around the reception hall. There was no furniture. Not even a hatrack. "Whose place is it?"

"Mine," Grimes said, shoving back a pair of sliding doors. "I bought it ten, maybe eleven years ago. When I bought it, it was crammed full of old furniture—Victorian stuff mostly. It was all kind of dinky, but what the hell, I liked it and so did my wife. She loves London for some reason. So we kept the furniture and used the place whenever we were over here—maybe four or five times a year. Well, about three months ago some guy from Kansas City comes through town, a dealer, and offers me as much for the furniture as I paid for the house. So what the hell, I sold it to him. All of it."

They had moved into a reception room that was furnished with a lamp, two folding camp chairs, and a bridge table. On the bridge table was a large bucket of Colonel Sanders fried chicken.

Grimes waved Dunjee toward one of the camp chairs and said, "Lunch."

Dunjee sat down, peered into the bucket, and selected a drumstick. Grimes reached down underneath the table into a paper sack and came up with two cans of beer. "No glasses," he said, handing Dunjee one.

"None needed."

They ate the chicken and the cool French fried potatoes and the sweetish cole slaw, which Dunjee didn't much like; and when they were through, Grimes dumped everything into a large plastic garbage bag, took it back to the kitchen, and returned carrying a thermos and two paper cups.

"Coffee," he said. "Black."

"Fine."

When the coffee was poured, Grimes leaned back in his chair and stared at Dunjee. "I never worked with you on anything like this," he said. "But I talked to some people who did when you were down there in Mexico. They say you work it funny."

"Funny?"

"Oblique might be a better word. They say you used to take an oblique approach."

"I always tried to use the smoothest path. Sometimes it was also the longest."

"What's your approach here going to be?"

"You're not supposed to make regular reports back to the White House, are you?"

Grimes shook his head. "The only thing I want to report back there are results."

"I have to get a line on a Libyan."

"Which one?"

"I don't know yet. I'm hoping for the one who was the London contact for Felix. But that may be hoping for too much."

"How're you going to do it?"

Dunjee smiled slightly and took a swallow of his coffee. When he continued to remain silent, Grimes sighed, and said, "Fifty thousand dollars, Chubb. It's got to buy a little encouragement."

After a moment Dunjee nodded thoughtfully and said, "The Csider woman."

"What about her?"

"I might have some use for her."

"How?"

"I don't know yet."

Grimes lit a cigarette, blew some smoke out, and fanned it away. "That other thing."

"You mean how I'm going to get a line on my Libyan?"

Grimes nodded.

"I'm going to see a guy I used to know in New York."

"When you were with the UN?"

"Uh-huh. He owes me a favor. Maybe even two."

"He British?"

"British."

"You're not going to . . ." Grimes let his question trail off.

Dunjee smiled. "I'll be . . . oblique."

"What'd this guy do?"

"At the UN?"

Grimes nodded again.

"He was a spy."

9

The Pimlico street number in Dunjee's small Leathersmith address book had been written there more than ten years before, and he was no longer at all sure that either it or the phone number he had tried several times that afternoon was still valid.

It was nearly three o'clock when he got out of the taxi in the rain, looked briefly up at the stern red brick example of 1913 architecture, hurried up its steps, and into the foyer. There was a double row of black buttons, and beside each button was a card with a name either written or printed on it. Dunjee noticed that most of the printed cards were engraved.

In the slot beside the button that belonged to flat three-E was an engraved card that read "Hugh Scullard," except that Hugh had been crossed out with green ink and above it had been printed "Pauline."

"Well, shit," Dunjee said, a little surprised that he had said it aloud, and pressed the three-E button. When nothing happened, he pressed it again.

He was about to press it a third time when a woman's voice said over the tinny foyer speaker, "What do you want?"

"It's Chubb Dunjee, Pauline."

"Who?"

"Chubb Dunjee."

There was a brief silence until the woman's voice said, "Do I owe you any money?"

"No."

"Then come up."

The buzzer rang and Dunjee went through the door. There was a small elevator with a glass-and-wrought-iron cage and a sign that read, "Lift Out of Order." Dunjee walked up four flights and knocked on the door of three-E.

A deadbolt was turned back. Then a second one. The door opened the length of its three-inch chain. An eye peered out—red-rimmed, bloodshot, with a lump of sleep granules collected in one corner.

Dunjee nodded and smiled at the eye. "Pauline."

"Well," the woman said. "Congressman."

The door closed, the chain was removed, and the door was thrown open. "Come in," the woman said. "It's a mess. And so am I."

Dunjee went in, closed the door, looked around, and said, "What happened?"

"What didn't?" the woman said.

Dunjee couldn't decide whether Pauline Scullard was moving in or out. Cartons of books were stacked in one corner of the room almost to the ceiling. A gray cat sat half asleep on the highest carton. A rolled-up rug lay before the grate. Several paintings leaned against one wall. The furniture—a couch, some chairs, a few tables, some lamps—was huddled together at one end of the room near the tall windows. There were shades on the windows but no curtains. The shades were drawn.

Pauline Scullard made a vague motion at the room. "I just haven't been able to cope—or something."

Dunjee took off his raincoat, looked around for somewhere to put it, and decided on one of the book cartons. When he turned back, the woman was pouring liquor into a glass. She handed the glass to him and poured another one for herself.

"Do sit down," she said. "Someplace. Any place."

Dunjee chose the couch. The woman picked up some magazines from a chair, dropped them to the floor, and sat down, tugging at her miniskirt, locking her knees primly together, and pointing her feet to the left.

"I have proper dresses. Three, I think. I wear them on Tuesdays and Fridays. Visiting days."

"Visiting days," Dunjee said.

"Yes."

"Where is he?"

"Hugh?"

"Hugh."

"Hugh's not here."

"How long have you been back?"

"You mean here—in this place? You know, we were frightfully clever to buy this place, or rather the lease. That was back in 'sixty-eight. It had ninety-two years to run then. Now it has—what? Seventy-eight years?"

"Nine," Dunjee said. "Seventy-nine."

"That many? Well, that should be quite enough to see us out nicely, don't you think?"

"What happened, Pauline?" Dunjee said patiently.

"You mean after New York?"

He nodded.

"Well, we went to Beirut and stayed there ever so long and after that we went to Berlin, but that didn't work out very well so we came home and, well, here we are, Mopsy and me."

"The cat."

"That's Mopsy up there on the books. Would you like a cigarette?" She reached into the pocket of the man's gray cardigan that was nearly as long as her ancient miniskirt and produced a package of Senior Service. Dunjee took one, although he seldom smoked, and lit both cigarettes. Pauline Scullard inhaled deeply, finished her drink in three swallows, and smiled.

"How silly of me. An ashtray." She rose and wandered around

the room until she found what she was looking for. "Here," she said and handed Dunjee an empty cat-food can. It hadn't been washed.

"Tell me about it, Pauline."

"Well, there's really not much to tell. We came back from Berlin five months ago, six now, I suppose—here, to this place—and then Hugh went crackers, and so now I wear one of my three nice dresses when I visit him on Tuesdays and Fridays." She smiled again, a strained, somewhat gray-toothed smile that Dunjee found a bit odd.

"He went crackers?"

"Yes, I'm afraid so. We had to tuck him away in this ever so nice looney bin out in St. John's Wood. Visiting days, Tuesdays and Fridays. It's private and terribly expensive and suddenly I'm very poor. Do you remember when I was rich? I mean, two thousand a year forever. Well, back then that was rich, wasn't it? I mean, I was almost an heiress."

"You're broke?"

She stared at him for a moment, then nodded. Dunjee decided that she was still an extremely attractive woman, despite her odd dress and tear-swollen eyes. Her complexion was still creamy, and hugging her head was still that same curly cap of straw-colored hair; and if she would only start brushing her teeth and quit weeping she wouldn't look much different from the way she had looked in New York a dozen years ago, although she must be thirty-seven now, perhaps even thirty-eight.

Dunjee sighed, took out his wallet, removed some hundred-dollar bills without counting them, and held them out to her. "Here," he said. "Buy yourself something pretty."

She looked at the money but didn't touch it.

"It's Monopoly money, Pauline. I didn't work for it."

"A loan?"

"Sure."

She took the money. "It'll be a while before I can—"

"I understand."

"You're very sweet, Chubb."

"Tell me about Hugh."

She picked up the Scotch bottle from the floor, poured some more into her glass, and held the bottle out toward Dunjee. He shook his head. She put the bottle back down on the floor.

"It started in Beirut," she said. "Then it got really bad in Berlin, so they sent us home and pensioned him off. We lived like this for almost two months. He wouldn't let me touch anything. He sat here in this chair by the window and looked out through the shade. He said he was waiting for them. When he slept, he slept on the couch. I brought him his meals on a tray over there by the window. He didn't eat much. So finally I went to see them, you know, *them,* and they sent a doctor over, a shrink, I think, and two days later they came and got him and put him away in that private looney bin. It's ever so nice and somehow I get dressed every Tuesday and Friday and actually go out there and see him. Paranoid-schizophrenic is what they say. I'm afraid it may be contagious."

"Could I see him?"

"Why?"

"I could take him some cigars. He used to like cigars."

"He's not all that well."

"Is he rational?"

"Most of the time. His doctor is Jewish. Hugh thinks he's with Mossad. I don't know what he'd think about you. Where've you been?"

"Mexico," Dunjee said. "Portugal."

"Was it nice?"

"Quiet."

"I suppose I could call, tell them you're an old friend. He doesn't have many, you know. All our old friends are now our new creditors."

"I'd like to see him this afternoon."

"All right. I'll ring them."

While she was making the call, Pauline Scullard looked down at the money she was still holding in her left hand. She seemed surprised at the sight of it. Cradling the phone against her left shoulder and ear, she used both hands to count the money. She counted it twice. When the call was finished, she turned to Dunjee and said, "You can see him at half past five."

"I'll take him some cigars."

"There's a thousand, four hundred dollars here, Chubb."

Dunjee smiled. "Buy yourself something pretty."

"A dress?"

"A dress would be nice."

It was an immense old house on a quiet street about halfway between Lord's cricket grounds and the place where the Beatles were once headquartered. The room in which Hugh Scullard sat on the bed opening the box of Cuban cigars faced the street. The room was on the second floor if you were American; the first if you were British. There were no bars on the window, no lock on the door, which was open.

Occasionally, a patient dressed in a bathrobe and slippers would shuffle by and glance in fleetingly, almost surreptitiously, as though afraid of being caught, and shuffle on. All of the patients seemed to be men. Middle-aged men.

Hugh Scullard, dressed in pajamas, a brown flannel bathrobe, and slippers, took a cigar from the box, sniffed it appreciatively, and offered the box to Dunjee, who shook his head and said, "I never learned to enjoy them, Hugh."

"Pity," Scullard said. "It's all right for us to smoke, but they won't let us have matches. There's an electric gadget down the hall at the nurses' desk that we have to use. Awful nuisance."

"Here," Dunjee said, and handed him a disposable lighter. "Keep it."

Scullard smiled. "If they find this, they'll probably take away my pudding for three days."

He used the lighter to get the cigar going, puffed on it several times, inhaling just a little, and then held it out and gazed at it with total pleasure.

"How'd she look?" he said.

"Pauline?"

"Pauline."

"She looked awful."

Scullard smiled again. The smile made him look younger, almost as young as he really was, which was fifty. Without the smile he looked sixty, perhaps sixty-five.

"Still no bullshit, right, Chubb?"

"Not unless I'm working."

"Are you?"

"Working?"

"Mmm."

"A little," Dunjee said.

"Not for them, I hope?"

"Who's them?"

Scullard nodded toward the window. "Take a look out there. Across the street there's a green car. A Volvo. There's a man in it, thirty-five, perhaps thirty-six, swarthy complexion, glasses. He's there every day."

Dunjee rose, crossed to the window, and looked out. There was a green car, a Volvo, and the man behind the wheel had a swarthy complexion. A woman wearing a gray raincoat and carrying an umbrella over her white nurse's cap hurried across the street and got into the car. The man kissed her. The car pulled away.

"He seems to be picking up his wife or girl friend," Dunjee said. "I think she's a nurse."

"Oh, she's a nurse all right," Scullard said. "Nurse Ganor. Now what kind of name do you suppose that is?"

"Irish?"

Scullard spelled it.

"I don't know," Dunjee said.

"Israeli."

"I guess I was thinking of Janet Gaynor."

"Nurse Ganor," he said, then added significantly, "Dr. Levin."

"He's your doctor?"

"I spotted *him* right away, of course."

"How?"

Scullard smiled mysteriously. "He made a slip. A very tiny one. I didn't let on, at least not to him. I told Pauline. She's arranging everything. By this time next week, we'll be back in Beirut."

"You're depending on Pauline?"

"Certainly. Why not?"

"Pauline doesn't look so hot."

"You think I've let her down, don't you?"

"Not at all. It's just that she's under a strain. Why don't you use somebody else?"

"Who?"

"The Libyans," Dunjee said, seizing his opportunity and wishing he were back in Sintra, or even Mexico. "You used to know a lot of Libyans in New York. Or some anyway. With all that oil money now, they've got their fingers in a lot of pies."

"The Colonel's dead."

"I know."

"Still . . ." Scullard let his thoughts slide away. "You were in Mexico."

"For a while."

"I heard. I even read about it somewhere. The Mordida Man. What happened?"

"They started swapping prisoners is what happened," Dunjee said. "Business fell off. In fact, there wasn't any business any more."

"Odd sort of business, I'd say."

"Very odd."

"About that other thing."

"You mean the Lib—" Dunjee stopped when Scullard held a finger up to his lips. Scullard then cupped the same hand to his ear and used his cigar to point around the room. Dunjee nodded. Scullard pantomimed writing. Dunjee took out his ball-point pen and an envelope and handed them to Scullard, who wrote something on the envelope and handed it back to Dunjee.

On the envelope Scullard had written, "Call Faraj Abedsaid—Cultural Attaché—Lib. emb. Tell him I be ready Thursday week. Pauline and Mopsy too."

"All of you, huh?" Dunjee said.

Scullard nodded his thin long head and sucked in his cheeks, which gave his head an almost skull-like look. His dark eyes were suddenly bright and excited.

"You're sure this is the right guy?" Dunjee said.

"He and I are in the same line of work, you might say. He's a petroleum engineer, a product of one of your own universities, I believe. Oklahoma. They do have a university in Oklahoma, don't they?"

"It's at a place called Norman."

"Tell him—" Scullard paused, then licked his thin lips, smiled, and said, "Tell him I think I know exactly where to drill."

"Okay," Dunjee said. "I'll tell him."

As Dunjee moved down the hall past the nurses' desk, a man in his thirties, wearing a neatly trimmed dark mustache and a three-piece suit stepped out of an office. "Mr. Dunjee?"

"Yes."

"I'm Dr. Levin. I wonder if you could spare a moment?"

"Sure."

"We might go in here," Levin said and led the way into the office, which contained a walnut table that doubled as a desk, two armchairs, and a couch. "Please," Levin said and indicated one of the armchairs.

When they were both seated, Levin smiled and said, "You're an old friend of Mr. Scullard's, I understand."

"We knew each other in New York."

"I suppose you noticed the change?"

"He's crazy as hell, isn't he?"

Levin smiled again, but this time it was a sad smile. "I don't share some of my colleagues' almost pathological aversion to the word, so I can agree with you. He is crazy as hell."

"Will he get any better?"

"I hope so."

"He thinks you're with Israeli intelligence. You and Nurse Ganor."

"Bernie Levin, the dread Mossad agent."

"He also thinks he's going to bust out of here next week."

Dr. Levin sighed. "Well, at least he still has plans for the future."

"I also gave him a cigarette lighter."

Dr. Levin sighed again and frowned. "I wish you hadn't done that."

"So do I," Dunjee said.

10

At six o'clock the next morning, Dunjee found himself in an after-hours club of sorts, a Greek place, tossing cheap white plates at the feet of the female singer. The singer was also Greek and a little past her prime, but she had a loud, true voice and a glorious smile and Dunjee found that he didn't at all mind the small mustache she seemed to be cultivating.

Dunjee was at the club with his two new best friends, another Greek and a Hungarian, both gamblers. The club was one of those outlaw places that open up around four in the morning after the gambling halls have closed. It was owned by a Mr. Tikopoulous who seemed to be very fond of his singer.

Dunjee had been cultivating his two new best friends for nearly ten hours. He had earned their oft-professed friendship, undeviating trust, and total loyalty by losing nearly two thousand pounds to them at a seven-card-stud table in the Embankment Sporting Club, which was located nowhere near the Embankment, but rather just off the Edgware Road.

Dunjee had lost his money skillfully, not quite methodically, even winning a hand now and again merely to make things look right, but losing nevertheless. The Greek and the Hungarian had taken nearly all of it. They had also gathered him to their collective bosom, clucked regretfully over his losses, and after a glimpse or two at the contents of his still fat wallet, suggested that his luck might change at an after-hours gambling den they just happened to know, which stayed open until shortly after dawn.

The illegal after-hours joint had been a small smutty place in Paddington run by a man who called himself Major Blake and hinted that he was a cashiered Guards officer with a strange and tragic past. The game at Major Blake's was five-card draw played with a stripped deck, and Dunjee had managed to lose another five hundred pounds at that, too, thus further cementing his already indisoluble bonds of friendship with the Greek and Hungarian, who now seemed determined never to let him out of their sight.

It was just after dawn when the game at Major Blake's had finally broken up, but the Greek and Hungarian's early morning rounds were still far from completion. They had insisted that Dunjee be their guest at Mr. Tikopoulous's place, where they could eat good Greek food, drink a little morning whisky, and throw cheap white plates at the feet of the singer.

It was the Hungarian who first noticed the young woman who was to lead Dunjee farther down the circuitous path to what he was looking for. She came in with another, slightly older woman just as Mr. Tikopoulous was delivering a fresh stack of plates to Dunjee's table.

"Well, look who's here," the Hungarian said. Mr. Tikopoulous turned, beamed in recognition, and hurried over to the two women, ushering them to a choice table near the small dance floor now littered with smashed crockery.

"Who's that?" Dunjee said as he took a plate from the new stack and tossed it toward the singer, where it shattered nicely at her feet. The singer smiled at him.

The Hungarian pursed his lips carefully, which was something he almost always did before delivering himself of one of his more weighty proclamations. Dunjee had discovered that the Hungarian never just said something. He instead issued declarations, edicts, and decrees. The Hungarian's name was Lou Zentai and he was called Hungarian Lou to distinguish him from Soldier Lou, another regular at the Embankment Sporting Club. Soldier Lou was an Englishman who had once done two hitches in the Foreign Legion, but didn't like to talk about it. Hungarian Lou, on the other hand, claimed to have been a freedom fighter in 1956 and bored everyone with tales of how brave he had been against the Soviet tanks.

"That," Hungarian Lou said, staring at the woman who had just come in, "is probably the most marvelous fuck in London."

He then looked at the Greek and let one eyebrow rise slightly. In response, the Greek's left eyelid dropped a fraction of an inch. They had agreed on something, although Dunjee couldn't quite decide what.

Dunjee turned his head to look at the woman more carefully. She had just enough weight on her small bones to escape being called lean, but it was a near miss. He watched her take off her jacket. Underneath, she wore a green silk blouse, its top three or four buttons carelessly left undone. Even from where Dunjee sat, the two small sharp breasts could be seen clearly through the thin silk. What he could see of her legs was slim and tanned. On her feet were green leather sandals. Her toenails were painted a bloody red.

The woman turned her head, caught Dunjee in his appraisal, and grinned. He would never see her smile. It was always that quick feral grin that revealed shiny, very white, curiously small teeth that looked extremely sharp. In repose, her full lips formed themselves into a child's pout. A spoiled child. She had a pretty chin and a very long neck and a nose that looked stuck up, but her best feature was her eyes. They were enormous, very brown, very moist, and quite wild. Had it not been for her pouty mouth, she would have looked perpetually startled. Instead, she just looked trapped. Dunjee thought he could guess by what.

"Looks expensive," he said as he turned back, took another

plate from the stack, and tossed it at the singer's feet, who rewarded him with yet another glorious smile.

"Not for you," the Greek said and smirked a little. The Greek's name was Anthony Perdikis. His profession was gambling. He also was part owner of a restaurant on the edge of Soho that he said he never went near. At forty-two, the Greek was sleek, black-eyed, bald, and just edging toward portliness.

Perdikis's smirk now turned into a warm and friendly smile. Too warm, too friendly, Dunjee thought. He was still smiling when he said, "Dear friend Chubb. You've had a terrible run of luck. Bloody terrible. But your bad luck has been our good fortune. So, Lou and I insist you accept our little gift of gratitude."

Perdikis turned and snapped his fingers for Mr. Tikopoulous, who hurried over. They spoke in Greek for almost a minute and it sounded to Dunjee the way Greek always sounded—as if some awful conspiracy were being hatched, possibly a revolution, at least a palace coup.

Mr. Tikopoulous, however, seemed delighted with whatever they were plotting, because he kept shooting sharp little glances at Dunjee and smiling and snickering a bit.

Eventually he went away but soon came back with a bottle of champagne and several glasses which he delivered with some ceremony to the table where the two women sat. They spoke briefly and Mr. Tikopoulous returned to Dunjee's table, bowed almost formally, and said, "The young ladies thank you, sir, most kindly for the wine and wonder if you'd care to join them in a glass."

"Our little gift of gratitude to you, friend Chubb," Perdikis said, his smirk back in place. "A little all-day-long gift from Lou and me."

Dunjee was about to turn it down with polite thanks when Hungarian Lou pursed his lips and delivered himself of yet another edict. "Keep away from her friends."

Dunjee immediately grew interested. "Why?"

"They're bad, that's why. Thieves, pimps, villains—that lot. All damn godawful bad."

"Well, she looks sort of interesting," Dunjee said. "There's just one thing wrong."

"What?" Perdikis said.

"I always pay for my own ladies."

The Greek managed to look hurt. "But she is our gift—Lou's and mine. It's all fixed."

Dunjee smiled and rose. "In the States, Tony," he said, making it all up, "it's considered bad luck to let anyone else pay for your woman."

Perdikis blinked at that, then nodded slowly. He was no longer offended. A gambler's superstition was something he could appreciate. "We'll see you tonight, of course."

"You bet," Dunjee said, picked up one of the last plates, and tossed it toward the singer, who gave him back another enormous smile.

When Dunjee reached the table, he looked down at the woman in the green silk blouse, but said nothing. He guessed her age accurately at twenty-five, and somehow he knew that within two years she would look ten years older than that.

She looked up at Dunjee with a careful stare, virtually an assessment. Then she made her lips and teeth form their foxy grin. "Too bad your taste in friends isn't as good as your taste in champagne," she said.

Dunjee sat down and poured himself a glass of the wine. "What's wrong with my friends?"

The woman shrugged. "What isn't?"

"Well, they won't be coming to my party."

"So it's *your* party now, is it?"

"My party."

"Just the two of us—or the three of us?"

Dunjee looked at the other woman. She was a pretty brunette, possibly foreign, with empty eyes and a soft, loose mouth.

"I think the three of us, don't you?" he said.

"Oh, absolutely," the woman in the green blouse said. "Three is much more fun than two. Much more. My name's Sloan. Vicki Sloan, and this is my friend, Sunday Smith. I'm not joking. That's really her name."

Sunday Smith seemed to feel that it was time for her to say something, so she said, "I like Americans," and ran her tongue slowly along her upper lip.

"What're you calling yourself this morning?" Vicki Sloan said.

"Dunjee. Chubb Dunjee."

She laughed. It was a loud laugh that started out soprano and wound up almost baritone. "You didn't make that up."

"Not at six in the morning."

"Chubb Dunjee," Sunday Smith said, as if it were her time to speak again. "That's really a super name."

The party got under way at almost half past six that morning in Dunjee's room on the sixth floor of the Hilton. It developed into a mild orgy that ended shortly before nine. The two women turned out to be more practiced than inventive, and during the French exhibition set piece Dunjee caught Sunday Smith yawning a little when she should have been writhing with lust.

By nine it was time to break the bad news and by then Dunjee had carefully made sure he was fairly drunk. It was something he'd never been able to fake very well. Vicki Sloan took the news hard. Extremely hard.

"What do you mean *you haven't got it?*" she said, almost screaming the last four words.

Dunjee looked up from the chair he had slumped into. He let his lips go loose and slack and grinned sloppily. "Temporary shortage of funds, love. That's all. You'll get your money. Only temporary."

She bent down over him naked, her two hands resting on the arms of the chair. Her face was less than a foot from his. He could smell her breath. It wasn't pleasant. Her eyes seemed furious, but when she spoke her voice was very low and quite controlled. "You owe us five hundred fucking quid, Jack."

Dunjee nodded agreeably. "Or a thousand dollars. Which-ever."

"When?" she demanded.

Dunjee wrinkled his forehead into thought. "When?" he repeated. "Yes, when? Well, noon, say. What about then? I'll have it by noon. Not to worry."

She stood up, shaking her head slowly as she gathered up her clothes and slipped into them. "I'm not worried," she said while dressing. "You're the one who'd better be worried. Where's your passport?"

"Get his fucking passport," Sunday Smith said.

Dunjee pretended that he couldn't remember where he had put it. All three searched the room until Dunjee finally looked under the mattress where he had slipped the passport earlier. "This what you want?"

Vicki Sloan snatched it away from him, examined it quickly, and then tucked it away in her purse. "If you want this back, you'd better be here at noon with the money. All of it."

"You'll be back at noon, huh?" Dunjee asked, knowing she wouldn't.

"Not me, love. Somebody else."

Dunjee decided it was time to get rid of them. He went around the two women to the door, turned back the locks, and unfastened the chain. "Well, I'll pay whoever shows up. Even offer him a drink—if he's a drinking man."

Vicki Sloan put her hand on the doorknob and stared up at him, still furious. "I wouldn't disappoint him, if I was you. He gets nasty vicious, he does, when he's disappointed."

She opened the door and went through it followed by Sunday Smith, who paused just long enough to say, "You don't have the money, Rollo, he'll cut your fucking heart out."

When they had gone, Dunjee closed the door and turned to survey his wrecked room. He thought about calling down for maid service, even for some breakfast, but decided against it, sat down on the bed, and lit a rare cigarette. A minute later he put the cigarette out and lay down. Three minutes later he was asleep.

He was still asleep when the determined knocking began on his door shortly before noon. It took several long moments before Dunjee became fully awake. He concluded that he felt somewhere between awful and terrible. He let the knocking go on for another few seconds, then rose and went into the bathroom to inspect himself in the mirror. He looked even worse than he felt—which was the way he expected to look. After splashing some cold water on his face and half drying it with a towel, Dunjee went to the door and opened it.

The man who stood there wore a gray tweed jacket and a ferocious scowl, but at the sight of Dunjee the scowl dissolved into a sad, lopsided grin. "God save us, lad, will you be dying on me this morning?"

"I might," Dunjee said. "Come on in."

The man followed Dunjee into the room and glanced around at the bottles and the smeared glasses and the twisted sheets. "Had a night of it, did we?"

"You her pimp?"

"I'm just a lost soul, brother, with the sad misfortune of being in love with a whore, and I'm fair dying for a drink." He took out Dunjee's passport and tossed it onto the writing desk. "My compliments."

Dunjee climbed onto the bed, reached up, and removed the air conditioning grille. He took out his wallet, put the grille back, and stepped back down to the floor. He opened the wallet as though to check its contents and let the man catch a glimpse of all the hundred-dollar bills it contained. "Let's have that drink," Dunjee said and started counting out ten of the bills.

The man turned toward the bottles. He was not quite as tall as Dunjee, but wider and at least seven or eight years younger. He had thinning blond hair and too much forehead and the sad eyes of a failed cleric. There was just enough chin and perhaps a bit too much mouth. He mixed the drinks deftly and handed one to

Dunjee, then raised his own glass and said, "To suicide, mate. I'm thinking you might drink to that this morning."

"I might," Dunjee said, formed the ten one-hundred-dollar bills into a small fan with one hand, and held them out to the man. There was a moment of hesitation before the man took the money and stuffed it down into his pants pocket.

"You overpaid, you know."

"I know," Dunjee said. "What's your name?"

"Harold Hopkins, sir, and notice how nicely I handle me aitches."

Dunjee nodded wearily, moved over to an armchair, and sank down into it. Hopkins sat on the edge of the bed. "I really love that bitch," he said. "Ain't that awful?"

Dunjee closed his eyes and leaned his head back. "How long were you inside, Harold?"

"Shows a bit, does it?"

"A bit. You're way too pale, even for London."

"Something fell off a lorry. I did fifteen straight without remission. Got out a fortnight ago."

"What fell off the truck, Harold?"

"A pearl necklace. Some gold and platinum bits and pieces. A few diamonds."

"I'm looking for somebody," Dunjee said, his eyes still closed.

"And who might that be?"

"A thief."

"Shame—an American gentleman like you."

"I'm looking for a good one, Harold," Dunjee said and opened his eyes.

After several moments Hopkins said thoughtfully, almost with dignity, "I'm a good one," and somehow Dunjee knew that he was.

11

When Thane Coombs, the Director of Central Intelligence, came into his large seventh-floor office in the Agency's Langley headquarters, he had to wake up the big bald-headed man who sat slumped asleep in the bolted-down armchair.

Six of the bolted-down chairs, all identical, formed a semicircle around Coombs's desk. They were the first thing he had ordered after being sworn in as DCI. The radius of the semicircle formed by the chairs was exactly six feet—which, Coombs had calculated, was exactly the distance needed to keep him from smelling the breath of others. As DCI, Coombs saw no reason why he should have to. He had a sensitive nose and wanted to use it to smell his roses—not breaths that reeked of cigarettes, alcohol, and decaying teeth, and especially not poor digestion brought on by ambition and fear and bad marriages.

As he walked over and snapped his fingers in the big man's left ear, Coombs wrinkled his nose because he could smell whisky and cigarettes and garlic and Scope and probably just a trace of marijuana. It was how the big man nearly always smelled.

The sleeping man's name was Alex Reese, and he awoke instantly without apology, but with his inevitable comment, "Must have dozed off there for a moment."

Reese could sleep anywhere, anytime, and often did. He stood six-four and weighed 270 pounds, and a lot of it, although not all, had settled around his gut. He was a man who scoffed at all gods and demons, held most of mankind in utter contempt, and wasn't particularly fond of animals. Nine years of his life had been spent with the FBI and twelve with the CIA. He drank a fifth of cheap whisky a day, much of it before noon, and had been hired by the CIA four times, fired three, and given two medals in private ceremonies, only to see them snatched back and locked away in the name of national security. He was forty-four years old, thrice married and divorced, and was now sexually inclined toward teen-age girls, whom he pursued shamelessly. Had it not been for his mind, he would have been impossible. His mind was extraordinary.

Coombs went behind his desk and sniffed suspiciously. "Tell me something," he said. "Do you ever bathe?"

"Every Saturday night," Reese said and then added because it was so old and awful, "whether I need it or not." After that he laughed his nerve-racking laugh which lay somewhere between a sea lion's honk and an old fox's sly bark.

Coombs sighed and sat down. Reese tried to hitch his bolted-down chair closer to Coombs's desk. The movement jarred the papers from his lap and they fell to the floor. Reese went down on his hands and knees to retrieve them. "What do you want to bolt these fucking chairs to the floor for anyway?" he said as he sat back down. "Afraid somebody's gonna crack a fart?"

Coombs closed his eyes and leaned back in his chair. "Just read what you have."

Reese picked up a legal-size sheet of paper from his lap and began reading an excerpt from a White House press conference that had been held twenty-two minutes before. He read in a bass monotone that was totally without inflection.

" 'Los Angeles *Times*: Mr. President, five days ago the Libyan delegation abruptly canceled its tour and flew back to Tripoli. My understanding is that the tour was canceled because your brother refused to let the Libyans go on a gambling junket to Las Vegas. Would you care to comment on that?'

" 'President: Not really. [Laughter.] I will say that I very much doubt that Bingo would ever try to prevent anyone from doing anything he wanted to do—especially gambling. As you know, my brother is something of a free spirit.' [Laughter.]

" 'United Press International: Mr. President, Frank Milroy, the Las Vegas Chief of Police, says your brother called him from Los Angeles to arrange maximum security for the Libyan delegation. But then the delegation never showed. Chief Milroy has been unable to reach your brother. My question, sir, is can you tell us where your brother is, or if he somehow offended or insulted the Libyan delegation?'

" 'President: That's two questions. First, Bingo doesn't check in with me; I check in with him. [Laughter.] I heard from him indirectly a few days back. He did not in any way offend the Libyan delegation, which, I understand, canceled the tour for reasons of its own.'

" 'Chicago *Sun-Times:* Could you tell us what those reasons were, Mr. President?'

" 'President: I'm afraid you'll have to ask the Libyan delegation that.' "

"He got off easy," Reese said as he put the paper back on his lap, took out a cigarette, lit it with a paper match, looked around for an ashtray, and, finding none, dropped the match on the carpet.

Coombs raised himself from his chair just enough to peer over the edge of his desk and make sure the match was out. As he sat back down, he said, "Quite remarkable. He managed to get through it without actually lying. What else?"

Reese didn't seem to hear the question. He was scratching his crotch and gazing up at the ceiling. "You know what? I think I got crabs."

"Give me strength," Coombs whispered.

Reese went on scratching earnestly until he smiled and sighed.

"Ahh! That's better." He looked at Coombs then, and the smile vanished. "You gave me this stack of shit when—five days ago? Yeah, five. You gave it to me because I don't leak and because I'm the only one who might bring it off. Well, I've come up with a few juicy items, but before we go into them I wanta talk about the payoff. I want London."

"Impossible."

"Fuck it then," Reese said and started to rise.

"Rome."

Reese sat back down. "London or nothing."

"Why not Rome? The climate is more salubrious, the food is infinitely better, the work is more rewarding. I'd far rather be chief of station in Rome than London."

"Pussy," Reese said. "They've got fourteen-, fifteen-year-old cupcakes in London who'll—"

"All right, London," Coombs said and whispered, "God forgive me."

"Wonderful," Reese said and split his face with a happy, yellowish smile. Above the smile was a big nose that leaned right, then left, then right again. On either side of it two secretive gray eyes gazed out on the world with what seemed to be total disbelief. Thick eyebrows like furry hedgerows guarded a forehead whose thought wrinkles went up and up, and then up some more until they reached where the hairline would have been, if there had been any hair, which there wasn't except for the grayish brown stuff that still sprouted around the ears and down on the nape of the neck. Below all this was an aggressive chin almost as big as a fist. It was an ugly, but somehow wise face, strangely medieval, and strangely corrupt.

"Item one," Reese said and flicked his cigarette ashes on the carpet. "Bingo's not in Libya any more."

"How do you know?"

"I got it off the Egyptians."

"Mercy!" said Coombs, making the word sound almost obscene.

90

"No choice."

"I don't accept that."

Reese didn't seem to care what Coombs accepted. "They came to me first. That slimy Wahab, remember him?"

Coombs nodded.

"He'd heard a rumor that the Israelis had snatched Felix. He wanted to know what we'd heard. I told him I'd look into it providing he'd check something out for me. Then I fed him this fairy tale about a prominent American who'd got lost or strayed in Libya. I told him I needed to know where the American was—exactly where. Well, we've got jack shit in Libya and the Gyppos know this, but still I thought my fairy tale maybe just might work. But when old slimy Wahab got back to me he was practically hysterical—giggling all over the place and smirking like Rumpelstiltskin. The 'prominent American,' he said, and I could just hear him wrapping the quotes around it, well, the 'prominent American' had been held in Tripoli for twenty-four hours and then moved—out of the country, except old Wahab, slick and slimy as he is, couldn't find out where. But he knows it's Bingo."

Coombs sighed. "How long?"

"Will he keep his mouth shut?"

Coombs nodded.

"Maybe a week. I told him there'd be a new 450 SE on his doorstep if he'd keep his mouth shut for a week and I'd break his fucking arm if he didn't. He might last a week; he might not."

Coombs nodded and made a note. "But the Egyptians now also think we have Felix?"

"Yeah, they think that because that's what the Libyans think. I let it lie."

"Good," Coombs said. "It's the only bargaining chip the President has." He put down his pencil and leaned back in his chair and inspected the back of his left hand. "Our task remains two-fold: first, find out who really has Felix and get him back, and second, determine exactly where the President's brother is being held captive." He shifted his gaze from his hand to Reese. It was a cold gaze, full of reproach, and the tone was even colder. "It would now seem that the sum total of our knowledge is that—one—Bingo McKay is no longer in Libya, although where he is, we haven't the slightest notion, and—two—you haven't even the vaguest clue as to where Felix might be or who might have abducted him."

"I'm working on that," Reese said and scratched an ear.

"Work a little harder."

"Another item," Reese said. "Paul Grimes."

Coombs's left eyebrow formed an interested arc. "Oh?"

"He saw the President just after you did, and then he started asking around town about Chubb Dunjee. Remember him?"

Coombs nodded thoughtfully. "Mexico."

"Yeah, Mexico. Well, Grimes flew to Lisbon and then took a taxi to Sintra, because that's where Dunjee was holed up. A day later, Dunjee flew into London."

"And Mr. Grimes?"

"He's there, too."

"Interesting. Mr. Dunjee. What's the current reading on him?"

"Whose?"

"The conventional wisdom."

"Everybody thinks he's a broken-down politician."

"And you?"

"Very smooth when he wants to be," Reese said. "Very slick. A side-stepper, an angle player. No pattern."

"A brilliant man?"

Reese thought about it. "Smart anyhow."

"Smart," Coombs said and made another note. "Well, let's do keep in touch with him. Loosely, of course."

"Right," Reese said, rose, and moved to Coombs's desk, where he held his inch-long cigarette ash threateningly over the polished surface until Coombs produced a small ceramic tray from a drawer. After Reese crushed out his cigarette he handed Coombs two closely typed pages.

"What's this?"

"Stray thoughts," Reese said. "Midnight musings. It's the only copy."

"Tell me."

"It's about the Libyan tour. Nobody's quite sure just how it got started."

"The Libyans asked for it."

Reese shook his head. "No they didn't."

Coombs frowned. "Let me think," he said. "The White House started dropping hints, as I remember. Or perhaps Bingo McKay did. It was really his show, his and the President's."

Again Reese shook his head. "That's not true either. I checked it out. It began as a rumor in New York, at the UN, as nearly as I can pin it down, although it's like trying to pin down a snowflake. But the rumor was simple. Oil for arms. The Libyans' oil, our arms. The same rumor popped up at almost exactly the same time in Rome, where all good Libyans still go for R and R. The Embassy there heard it, and then suddenly it becomes more than a rumor. It turns into a nice little story on page twenty-six of the New York *Times,* with a Rome dateline, which says that the Libyans have no intention of making a window-shopping tour of the U.S. The State Department replies politely in about two or three hundred words that the Libyans haven't been invited. And the whole thing dies—for about a week."

Coombs nodded, as though remembering. "Then what?"

"It was born again."

"A resurrection?"

"Just about."

"Who was . . . present?"

"The Ambassador in Rome, for one. He heard in a roundabout way that the Libyans were having second thoughts."

"He heard this from whom?"

"The Nigerians. The next thing you know there's a carefully drafted answer to a carefully planted question at a regular State press conference, which, in effect, says that State wouldn't have any objection to a *private* Libyan window-shopping expedition. Well, the guy over at State hardly gets the words out of his mouth before a couple of oil companies down in Houston issue an invitation to the Libyans. Other oil firms chime in, and Bingo McKay becomes the unofficial tour leader and the trip is on."

Coombs frowned as though having difficulty in adding up a column of figures. "How long did all this take?"

"From start to finish—about three months."

"But it died once."

"Twice, in fact."

"And the Nigerians were present at both resurrections?"

"Both."

"Have we talked to them?"

"I did. Both here and in New York. As best as their UN people can pin it down, they first heard the rumor from Gambia—although they won't bet the rent on that, because they think the rumor may have been floated simultaneously in Rome."

"Gambia," Coombs said thoughtfully. He stared at Reese and repeated to himself, "Gambia."

Reese said nothing. Instead, he lit another cigarette and said, "You got anything to drink around here?"

"Interesting," Coombs said, producing a pint bottle of California brandy from a bottom drawer. He put it next to the silver water thermos on his desk and watched disapprovingly as Reese poured a large measure into a glass. "We shouldn't forget that while the Libyans went window-shopping here," Coombs said, "Felix was being kidnapped in London. A coincidence perhaps, although I have long been convinced that nature abhors them, just as it does vacuums. They're unnatural."

"But they happen," Reese said, finishing off the brandy.

Coombs shrugged and in a thoughtful voice said, "Gambia," again.

"You finally get there after all, don't you?"

"Dr. Joseph Mapangou."

"A nasty little shit."

94

"But a useful conduit, I understand," Coombs said.

"So's an open sewer. Useful, I mean."

"Yes, well, I think someone had best have a chat with Dr. Mapangou." He looked at Reese. "What tribe is that, by the way?" he asked, hoping that Reese wouldn't know, but realizing that it was a vain hope.

"Mandingo," Reese said promptly. "If he wasn't a Mandingo, he wouldn't have made it to the UN."

"You *will* talk to him, won't you?"

"Mapangou?" Reese said. "Sure, I'll talk to him."

12

The retired Maltese smuggler was already past seventy and probably needed glasses, but his eyes were still keen enough to recognize easily the ninety-two-foot yacht with the raked stack. Not many of today's yachts had stacks raked like the one that had docked that morning. The old man remembered the yacht well, from when it had been built in Valletta under British supervision twenty-five years ago. Or was it twenty-six?

They had built it for the King, he remembered. The King of Libya. He tried to remember the King's name, but couldn't, so he gave up and felt content just to sit there on the quay with his back against the sun-warmed wooden crate and let his mind wander as he watched the three customs officials file aboard the yacht.

When the three customs officials hurried off the yacht less than ten minutes later, the old man suspected that each was probably richer by a few quid. He couldn't blame them. After all, who could really devote himself to a job that required harassing the rich and the powerful? And certainly the Libyans were now both.

The old man didn't much care for the Libyans, who had been swarming over Malta in recent years with their big talk and their big plans and their oil millions—although the big talk had lessened in recent months. But still he didn't much care for them—or the British or the Italians or the French, for that matter. The Krauts, too, he decided. They were all over the place nowadays. He didn't like them either.

The old man had long felt that there were still too many foreigners on Malta. Always had been. Now there were the Libyans and the German tourists and even the Americans with that dungaree factory of theirs. Not so many British any more, though. Not like twenty-five years ago when the British had built that yacht for King Idris.

The old man was pleased when the name of the deposed Libyan King came back to him so easily. But he knew that was the way it always worked. Try to think of it, and you couldn't. But let your mind go free, let it wander, let it soar a little like a gull riding the air, and it would pop right into your mind. Always. Well, nearly always.

The old man twisted himself into an even more comfortable position against the warm crate, took out a cigarette, and lit it with a French lighter. His name was Mario Cagni, but for years most people had called him Jimmy—or rather Jeemee—because of that American film actor, the one who always played the gangster who got killed, although the actor spelled his name differently—and pronounced it differently, too. But nearly everyone still called the old man Jimmy, although many, especially the young, no longer remembered why—or cared.

Cagni had been a smuggler—and a good one—for more than fifty years, and his interest in boats was more than casual. Retired now and living with his widowed daughter, who couldn't stand him underfoot all day, the old man spent much of his time down on the waterfront near the boats that for so long had been such an essential tool of his profession.

He had almost decided to rouse himself and head for his favorite cafe and his regular mid-morning cup of coffee when the Japanese went aboard the Libyan yacht. Cagni found that interesting. Not extremely so, perhaps, but interesting enough to keep him on the quay with his back against the warm crate and his eyes on the yacht. He lowered his eyes just long enough to take out a pencil and a scrap of paper and write down, "1 oriental (maybe jap?) 6 ft. w/ camera 10:17 a.m." Then he settled back with another cigarette to see if anything else interesting might happen.

At ten-twenty the German went aboard. At least he looked German to Cagni—all that blond hair, pale skin, and no neck. So he wrote down, "1 kraut (dutch?) 10:20 a.m. 12-13 stone, 5-10, tres blanc."

Cagni prided himself on his languages. He more or less spoke four, not including Maltese, and none of them particularly well. He prided himself most of all on his French, which had proved useful in his trade, especially when dealing with the Corsicans. And it was French he used to describe the young dark-haired woman who went aboard the yacht at ten forty-eight that morning. Cagni wrote down that she was "tres jolie."

After that, Cagni waited until half past eleven, but when nothing else interesting happened, he rose, stretched, and decided to go find the Pole and see whether he could sell him what he had seen.

During the reign of King Idris I, the yacht had been called *Sunrise I,* and the name had been lettered in gold on her stern and bow in both Arabic and English. Now she had been renamed the *True Oasis,* out of Tripoli, and all this had been gold-lettered in both English and Arabic in accordance with standard international maritime practice, although the English was noticeably smaller than the Arabic.

Down in the small cabin next to what once had been the royal stateroom, Ko Yoshikawa had his right eye pressed against the fish-eye security viewer that had been inset into the bulkhead. Through it Ko could watch as Dr. Abdulhamid Souri changed the dressing on the left side of Bingo McKay's head— the side where he no longer had an ear.

Since the abduction of Felix, Ko had assumed command of the fragmented Anvil Five after an election of sorts had been held in Rome. When the subject of who should lead the terrorist group had come up, Ko had been elected by acclamation, the votes consisting of a bored nod from the lashless German, Bernt Diringshoffen, and an indifferent shrug from the Algerian-born Françoise Leget.

In Rome they had screened four possible recruits to Anvil Five—three Italian communists and an American movement veteran. All had been rejected, the Italians because of provincialism, which meant that they had hinted they would like to be home in time for dinner every night, and the American because of dilettantism, which, in translation, meant he was strung out on hashish and Quaaludes and needed money to support his habit.

Ko turned from the fish-eye viewer to look at the lean, jittery Libyan with the tic near his left eye who perched on the edge of the steel-framed chair. The lean man was Ali Arifi, the Libyan Minister of Defense.

"You actually cut it off, didn't you?" Ko said as Diringshoffen rose and took his place at the viewer. Françoise Leget sat on the edge of the cabin's bunk smoking, her movements nervous and irritable.

Since Ko's question had been rhetorical, Arifi saw no need for a response other than a nod.

"And the Americans' reply?" Ko said.

"President McKay insists on talking to his brother before he will enter into any negotiations. Or so the Nigerians say."

"Felix is dead," Françoise Leget said.

Arifi looked at her in surprise and then at Ko. "She had a dream," Ko said. "In it, Felix was put into an American car and crushed into a cube by a car smasher. She believes in dreams."

So did Ali Arifi, but he saw no need to mention it. Instead, he looked at his watch and said, "I must be going."

"We should make them let us talk to Felix," Françoise Leget

said and stabbed out her cigarette. "It was a Chevrolet. The car Felix died in."

No one paid any attention to her. Bernt Diringshoffen turned from the viewer, an amused smile on his face. "They really cut it off," he said.

"The Nigerians will be handling the negotiations, right?" Ko said to Arifi.

Arifi nodded. "Their Ambassador to America is flying into Rome. A man called Dokubo. Olufemi Dokubo. He seems a sensible type, if a bit self-centered."

"You know him?"

"Yes."

"And Abedsaid is flying down from London when?" Ko was referring to Faraj Abedsaid, the Cultural Attaché in the Libyans' London Embassy.

"Sometime tomorrow," Arifi said. "He will be in full charge of our negotiations."

"We're wasting our time," Françoise Leget said. "Felix is dead."

"Shut up, Françoise," Ko said without looking at her. She turned and moved to the fish-eye viewer.

"The Americans aren't going to let us talk to Felix," Diringshoffen said. "They don't work that way."

"The Colonel insists on it," Arifi said. "He was adamant."

"Is he . . . upset?" Ko asked.

"He is furious."

Ko nodded, as though not surprised. "I think," he said, "I think we should give them some proof that McKay is still alive. A Polaroid picture of him holding today's newspaper should do. Then we could insist on similar evidence of Felix's well-being."

"Where is the woman?" Françoise Leget said, turning from the viewer.

"In the cabin on the other side of the stateroom," Arifi said.

"Do you let them have time together?"

"We let them have a few moments together earlier today."

"You should keep them separated," Françoise Leget said. "You should keep them separated and shackled and blindfolded most of the time. It destroys their morale."

The tic at the edge of Arifi's left eye began to throb. "Yes, well, you people are the experts in such matters. That is why you will be in charge of security."

"What about the crew?" Ko said.

"They and the soldiers are instructed to obey your orders and none is allowed ashore."

"Customs?"

"Generously bribed—but not so generously as to create suspicion."

"How long can we remain here in Valletta?" Ko asked.

"As long as necessary," Arifi said. "Rome is an easy flight. Communications with the Colonel in Tripoli are excellent. And the Maltese are both incurious and hospitable."

"How do we know your security is as good as you say it is?" Françoise Leget said around a cigarette that she was lighting.

"At least," Arifi said stiffly, "we have no informers in our midst."

Françoise Leget flushed and started to say something, but changed her mind and puffed furiously on her cigarette instead.

"Well," Arifi said as brightly as he could manage, "shall we drop in on Mr. McKay?"

It was Ko who took the Polaroid picture of Bingo McKay sitting in a chair and holding that day's front page of the *International Herald Tribune* up under his chin.

"Prove I'm still alive and kicking, huh?" he said.

"Yes, Mr. McKay," Arifi said. "That's the general idea."

"And these folks are what's left of that Felix bunch you told me about?"

"They will be in charge of security."

"They look like a right nice bunch of folks," Bingo said and winked at Françoise Leget.

"Does your ear pain you, m'sieu?" she said.

"Why, no it don't, little lady, but it was right nice of you to ask. Old Doc Souri here turned out to be a real fine ear slicer. Ever I want my other one cut off, I'll sure know where to go."

"I will be leaving you now, Mr. McKay, and returning to Tripoli," Arifi said.

"Well, it's sure been real nice talking to you, Minister. But like I said, you oughta do something about that tic—get the doc here to give you a shot or something before you go."

Arifi's left hand moved up to his left eye where the tic throbbed busily. "Goodbye, Mr. McKay."

"By the way, Minister, wouldn't be any chance of me getting a little drinking whisky just to keep the chill off, providing, of course, it don't cause you any religious problems. Wouldn't wanta do that."

"I'll . . . I'll see to it," Arifi said and hurried from the stateroom.

Bingo McKay stretched, smiled, and winked again at Françoise Leget. "Not on the Riviera, are we, little lady?" he said. "Reason I asked is you called me m'soo and that's French and so I figured maybe we were docked at Cannes or someplace nice like that."

Ko smiled, shook his head, and said, "Nice try, Mr. McKay."

McKay smiled back. "Call me Bingo."

The Pole that Mario Cagni, the retired smuggler, had gone in search of was actually a third-generation American from Pittsburgh with the Polish name of Frank Krystosik. He was in Malta as a systems analyst for the Alamo Manufacturing Company, which turned out Puncher blue jeans, and was the largest single private enterprise on the Maltese Islands. Krystosik was also a part-time spy for the CIA. At least, that was how he thought of himself. The CIA chief of station in Rome considered Krystosik to be an extremely low-grade asset of doubtful value, while CIA headquarters in Langley was scarcely aware of his existence.

Mostly, Krystosik was a filer of sporadic reports on the Libyans and their economic encroachment on Malta, which had been going on for several years. None of his stuff was particularly useful, and there was little of it that couldn't be found in either *The Economist* or the Rome dailies. But once in a great while Krystosik would turn up something mildly interesting and for that reason the Rome chief of station kept him on and even sent him a little money from time to time.

Krystosik used the money to set up what he thought of, but never revealed to another living soul, as the Krystosik Net. It was composed mostly of old smugglers like Cagni and retired British non-coms who had settled in Malta with their Maltese wives. They had discovered that almost anything they fed Krystosik, real or imagined, was good for at least a lunch and a pint or two and sometimes even a few pounds. The Krystosik Net would have been far larger had not the old smugglers and ex-non-coms jealously guarded its membership rolls. Attrition in the ranks of the net came about only by death or jail, and new members had to be voted in. There was a fairly lengthy waiting list.

Krystosik often used his lunch hour to rendezvous with his agents—a practice that was encouraged by the agents after they found that Krystosik could be counted on to pick up the check.

Cagni and Krystosik met at one o'clock that day in a cafe—not Cagni's regular place, but a far more expensive one that prided itself on its veal. Cagni had just had the veal and was now on his third glass of wine. Krystosik made it a rule never to drink with his agents. He had many rules like that, many of them borrowed from the complete and carefully collected paperback works of David St. John, the pseudonym of a convicted Watergate burglar.

At thirty-two, Krystosik was single, pudgy, and losing his hair. Because of his weight he had had only a salad for lunch. As Cagni finished his veal, Krystosik took off his tinted glasses, polished them, and then repolished them. He polished them yet another time, put them back on, and said, "Well, what've you got?"

Cagni used his right elbow to inch a folded newspaper toward

Krystosik. He had rescued the paper from a trash can and slipped his morning notes into it. Krystosik liked folded newspapers, and duplicate plastic briefcases, and twin cigarette packages—all examples of what he thought of as tradecraft. Cagni tried to please him.

Krystosik nodded significantly and let his right hand fall casually on top of the folded newspaper. Cagni swallowed the last of his third glass of wine and signaled for another.

"A Jap and a Kraut," he said after the wine had come. "Or maybe a Dutchman, and a woman, maybe French, maybe Spanish. All going aboard a Libyan yacht this morning within an hour of each other. What do you think of that, hey?"

Krystosik pushed out his lower lip and nodded significantly, indicating that he wasn't at all surprised by this new turn of events and their obviously dire implications. "It figures," he said.

"What does?"

But Krystosik only shook his head cryptically. Cagni wondered whether he should risk ordering yet another glass of wine, but decided against it. No need to go to the well too often. "It's the *True Oasis,*" he said.

"What?"

"The name of the yacht. It used to be *Sunrise One,* but now it's the *True Oasis.* I wrote it all down in there. Should be worth a little extra something, hey?"

Krystosik picked up the folded newpaper with his left hand and reached into his pants pocket with his right. He rose and extended his right hand to Cagni. It was now almost clenched into a fist because of the bill he was trying to palm, but Cagni was used to the American's clumsiness. The old man palmed the bill smoothly, transferred it to his own pocket, then picked up the luncheon check and handed it to Krystosik. "You almost forgot this."

Once outside the cafe, Cagni looked at the bill. An American twenty. The man's a complete fool, he thought happily, and headed back down toward the waterfront to the warm wooden crate where he would wait and watch some more.

That evening at the Alamo Manufacturing Company, after everyone had gone for the day, Krystosik locked the door to his office, unzipped his portable Lettera typewriter, and proceeded to translate Cagni's note into what he considered proper espionagese.

When he was through typing he carefully burned Cagni's notes in an ashtray, went into the men's room, and flushed the ashes down the toilet. He then went back to his office and typed out the Rome accommodation address on a plain white envelope.

With luck, the letter would be in Rome the day after tomorrow and delivered the day after that, depending on the mood of the Rome postal workers. Actually, it was to take four days for the letter to reach the Rome accommodation address. And it wasn't until a day later that the CIA chief of station there finally saw it. But by then Chubb Dunjee had already arrived in Rome.

13

The apartment building was fairly new—new for South Kensington anyway—and the Saudi who owned it was from Jidda on the Red Sea. Although the rents were well up in the stratosphere, it didn't seem to bother any of the tenants, nearly all of them from the Middle East, and there was a long waiting list, possibly because the place was completely staffed by Arabic-speaking personnel who were, to a man, impecunious if distant members of the Saudi landlord's enormous family.

Holding down the reception desk when Chubb Dunjee and Harold Hopkins, the thief, walked in at 2 P.M. wearing their gray coveralls with "Belgravia Locks Ltd." stitched in red across their backs, was Saleh Khoja, the landlord's twenty-seven-year-old third cousin on Khoja's father's second wife's side.

Hopkins, followed by Dunjee, moved over to the desk, set his tool kit down, fumbled in his breast pocket for a folded sheet of paper, and spread it out on the countertop. He looked at Khoja suspiciously.

"You in charge, mate?" Hopkins said in the extra loud voice he always unconsciously used when addressing those who came from across the sea.

Khoja leaned on the counter and looked off into space. "I am in charge," he said.

"I got an order here to install two new deadbolts on 531," Hopkins said, reading from the form, which was headed "Work Order, Belgravia Locks Ltd." Hopkins squinted at the name written on the form. "Mr. Faraj Abedsaid, if that's how you pronounce it."

"I know nothing about it," Khoja said and yawned.

"You know nothing about it, huh?"

"Nothing."

Hopkins nodded as if that was exactly what he had expected and turned to Dunjee. "You hear that, Ralph? He don't know nothing about it. He just works here. He's just the chief counter holder-downer."

Dunjee shrugged.

"Let's go," Hopkins said and picked up his tool case.

"You cannot go up," Khoja said, examining the fingernails on his left hand. "It is not permitted."

Incredulity spread over Hopkins' face. "Up! You hear that, Ralph? Abdullah here thinks we're going *up*. We're not going *up*. We're going back to the shop and ring up Mr. Abedsaid at the Embassy and tell him it's a no go at Cameldrivers' Towers and he can bloody well wait another two months to have his locks changed, and if somebody keeps on breaking in and stealing things, then maybe he better talk to the man in charge, which is you, idn't it?"

Khoja frowned. "Stealing?"

"Got the stereo the other night, they did. Right, Ralph?"

Dunjee nodded.

"I had not heard," Khoja said.

"Well, he's not going to be spreading it around now, is he? Not likely." Hopkins gave the counter a pat of finality. "But you can explain it all to him. Just tell him we wouldn't go up without your okay. Tell him to give us a ring. We can be back in a month or two." Hopkins turned away.

"Wait," Khoja said.

Hopkins turned back.

"I can ring him."

"Ring him?"

"Yes. The telephone. Here."

"Well, that's an idea now, isn't it? You got his private number?"

"Private number?"

"At the Libyan Embassy. Here." Hopkins dug out the work order and again spread it in front of Khoja, pointing to a telephone number.

"Ah, yes. His private number."

Hopkins and Dunjee watched Khoja dial the number. It was answered on the second double ring. Khoja started out hesitantly in English and then with obvious relief switched quickly into voluble Arabic. The conversation went on for several minutes.

After Khoja hung up he turned back to Hopkins. "You can go up."

"You talked to him, did you?"

"To his assistant."

"Miss Salem?"

"You know her?"

"She's the one who called in the order."

"She gave me instructions," Khoja said. "You are to clean up afterwards. You are to leave no mess. She was very firm."

"We never leave any mess, Jack," Hopkins said and turned toward the elevator.

It was a two-room apartment, or possibly three, counting the small kitchen, which contained some cheap china and stainless steel flatware, a few glasses, and by way of nourishment two containers of frozen orange juice and a jar of instant coffee.

Dunjee watched Hopkins work. Hopkins was both methodical and fast. The kitchen took him only two minutes, and his search included a careful inspection of the oven as well as a fast but thorough look into the small space behind the refrigerator.

Hopkins moved into the living room shaking his head. "Nothing—except it'd be ducky if I knew what the hell I was looking for."

"I don't know," Dunjee said.

A small kneehole desk was positioned in front of the windows. Hopkins crossed over and tried the drawers. They were locked. He took a small length of thin steel from his pocket and with a quick move that was almost too fast to follow snapped the desk lock open. He looked up at Dunjee. "You take the desk," he said.

Hopkins began his search of the living room while Dunjee sat behind the desk and started opening drawers. In the bottom drawer was a thick unsealed envelope. In it was a sheaf of five- and ten-pound notes. Dunjee tossed them onto the desktop. "Here," he said.

Hopkins rolled back a small, cheap Oriental rug he'd been looking under, moved to the desk, picked up the envelope, and looked inside. "Nice," he said and stuck the envelope down into his coverall pocket.

The rest of the desk's contents included a Lloyds Bank checkbook, blank envelopes, stationery, stamps, some dried-out ballpoint pens, and a small key which Dunjee tossed onto the desktop. "What's this for?" he said.

Hopkins came over to look at it. "A tin box. Or maybe a briefcase. I'll try the bedroom."

While Hopkins was gone, Dunjee reopened each of the desk's seven drawers and ran his hand under their bottoms. He then took each drawer all the way out to see whether anything had been taped to their ends. He was putting the last drawer back when Hopkins came in from the bedroom carrying a small gray steel box.

"In the wardrobe," he said. "Back behind the luggage."

Hopkins used the key to open the steel box. When he saw what its contents were, he wrinkled his nose and spun the box around so Dunjee could look. The box's contents consisted mostly of pictures, eight-by-ten glossies. The pictures were of nude young girls, most of them in their early teens. All were engaged in various homosexual practices. All looked very English. Dunjee sighed and started examining each picture, both back and front. There were forty-two pictures. On the back of the thirty-ninth picture was the name Frank and a phone number written in pencil. With another sigh, Dunjee copied it down into his address book.

The rest of the steel box's contents consisted of papers for a 450 SLC Mercedes; a .25-caliber Colt automatic, loaded; a switchblade knife with a six-inch blade and a broken spring; a cheap souvenir metal model of the Eiffel tower; a small suede drawstring bag that felt heavy, and a breast-pocket-size notebook whose leather cover was embossed in gold with "Organize Your Day."

Dunjee thumbed through the notebook. What few entries there were were written in Arabic. He put the notebook into a coverall pocket, picked up the drawstring bag, opened it, and dumped its contents on the desk. Twenty gold Krugerrands spilled out. Dunjee had just finished stacking them into two neat piles when Hopkins came out of the bedroom again shaking his head. At the sight of the gold he stopped shaking his head and smiled.

"Makes you want to go to church, doesn't it?" Hopkins said as Dunjee shoved the two stacks of gold coins toward him.

"What about this?" Dunjee said, indicating the .25-caliber pistol.

"You mean if I were on me own?"

Dunjee nodded.

"I'd take it. Might fetch a few quid."

Dunjee shoved the pistol into a hip pocket, repacked the contents of the steel box carelessly, and handed it to Hopkins, who took it back into the bedroom. He came out just as the polite knocking at the door began.

They looked at each other. "I'm not looking to go back inside, friend," Hopkins said and held out his hand. Dunjee took the pistol from his hip pocket and handed it to him.

Hopkins moved to the door, the pistol in his right hand and behind his back. He used his left hand to open the door.

"Well?" Hopkins said.

Dunjee thought that the voice in the hall seemed to be all adenoids. "He told me to bring it up."

"Who told you?" Hopkins said.

"The wog at the desk."

"Bring what up?"

"The tickets. You Mr.—wait a sec—Abedsaid? You don't look like no Mr. Abedsaid."

"What kind of tickets?" Hopkins said.

"Airline tickets. These."

"I'll give 'em to him," Hopkins said.

"You gotta sign."

"Me guvnor does all the signing," Hopkins said and opened the door wide enough to let in a skinny fifteen-year-old with a face full of angry pimples and know-it-all brown eyes. The eyes swept the room and settled on Dunjee. "You the signer?"

Dunjee nodded.

The messenger handed him a thick blue envelope, produced a receipt book, found the right page, and offered it to Dunjee along with a ball-point pen. Dunjee read the receipt carefully and then signed "Arsène Lupin" on the indicated line and handed it back. The youth read the name, moving his lips. He stared at Dunjee. "That French?"

Dunjee smiled.

The messenger turned to Hopkins. "What's the matter, don't he speak English?"

Hopkins jerked his head toward the door. "Out."

"What about me generous gratuity?" the messenger said. "That's how I take care of me old mum. We'd starve, we would, sir, mum and me, if it wasn't for generous gratuities."

Hopkins dug down into his pocket, found fifty pence, and slapped it into the youth's outstretched palm. "Out."

"Leggo my arm," the youth said as Hopkins steered him

111

through the door and slammed it shut. He moved back to the desk, took the pistol from his pocket, and offered it to Dunjee.

Dunjee again put the pistol away in a hip pocket, picked up the thick blue envelope, ripped it open, and examined the enclosed ticket.

"Where to?" Hopkins asked.

"Rome," Dunjee said. "First class."

14

They had slipped the Belgravia Locks Ltd. coveralls off in the Volvo Dunjee had rented and stored them in the car's trunk. Back up in his room at the Hilton, Dunjee dialed a number while Hopkins counted the Krugerrands.

"What's gold bringing?" Hopkins asked.

"Eight-oh-two, the last I noticed," Dunjee said and listened to the phone ring. It was answered just before the third ring by Delft Csider with her usual noncommittal "Yes."

"You were great," Dunjee said.

"I got tired of waiting in that phone booth."

"Sorry," he said. "How are you at wheedling?"

"Try me."

"There's an Alitalia flight to Rome tomorrow morning at eight forty-five, flight 317. I want seat three-B for myself in first class. And I want the two seats just across the aisle from me for my secretary, D. Csider, and my associate, H. Hopkins. Hold on." He looked at Hopkins. "You got a passport?"

"Rome?" Hopkins said.

"Rome."

Hopkins thought about it. "I got a passport," he said.

"He's got one. Second, I need something else from that instant printer of yours who did the locksmith thing."

"What?"

"A couple of dozen letterheads. Make them read 'Anadarko Explorations, Inc.' Think up some address and phone number for Tulsa. I want letters typed on each one—some long, some short. My name below as president."

"Anyone going to be reading the letters?"

"Maybe just the salutations. They should include a lot of names and addresses in Kuwait, Oman, and maybe Nigeria."

"Anything else?"

"Is Grimes around?"

"He'll be back at four."

"Tell him I'll either see him or talk to him then."

"I'll tell him. Where do you want to stay in Rome?"

"Some place expensive."

"The Hassler do?"

"Perfect."

"I'll try," she said. "What else?"

"Let's have dinner."

"Seven?"

"Fine. I'll either see you or call you by five."

After they said goodbye, Dunjee hung up the phone and turned to Hopkins. "Five thousand for Rome plus expenses."

"Rome, is it?"

"Rome."

"Might see the Colosseum."

"Don't bank on it."

"Be too busy, will we?"

"I don't know."

Hopkins stacked the twenty Krugerrands into one pile. "At 802 an ounce that's 16,040 dollars. There was another nine hundred quid in that envelope you found. You want a slice?"

"No."

"You're making me rich, Mr. Dunjee, sir."

"I know."

Hopkins used his forefinger to knock the pile of gold coins over. "When will we be getting to the nasty part?"

"Maybe in Rome. Maybe not. I don't know."

"Never been to Rome."

"You'll like it."

Hopkins nodded. "I'll go. You know why?"

"Why?"

"Because I'm greedy, I am."

"Everybody is," Dunjee said, took out his address book, and turned to the page where he had written the name "Frank" and a telephone number. He stared at the number for several moments, then shrugged, picked up the phone, and dialed.

When a man's voice said hello, Dunjee said, "Frank?"

"Frank, is it?" the man said.

"That's right."

"The Kraut, you mean?"

"Frank won't like that."

"What?"

"You calling him a Kraut."

"You're a Yank, aren't you?"

"Right."

"I never knew a Yank yet who minded being called Yank, so why should a Kraut mind being called Kraut?"

"Well, you know Frank."

"I know he owes me fifty quid in rent and I've got his stuff locked away in the bin down in the cellar and if that's what you're calling about, I'm thinking you'd better be bringing it along."

"Fifty? Frank didn't say it'd be that much."

"Fifty it is. I keep records. All down in black and white."

"Well, Frank wants his stuff, so I'll come up with it somehow. You take a check?"

"No checks."

Dunjee sighed. "I guess you'd better give me that address

again. Frank wrote it down on the back of a napkin and you know how Germans write—all spikes and squiggles."

The man on the telephone recited an address and Dunjee wrote it down. "I'll be there in half an hour."

"With the fifty quid."

"With the fifty quid."

After he hung up, Dunjee showed the address to Hopkins. "Bayswater," Hopkins said. "Not far—maybe five minutes. Who's Frank?"

"I haven't the slightest idea. He seems to be German and his name was written on the back of one of those girlie pictures."

"So what's the fifty quid going to buy?"

Dunjee shrugged. "Let's go find out."

The old house was on a dead-end street called Caroline Place. The landlord was a fifty-six-year-old man whose bulging brown eyes gave him a perpetually startled look, which may have been caused by a bad thyroid, or by the awful surprise that life had handed him. His name, he said without being asked, was Mr. Thumbolt and wasn't it too bad how the niggers were ruining the country. "I keep 'em out of here though," he said, adding sadly, "Most of the time."

"You said fifty," Dunjee said.

"Fifty. Twenty-five per. In advance. He missed one week and I didn't think nothing about it because he was always in and out—you know, sleeping here only one, two, maybe three nights a week. But after he didn't show for eleven straight days and no word, well, I packed him up and locked him away in the bin."

"Frank said he owes only one week."

"I got it down in black and white."

"Let's take a look," Dunjee said.

Mr. Thumbolt limped to a desk in the cluttered ground-floor bed-sitter and flipped open a gray ledger with red leather corners. "Right here," he said, jabbing his finger at a name. The name was Frank Glimm, and Dunjee ran his eyes over the dates of payment and learned that Glimm had been renting the third-floor bed-sitter for three months.

"That's not two weeks," Dunjee said. "That's eleven days."

"One day to move him out and clean it up, right? Another day to show it, right? Another day before the new one can move in, right? That's three days. Three plus eleven is fourteen. Two into fourteen makes seven. Seven days in a week at twenty-five per, times two, makes fifty."

"Frank isn't going to like this, is he, Ralph?" Dunjee said to Hopkins.

"He'll scream," Hopkins said. "Close, Frank is. Very close."

"Tell him to come scream at me," Mr. Thumbolt said.

Dunjee took fifty pounds from his pocket in one- and five-pound notes and counted them slowly onto the desk. "There's your fifty. Where's his stuff?"

"Bit of a walk," Mr. Thumbolt said and limped out of the room and down the hall. Dunjee and Hopkins followed. "Got this in Africa, I did," Mr. Thumbolt said, giving his limping left leg a slap. "Bloody Krauts anyway."

At the end of the hall he opened a door, switched on a light, and started down a flight of stairs. The cellar was crammed with discarded furniture. In one corner old bed slats had been used to build a floor-to-ceiling bin. The bin was full of suitcases, trunks, and cardboard boxes tied with string. Mr. Thumbolt produced a ring of keys and used one to unlock a padlock on the bin's chicken-wire door.

"I flog everything they leave behind but the luggage," he said. "Chap over in the Portobello Road gives me a price. Wirelesses, gramophones, irons, pots and pans, things like that. One of these days I'm going to flog this lot off." He pointed to two large suitcases, not new. "That one and that one."

Dunjee took one; Hopkins the other. Both were heavy.

"Frank said something about a cardboard box," Dunjee said.

"No box," Mr. Thumbolt said firmly.

"No box. I'll tell him that."

"What about the wireless," Hopkins said. "Frank said he had himself a nice little Grundig."

"He's a liar," Mr. Thumbolt said. "No pots, no pans, not a dish, and just a couple of glasses. He says he had a wireless, you tell him I say he's a liar."

"I'll tell him," Hopkins said.

"What about mail?" Dunjee said as they went back up the stairs.

"No mail. Never got any mail."

"Well, he was never one to write," Hopkins said.

The suitcases weren't locked. They opened them on Dunjee's bed in the Hilton. There was nothing in the first suitcase except clothing—most of it of Italian and French manufacture. It had been packed carelessly. None of it was expensive. Dunjee went through each pocket, turning them inside out when he could, and even checking the waistbands of the trousers. He found nothing except three French francs.

Hopkins found the heavy steel box in the second suitcase. There were scratches around its lock. It looked as though some-one had used a screwdriver or a chisel in an attempt to pry up one corner. The attempt had failed. There were four round dents in the top of the box where it had been struck by some-thing, possibly a ball-peen hammer.

"How'd you know there was a box?" Hopkins said.

"I didn't."

"You asked him about it."

"I asked him about a cardboard box."

"Well, he sure had a go at this one. Nice little box." He weighed it in the palm of one hand. "Quarter-inch steel, or I'm a liar."

"What about the lock?"

Hopkins used both hands to raise the box up to eye level. He stared at the lock. "Very pretty. Looks German. Or Swiss. They make 'em and the French buy 'em to hoard their gold in. Or so I hear. No gold in this one though. Not heavy enough."

The steel box was not quite as large as those that cigars come in and not nearly as deep—no more than an inch or so. Hopkins put the box back down on the bed, took out his wallet, and selected a steel pick. He knelt and began to probe the lock with his pick. "Tricky little bastard," he said. "It's Swiss."

"How can you tell?"

"I can tell."

Dunjee lit his third cigarette of the day. It took him seven minutes to smoke it. A minute after he had ground it out in a tray Hopkins said, "Ah!" He looked up at Dunjee. "It's open," he said.

"It's not open."

"All you have to do is lift up the lid."

"Well, lift it up."

"I'm going to take a stroll down the hall, mate."

"You want me to lift it up?"

"That's up to you," Hopkins said. "When I was inside, a pal of mine told me about a box like this. Described it exactly, he did. Last thing he ever saw."

"Blind?"

"Blind. Boom, it went. Little glass fragments. Acid all over his face and in his eyes. He was a right mess."

"Take your walk," Dunjee said, went over to the bed, picked up a pillow, and placed it over the box.

"Well, I'll just go over here in the corner."

Dunjee felt around underneath the pillow until he had a grasp on the lid. He pressed the pillow down hard, turned his head, and squeezed his eyes shut. He relaxed his pressure on the pillow, lifted the lid up quickly, then slammed it and the pillow down again, his eyes still closed. Nothing happened. Dunjee backed quickly away.

"You lift it up?" Hopkins said.

"I lifted it."

"How far?"

"An inch. At least an inch."

"Not to worry then." Hopkins crossed over to the bed, tossed the pillow aside, turned the box around, and lifted the lid. "Aw shit," he said, turning away in disgust.

"More pretty girls?" Dunjee said.

"How'd you know?"

"I didn't."

Dunjee sat down on the bed, took the pictures out, and looked at each one, both back and front. These were five-by-seven glossy prints. Some were the same poses and participants as he had seen in the box in Abedsaid's apartment. Others were different. There were twenty-four of them. Dunjee put them aside.

There were two envelopes in the box. One was sealed; the other wasn't. In the unsealed envelope were six Polaroid color pictures. They showed some people at a sandy beach, all of them in swimsuits. There were two women and two men. One of the men was Oriental. The other man was pudgy with unkempt hair that came down almost to his jaw line. The pudgy man wore sunglasses. Five of the pictures were of the group of four. The sixth picture was of a man lying naked in a bed. He was smiling at the camera and pointing at his erection. The smiling man was blond, in his late twenties, and looked hard-muscled.

"Want to see what Frank looks like?" Dunjee said, holding out the picture.

"Shame on him," Hopkins said. "He hasn't got all that much to be smiling and pointing about. How do you know it's Frank?"

"I'm guessing."

Dunjee ripped open the sealed envelope. Inside were twenty-five very new, quite crisp hundred-dollar bills. "You got lucky again, Harold," he said and handed the bills to Hopkins.

"Lord love us," Hopkins whispered and started counting the money.

Dunjee looked again at the front of the envelope that had contained the money and then at its back. He took a final look inside. Down in the far left corner was a folded piece of paper, no larger than a postage stamp. He unfolded it carefully. It was a ruled piece of paper, apparently torn from a spiral notebook. On

120

it written in pencil were two capital letters, "G. G." Then an address: "18 via Corrado."

Hopkins looked up from his money. "Anything?"

"An address."

"Where?"

"Rome," Dunjee said. "If we're lucky."

Hopkins looked down at the money in his hand, then over at the open metal box, and then back at Dunjee. He shook his head slowly. "You've got luck you don't even know about yet, mate."

15

The Boeing 727 from which the man called Felix had fallen a little more than a mile into the sea landed at Newark International Airport at 7:04 P.M.—approximately the same time that the apartment of Faraj Abedsaid, the Libyan Embassy's Attaché (Cultural Section), was being burgled in South Kensington.

The 727 landed at Newark rather than at Kennedy International because harassment of the plane's passengers and crew was only pro forma at the New Jersey airport. Some time back its officials, both municipal and federal, had discovered that if they merely fumbled through the motions of carrying out their duties after the plane landed, a plain white envelope would arrive in the mail at each of their homes three days later—or sometimes four—depending on the postal service. In each envelope would be five hundred-dollar bills.

So now when the 727 flew in from the island Democratic People's Republic, the plane's crew and passengers were almost feted. In fact, one U.S. customs officer had been overheard saying to a colleague, "Get out of the way, nigger. Here comes Mr. Keeling. Lemme at him." And Franklin Keeling, the ex-CIA man, had been taken into the search room, given a perfunctory pat or two, and a nip from the customs officer's half pint of vodka. Similar treatment was also awarded Jack Spiceman, the ex-FBI agent, and the plane's sixty-three-year-old pilot and sixty-five-year-old co-pilot who once had flown for Pan Am and TWA respectively.

When the 727 had flown into Newark International that first time nearly two years ago, the U.S. government had tried to scize it on the presumption that it would help pay up at least some of the $22 million in back federal taxes, which was the IRS's mysterious estimate of what was owed by Leland Timble, the exiled bank robber and computer genius.

Timble had bought the 727 for cash in 1979 from the estate of an overdosed rock star. What the U.S. government hadn't then known was that Timble had quickly sold the plane for one dollar to the island Democratic People's Republic and immediately leased it back for a million dollars a year.

The plane now composed one-fourth of the island Democratic People's Republic's air force, the other three-fourths consisting of a DC-3 with clapped-out engines and two small Cessnas. Seventy-five percent of the annual million-dollar leasing fee went into the Republic's coffers. The other 25 percent was spread around among the Prime Minister, the Minister of the Interior, the Minister of National Security, and the Prime Minister's brother-in-law, who had resigned his bartending job to become Minister of Air and Space.

While pondering the legality of the transaction, the U.S. government had detained Keeling and Spiceman, as well as the two superannuated pilots, in a cheap motel near the airport. Keeling and Spiceman had used the time to ingratiate themselves with the airport's key personnel, both federal and municipal. Five days later the U.S. Attorney General himself had ruled—reluctantly, it was said—that the buy and lease-back transaction was perfectly legal. Spiceman, Keeling, and the two pilots were released. By then the ingratiation process had cost Keeling $9,769. He itemized it on his expense account as "hospitality for others."

As was their usual practice, the elderly pilot and co-pilot went through customs and immigration first. Later that evening the pilot would bowl a few lanes while the co-pilot sought out the nearest meeting of Alcoholics Anonymous. Afterwards, they would meet for a late dinner, go back to the airport, and sleep on the plane. Both were divorced—the pilot thrice, the co-pilot four times. Their combined monthly alimony payments came to nearly four thousand dollars, and neither had much to do with women any more.

It took Keeling and Spiceman longer to get through the airport because they had to butter up various officials and inquire about their families. Once outside, they climbed into the rear of a waiting rented stretched Cadillac limousine.

As the limousine pulled away, Keeling pressed the button that lowered the dividing glass and said, "How are you, Henry?"

"Just fine, Mr. Keeling," the driver said.

"You bring the dry ice?"

"It's up here in the Styrofoam thing."

Keeling reached into his breast pocket, brought out two metal tubes, the kind that cigars sometimes come in, and handed them to the driver.

"Jesus, they're cold!"

"They're frozen," Spiceman said. "We want to keep 'em that way."

"Yes, sir," Henry said, opened the Styrofoam container, and carefully placed the two metal tubes on the steaming dry ice. After making sure that Henry refastened the lid securely, Keeling pressed the button that raised the dividing window, and leaned back in his seat to enjoy the ride.

The co-pilot arrived ten minutes early at the AA meeting, which was being held that night in the basement auditorium of the nearby Sinai Temple. He poured himself a cup of coffee, picked out two sugar cookies that looked home-baked, and went in search of a pay phone, which he found in the hall.

He ate one of the cookies first, took a sip of the coffee, looked at his watch, put the coffee and the remaining cookie down on a chair, dropped some coins into the telephone, and dialed a number, which was answered with a hello halfway through the first ring.

"Room 542," the co-pilot said. "The Gotham, ten P.M., Mr. Minder."

"Minder?" the voice that had said hello asked.

"Minder."

"Thank you," the voice said, and the phone went dead.

The co-pilot picked up his coffee and the cookie, which he ate as he wandered back into the auditorium. It was beginning to fill up. The co-pilot's practiced eye spotted the fresh fish coming through the door. The fish was a shaky forty-two-year-old male who looked pale and sick and terribly frightened. The co-pilot guessed that the fish was less than a week off a six-month drunk.

The co-pilot's mouth spread itself into a wide, warm smile as he moved over to the fish, stuck out his hand, and said, "Hi. I'm Don. How's it going, pal—a little rough?"

The man who had taken the telephone call from the co-pilot was Gambia's permanent representative to the United Nations, Dr. Joseph Mapangou, who lived far above his means in a $2,150-a-month one-bedroom-with-den apartment on East 60th, which almost, but not quite, commanded a view of Central Park.

During his nine years in New York, Dr. Mapangou had built the reputation of being one of the UN's most charming and lavish hosts. There was some small argument over whether he actually spent more than the Kuwait delegation, but there was no argument at all over his ranking as the UN's most delightfully wicked gossip.

As the principal representative of Africa's smallest nation, Dr. Mapangou's official duties and obligations were minimal, almost non-existent, and he had spent his first two years at the UN simply making friends, which he did with remarkable ease. For

Dr. Mapangou was a naturally gregarious man, totally without pretense, who found everyone equally fascinating. He also was a true democrat, perhaps the only one accredited to the UN, and certainly the only delegate who still believed that the organization was really the parliament of the world.

It was perhaps because of his innocence that others confided in Dr. Mapangou. They told him their most awful secrets even though they knew he simply could not keep his mouth shut. And because he revealed everything he knew to others, they, in turn, confided in him even darker secrets, which he cheerfully recounted to anyone who would listen.

The Italians, of course, had been the first to recognize Dr. Mapangou's true value. The Italians were having a minor but irritating problem with a stubborn delegate from Somalia. Over an expensive lunch at Lutèce, the Italians had whispered to Dr. Mapangou about the Somalian delegate's shocking peculations. By nightfall it was all over the UN. By the next morning it had reached Mogadishu, and by that afternoon the Somalian delegate had been ordered home, much to the Italians' immense satisfaction.

Indeed, so grateful were they to Dr. Mapangou for his small favor that the Italians sent him an expensive silver coffee service. Dr. Mapangou immediately pawned it for four hundred dollars, which he needed to help pay the rent on the third-floor walk-up in the East Village where he then lived.

During the next few years, Dr. Mapangou became the UN's unofficial clearinghouse for rumor and innuendo of the base, vicious, and scurrilous kind. He was valued and even respected for two qualities: first, his meticulous accuracy, and second, his refusal ever to reveal his sources. Because of all this, he was not only tolerated but indeed encouraged by the spies and rumor-mongers who made extensive use of his services and rewarded him with expensive and easily pawnable gifts that Dr. Mapangou used to help finance his increasing social responsibilities.

On the anniversary of his seventh year at the UN, Dr. Mapangou found himself immensely popular and nearly ninety thousand dollars in debt—all because of his lavish hospitality. The exact figure of his debts was $89,831.19, and it stared up at him in red from the Litronix pocket calculator that rested on his desk next to the stack of bills and nasty letters from assorted collection agencies.

It was the morning after the party he had given himself in observance of his seventh anniversary with the UN and he was still in his pajamas. Around him in his East Village living room was all the depressing evidence of the previous night's party. During the party he had gleaned one delicious item that he knew would be worth at least a thousand dollars to the East Germans. But what good would a thousand dollars do? Dr. Mapangou pressed the C button on the calculator, which erased the hateful $89,831.19 figure. Three tears began to roll down his plump cheeks as he picked up his breakfast, which consisted of a piece of stale toast that he dipped into the remains of last night's caviar. He was still sniffing back his tears and chewing on the toast and caviar when the pounding began at his door.

Dr. Mapangou didn't bother to put on a robe. Instead, he wiped away the tears with a used cocktail napkin and went to the door in his pajamas. He knew who it was. It was the police. They had come to seize him, to clap him into some kind of debtors' prison. He opened the door. A big man with a rubbery face stood there. In his hand was an attaché case.

"You Dr. Joseph Mapangou?"

Dr. Mapangou tried to smile but couldn't. "I will get dressed," he said and turned away.

"What for?" said the man as he came in and closed the door.

"I cannot go like this."

"Go where?" the man said and moved over to the switch on the television set. "Where's your bathroom?"

Dr. Mapangou pointed. The rubbery-faced man went in and turned on all the taps in both the bath and the basin. He then lifted the top off the toilet and did something to the float bulb inside that made the toilet run and gurgle.

After that he came back into the living room, looked around, and moved to the desk, where he shoved the stack of bills and the Litronix calculator to one side. He placed the attaché case on the desk and glared at Dr. Mapangou.

"My name's Arnold," lied Franklin Keeling, the ex-CIA agent. "You're going to work for me."

"Work? I? Well, I mean, doing what?"

Keeling opened the attaché case. "What do you care?"

The case was packed with greenish pieces of paper. But then Dr. Mapangou fumbled his glasses from the pocket of his pajamas, put them on, blinked a few times, and discovered that the greenish pieces of paper were actually hundred-dollar bills. There seemed to be a simply enormous number of them.

All that had happened two years ago. The hundred-dollar bills in the attaché case had enabled Dr. Mapangou to erase his debts and to lease the apartment on East 60th, which he dearly loved, and to continue and even increase both the number and quality of his social engagements.

And every Friday morning at nine o'clock Dr. Mapangou would sit down at his new custom-made pecan desk, take pen in hand, and report in careful detail every item of gossip and rumor that he had heard during the week. When the report was done, he would seal it in a plain envelope, take the subway to East 12th Street, and drop it off with a blind man who ran a candy store. On the first Friday of every month the blind man would hand Dr. Mapangou an envelope. Sometimes it would contain instructions from the man called Arnold. Sometimes not. But it always contained fifty hundred-dollar bills.

After the call came from the co-pilot, Dr. Mapangou canceled the dinner for eight that he had scheduled at the Four Seasons, soaked for an hour in his tub, dressed carefully in a dark blue worsted suit, and resolved to walk to the Gotham Hotel to save money. Dr. Mapangou was often guilty of such small, mindless false economies, and he often twitted himself about them.

Nevertheless, he walked, arriving at the Gotham promptly at

10 P.M. He failed to notice the black Mercury sedan that crept along behind him. The car trailed Dr. Mapangou all the way to the Gotham. When Dr. Mapangou entered the hotel, the driver got out and gave the doorman a twenty-dollar bill to let him park the Mercury on 55th Street just past the hotel's entrance.

Dr. Mapangou took the elevator up to room 542, which was registered to a Mr. Minder, but actually occupied by Franklin Keeling, formerly of the CIA, and Jack Spiceman, formerly of the FBI. The meeting of the three men lasted thirty-two minutes.

After Dr. Mapangou left room 542, he rode the elevator down, left the hotel, and—still seized by his fit of economy—decided to walk back to his apartment. In his left hand he carried an insulated paper sack, the kind that is used to get ice cream home before it melts.

It wasn't until he had reached 60th Street that the Mercury sedan pulled up beside him and the big man with the bald head got out. The big man was Alex Reese, who intended to become the CIA's chief of station in London, if everything worked out just right.

"Dr. Mapangou," Reese said in his harsh bass voice.

Dr. Mapangou turned.

"What've you got in the bag, Doc?"

"It—it is ice cream. Yes, ice cream. Chocolate."

Reese reached over and took the bag away from Dr. Mapangou. "Come on, I'll give you a lift."

"I—I really would prefer to walk."

"Come on," Reese said, managing to turn the two words of invitation into a threat.

Dr. Mapangou climbed into the front seat of the sedan. Reese got behind the wheel. The car pulled away. "Let's take a little drive," Reese said.

Driving with one hand, Reese opened the insulated ice cream bag and then switched on the sedan's map light. He reached into the bag and took out a frozen metal cylinder, the kind that cigars

129

sometimes come in. The cylinder was sealed with Scotch tape. At a stop sign, Reese peeled it off.

"Ice cream, huh?" he said to Dr. Mapangou. Dr. Mapangou said nothing.

Reese twisted the cap from the metal cylinder and shook its contents out into the palm of his left hand. The contents consisted of a single human forefinger, frozen solid.

Reese stared at it for a long moment, then looked at Dr. Mapangou and smiled. "You and me, Doc—you and me'd better have a little talk."

Dr. Mapangou licked his lips nervously, nodded slightly, and was surprised to discover that, despite everything, he was quite looking forward to it.

16

The meeting between Paul Grimes and Chubb Dunjee took place at 4 P.M. that day in London in the sparsely furnished reception room of Grimes's house that faced out onto the small green park with the black iron fence around it.

Grimes was bent over the card table examining the six photographs that Dunjee had removed from the steel lock box, which he had found in one of the two suitcases that had been ransomed from the landlord in Bayswater. Five of the pictures showed the two men and two women in swimsuits on a beach. The sixth picture showed the naked smiling man lying on a bed and pointing at his erection.

"The guy with the hard-on took the beach pictures, right?" Grimes said. "That's why he isn't in any of them."

"Probably," Dunjee said.

"Well, this one," Grimes said, pointing, "this tubby guy with all the hair is definitely Felix. Let me show you."

Grimes took out his wallet and removed a two-by-three-inch picture, which he handed to Dunjee. The picture, grainy and a little out of focus, portrayed a man with an open mouth and startled eyes. "That's Felix. It's the only picture there is of him except for some when he was five and six years old."

"How'd they get it?" Dunjee said.

"He was coming out of a bank they'd just robbed in Brest. A Belgian tourist was taking a picture of his wife. Felix stepped into the picture. The tourist got shot. He died a couple of days later. Three months after that his wife finally got around to having the film developed. She turned it over to the Belgian cops. It took another two months before somebody woke up and figured out who the guy in the picture really was."

"Not much of a resemblance," Dunjee said, comparing the face of the startled man with that of the plumpish man on the beach.

"There's enough," Grimes said. He put his finger on the bare stomach of the Oriental man, who was also in the picture with Felix and the two women. "This guy is Ko Yoshikawa. Japanese. He went to Stanford. The thin broad next to him is dead. Her name was Maria Luisa de la Cova, and some kids found her strangled to death out in Hammersmith. She used to be Felix's girl friend. The other woman with the figure is Françoise Leget. French—or Algerian, I guess. It's where she was born anyway."

"And the guy with the hard-on is German, right?"

"Right," Grimes said. "Bernt Diringshoffen. From Hamburg. About thirty-two now."

"He's the connection," Dunjee said.

"With the Libyan?"

Dunjee nodded. "They both like girls. Young ones. Very young. Or pictures of them anyway."

"How're you going to work it?"

"I'm going to sit next to the Libyan on the plane to Rome tomorrow and see what happens."

"You sure something will?"

Dunjee said nothing, and after a moment Grimes said, "Yes, well, I almost forgot. That's what you're good at, isn't it?"

"That's what I'm good at."

"You sure you need Delft?"

"I'm sure."

"And what about this other guy you're taking along? This Hopkins. Who's he?"

"A thief."

"Jesus. Why a thief?"

"They come in handy," Dunjee said. "Sometimes."

Grimes shook his head sadly and waved a hand at the photographs on the table. "You need these any more?"

"No."

"I'm flying back tonight and meeting with McKay in the morning. I'll give them to him. They'll be our progress report—such as it is. He can turn them over to the FBI or the CIA, and maybe they can do something useful with them—like figuring out what beach they were taken on. Although I don't know what the hell good that would do now."

"None," Dunjee said. He gathered the photographs up and handed them to Grimes. "Do they know about me?"

"Who—the CIA?"

Dunjee nodded.

"I don't know. You want me to find out from McKay?"

"Tell him I want hands off."

Grimes nodded thoughtfully. "All right. Anything else?"

"What if I need a lot of money all of a sudden?"

"Talk to Delft," Grimes said. "She knows what to do."

The restaurant was in Chelsea, one of those French places that last for a year or two, sometimes three, in the King's Road in that stretch between Oakley Street and Sloane Square. This one was called Gustave's, but Gustave was long gone, having sold out to a Greek at the crest of the restaurant's popularity, which had occurred exactly eleven months after it had opened for business. The Greek was now looking for a buyer and thought he might have a couple of Indians lined up.

The tables on either side of the one that Delft Csider and Chubb Dunjee sat at were deserted and had been for nearly thirty minutes. A mildly attentive waiter drifted by occasionally to replenish their coffee cups. They both had ordered the trout, which had been surprisingly good. Instead of dessert, Csider had asked for a Drambuie; Dunjee a brandy.

"That's it then," she said. "I just hand you letters to sign and call you Congressman."

"That's it."

"And what do you do?"

"Ignore him."

"What if he ignores you?"

"He won't," Dunjee said. "He'll either be curious, or suspect it's a setup, or both."

"Then what?"

"Then he discovers that he can use me—or exploit me, probably. I resist; he implores; I give in."

She shook her head. "I don't believe it."

"It's the way it works."

"Why aren't you still in Congress, if you're so smart?"

Dunjee grinned. "My wife ran off with the Weathermen. For some reason, my constituents didn't think that was such a hot idea."

"Did you like it?"

"Being a Congressman?"

She nodded.

Dunjee thought about it—or at least seemed to. "Sure. I liked it. It was a good job. Back then in 'sixty-eight, it paid thirty thousand a year plus perks. The year before I was elected, I was a $10,176-a-year Army captain."

"They gave you a string of medals, didn't they? That's what Grimes says."

"They gave me a string of medals."

"For what?"

"For killing people. Rather small people. They seemed to think it was important and necessary. The people who gave me the medals, I mean."

"But you sent them back."

"That was later. I took them and kept them awhile, and then got drunk for a while and sent them back. As gestures go, it was pretty sophomoric."

134

"All those rather small people were still dead."

"Still dead."

"But it got you in the papers."

"And on television. Don't forget television. They liked the way I looked on television."

"Who?"

"The guys who came to see me. They were a couple of movers and shakers who wanted to know whether I'd like to be a U.S. Congressman. I was twenty-eight and broke. My opponent in the primary was seventy-two and rich and a little senile. I was hungry. He wasn't. So I won. He had been in Congress for forty-two years, and when he lost they say it broke his heart. I got elected because I said I was sorry about all those rather small people I'd killed. Back in 'sixty-eight that was one hell of a platform—at least in my district. I had all the crazies in my district."

Delft Csider took another sip of her Drambuie. "Where'd you meet Grimes?"

"At school. UCLA."

"But you knew him after that."

"He was one of the two movers and shakers who came to see me about whether I'd like to be a U.S. Congressman."

"I was wondering. He knew your wife, didn't he?"

"He knew her."

"What was she like?"

"Very pretty, overly intelligent, deeply concerned, highly motivated—and very much a pain in the ass. Her father was a vice-president of the old Mine, Mill, and Smelter Workers. Her mother was an actress who got blacklisted. A very political family. An uncle once socked Joe McCarthy on the jaw—or so he claimed. My wife was born in 'thirty-nine and always said her earliest memory was of attending a Second Front Now rally in New York when she was three—or maybe four. Her proudest moment came in 'fifty-two, when she watched her mother on television tell the House Un-American Activities Committee to go fuck itself. I turned out to be something of a disappointment to Our Nan, as Grimes calls her."

"For some reason you don't strike me as the typical politician."

Dunjee shrugged. "They come in all sizes and shades. The president of Mexico writes novels. Or did. The Senate Majority Leader plays the fiddle and sings. There've been Senators and Congressmen who've been astronauts, actors, and athletes. When they get too old for that, they sometimes become politicians. It's a good way to keep answering a question that nags a lot of people: Who am I? If you're a politician, you can say, I'm the Mayor or the State Treasurer or even the President of the United States. And if you can get a majority of the people to agree with you, then that's what you are and there's a sign on the door to prove it."

"What are you now?"

Dunjee smiled. "A philosopher."

"That doesn't require an election, does it?"

"Self-appointed. Or self-anointed might be better. What about you? Have you got a handy label?"

"As I said, I'm the back-up."

"And before you were the back-up?"

"I did this and that—here and there."

"Since you're the back-up, you mind if I ask where here and there was?"

"I don't mind," she said and finished the last of her Drambuie. She then lit a cigarette and blew the smoke to one side. "I'm thirty. I might be thirty for a couple more years. I haven't decided yet. My mother and I came out of Hungary in 'fifty-six. I was five. I don't know what happened to my father, except that he was killed. We never did find out how. We went to Vienna and stayed there a year. I learned German. After Vienna, we went to Genoa. Two years there. I learned Italian. Did I mention that my mother was a nurse? She married a doctor in Genoa. A Lebanese. A nice man. We went to Beirut. I learned Arabic. And French. The doctor died two years later of cancer. He left a little money, but not much. At the time, nurses were needed in Berlin, so we went there. I don't suppose I ever really learned any language. 'Absorbed' is probably more accurate. I'm a parrot. We were in Berlin from 'sixty-one to 'sixty-four. There was a growing shortage of nurses in the States. So we decided to go there. I was thirteen then. We taught ourselves English in six months and went to San Francisco. My mother worked as a private nurse. For the rich mostly. She was very good. We usually lived with them. The rich, I mean. My mother died of a stroke in 'seventy when she was forty-one. I was nineteen."

"A lot of moving around," Dunjee said. "A lot of schools."

Delft Csider smiled slightly. "I never went to school."

"Never? Not even kindergarten?"

"Not even kindergarten. Don't look so surprised."

"Everybody goes to school."

"Not everybody."

"What about—"

"Truant officers? That's what you were going to ask, wasn't it? Everybody does."

Dunjee nodded.

"Truant officers don't go looking for neatly dressed, solemn little girls who spend their school hours in public libraries. That's where I hung out when my mother worked days. When she worked nights, which she mostly did, I stayed home with her. She was my . . . best friend, I suppose you could say."

"Didn't you ever want to go to school?"

"Why?"

"I don't know. For an education, I suppose."

"Are you saying I'm not educated?"

It was an apologetic smile that Dunjee gave her. "No. I'm not saying that."

"I'll give you the rest of it. I find long division still a little murky, but who cares now that you can buy a calculator for nine dollars. I'm weak in baseball and American football. But I'm a whiz at geography and history and politics and how the rich live.

I took a post-graduate course in that, you might say. After my mother died, I lived with a very rich, very elderly man. We traveled. I'd picked up enough nursing skills to give him his shots and check his blood pressure twice a day. The old man was interested in politics. He liked to back winners. That's how I met Grimes. He came by to pick up some money from the old gentleman in 1976. Quite a lot of money. We talked, Grimes and I. He didn't seem to care whether I'd ever gone to school or not. But he said if ever I left the old man and needed a job, to come see him. The old man died six months later. I went to see Grimes and I've been working with him ever since."

"Doing what he does."

She nodded. "Learning how to do it, anyway. He says I do it rather well. What about it, philosopher? Do I measure up?"

Dunjee smiled again. "Sure," he said. "You'll do fine."

It was cool when they came out of the restaurant. Delft Csider wore a wraparound camel's-hair coat. She turned the collar up and started to her left. Dunjee touched her arm. "Wait here a second," he said.

He put his hands deep into the pockets of his brown tweed topcoat and moved down the sidewalk twenty paces or so until he came to the parked green Jaguar sedan with the two men in the front seat. He stood next to the window of the car until one of the men rolled it down.

"You want something?" the man said in an accent that came from somewhere east of Texas and west of Georgia.

Dunjee nodded. "Tell whoever sent you to pull you off—or I pull out. You got that?"

They stared at each other for a moment and finally the man nodded and rolled the window back up. Dunjee turned and moved back to Delft Csider.

"Who was that?" she said.

"Kibitzers," Dunjee said.

17

Up in Dr. Joseph Mapangou's dearly beloved apartment on East 60th Street, Alex Reese lowered himself into the chair behind the custom pecan desk, put the ice cream bag down on the leather-edged blotter, and stared balefully at Dr. Mapangou, who stood nervously before him, not at all sure whether he needed permission to sit.

"What've you got to drink?" Reese demanded.

Dr. Mapangou smiled. Now he could be host—a familiar and comfortable role. "Some very nice whisky perhaps? Or some excellent brandy?"

"Whisky," Reese said. "About that much." He held his thumb and middle finger about two inches apart.

Dr. Mapangou poured the drinks quickly, the whisky for Reese and a smaller measure of brandy for himself. "May I sit?" he said as he put the drinks down on the desk.

"Sit," Reese said, drank off half of the whisky, and took the metal cylinders out of the ice cream bag. He opened both cylinders and shook their contents out on the blotter. Two frozen severed fingers pointed accusingly at Dr. Mapangou, who shuddered.

Reese bent forward slightly to examine the fingers more carefully. "Bit his nails, didn't he?" he said and again turned his baleful stare on Dr. Mapangou.

Dr. Mapangou seemed to feel that the question required an answer, so he bent forward, gave the fingers a quick inspection, nodded slightly, and hastily drank some of his brandy.

"You got an ink pad?" Reese said.

"I beg your pardon?"

"An ink pad. You know." Reese pounded a fist from side to side on the desk as though demonstrating how documents should be stamped to someone who had never heard of documents.

"In the second drawer on the left," Dr. Mapangou said, suddenly convinced that Reese would have made a perfect district officer in some repressive African colonial regime.

Reese found the ink pad as well as two sheets of smooth white paper. Dr. Mapangou watched as Reese inked the severed fingers carefully and then rolled each one onto a separate sheet. Reese tenderly put the sheets away in a used manila envelope that he had found in the desk's middle drawer.

"Wash 'em off," he said and used his own middle finger and thumb to flick the two severed fingers across the desk toward Dr. Mapangou.

Again, Dr. Mapangou said, "I beg your pardon?"

"You know," Reese said, dry-washing his own hands. "Washee, washee."

Dr. Mapangou gingerly picked up the two fingers and moved to his wet bar, where he washed the ink off them with a bar of lavender-scented soap. After that he dried them with a paper towel and turned back to Reese.

"They're beginning to thaw, I believe," Dr. Mapangou said.

"You got any aluminum foil?"

Dr. Mapangou nodded.

"Wrap 'em up good in that and pop 'em into your freezer."

After finishing his chores in the kitchen, Dr. Mapangou returned to the living room and sat back down in front of the desk.

140

He watched as Reese drank more whisky, looked around the room, and nodded appreciatively at what he saw.

"You got a real nice place here," Reese said. "How much does it run you?"

"Twenty-one-fifty a month."

"No kidding? That much. Tell me about the fingers, Doc."

"I did not know what they were."

"You didn't, huh?"

"No."

"Let's see now. You left here about a quarter to ten, walked to the Gotham, went in, stayed about half an hour, and came out with a couple of frozen fingers in cigar tubes all nice and insulated in an ice cream bag—except you didn't know what they were, right?".

"That is correct."

"What'd you think they were?"

"I was not told."

Reese nodded. "What room did you go up to? Remember, I'm gonna check it all out."

"Room 542."

"And whose room was that?"

"I was told that it was a Mr. Minder's."

"Is that who you saw?"

"No."

Reese sighed. "Okay. Who did you see up there in room 542?"

"Mr. Arnold," Dr. Mapangou said. "And Mr. Benedict."

"Arnold and Benedict."

"Yes."

"Tell me about Arnold and Benedict. They white folks?"

"Americans."

"What're their first names?"

"I do not know. The only names they ever gave me were Arnold and Benedict."

"All right, we'll let that slide. What did Arnold and Benedict want you to do?"

141

"They wanted me to deliver the two . . . cigar tubes."

"They did, huh?"

"Yes."

"Who did they want you to deliver them to?"

Dr. Mapangou picked up his brandy and took a swallow, thinking, Now it's going to become unpleasant. He sighed and put the brandy glass back down on the desk.

"They wanted me to deliver the cigar tubes to certain members of the Libyan and Israeli delegations. One each."

"Which members?"

"To Fathi Ashour, who is Libyan, and to Gad Efrati. He, of course, is Israeli."

And what were you supposed to tell Brother Ashour and Brother Efrati after you delivered them the sliced-off fingers?"

"I did not know about the fingers."

"Okay. You didn't know. But what were you supposed to tell them?"

"The same thing."

"Which was what?"

"I had to memorize it."

"You mean Arnold and Benedict made you memorize it?"

"Yes."

"What was it?"

"I was to tell both Ashour and Efrati this, exactly: 'If you want the rest of the merchandise, the price will be ten million dollars. Upon receipt of the money, the merchandise will be returned undamaged within twenty-four hours. Dr. Mapangou will serve as intermediary.' That is the end of the message I had to memorize." Dr. Mapangou quickly gulped down the remainder of his brandy.

Reese nodded his big head thoughtfully. He leaned across the desk toward Dr. Mapangou and dropped his big bass voice to a confidential rumble. "Tell me something. What do you think the 'rest of the merchandise' is?"

Dr. Mapangou swallowed noisily. "I do not know."

142

"Come on, Doc. You deliver them each a finger. Now what do you think belongs to a finger?"

"A person?" Dr. Mapangou whispered.

"A person!" Reese said, trying to sound surprised and not succeeding too well. "That's very good. In fact, for a jungle bunny, that's damn good. Now why didn't I think of that? A *person!*"

Dr. Mapangou tried to smile. "Perhaps a little more whisky?"

"Sure. Why not." Dr. Mapangou rose as Reese locked his hands behind his big bald head and stared up at the ceiling. "A person. Now what person would both the Israelis and Libyans be willing to pay ten million bucks for, providing he was returned in good condition?"

"Perhaps the person is a she?" Dr. Mapangou said, setting the whisky down in front of Reese.

"A she, huh? Well, that's an idea, except I don't think a she would have thick, stubby fingers like that with the nails chewed down to the quick and the cuticles all shot to hell. No, I think it's a he. That's what I think."

He's playing with me, Dr. Mapangou thought sadly. He thinks I am a fool and now he is going to make me do something awful. For the first time, Dr. Mapangou found himself wishing he had never come to New York.

"You know what I'm gonna do with those two pieces of paper that I've got in this envelope," Reese said, smacking the manila envelope with his left hand.

Dr. Mapangou shook his head no.

"I'm gonna take these down to Washington and then I'm gonna compare 'em with a set of fingerprints that the French got out of a hotel room in Paris and I'll bet you six boxes of fig newtons that they match up exactly. And you know who those fingerprints that the French got out of that certain hotel room in Paris belong to?"

Again, Dr. Mapangou shook his head no, dreading what Reese would say next.

"Why, they belong to Gustavo Berrio-Brito, that's who. The well-known freedom fighter. The guy everybody calls Felix. You've heard of Felix, haven't you, Doc?"

"Yes," Dr. Mapangou whispered. "I've heard of him."

Reese stared at Dr. Mapangou for several moments. When he finally spoke, his deep voice was soft and curiously gentle. "You better tell me the rest of it, Doc. All of it. You know I'm going to get it out of you one way or another."

Dr. Mapangou stared down at the blotter on his pecan desk. Two tears rolled down his cheeks. A moment later he began to talk in an indistinct, choked voice. It was so low that Reese had to lean forward to hear.

Dr. Mapangou began at the beginning, back when he was $89,831.19 in debt and his creditors were closing in and the man called Arnold appeared suddenly, as if by magic, like some rubbery-faced good fairy, bearing the attaché case full of greenish pieces of paper that turned out to be hundred-dollar bills once Dr. Mapangou had slipped his glasses on.

"This guy Arnold," Reese said. "What did he look like?"

Dr. Mapangou gave a detailed description of Franklin Keeling, the ex-CIA man, and his constantly exasperated expression, and his sometimes tortured syntax.

"Did he do this a lot?" Reese said and wiped his right hand hard across the bottom half of his face.

"Yes, he does that frequently."

"And when he talks do his hands move around a lot like this?" Reese made his hands flutter about above the desk blotter.

"Like fat butterflies," said Dr. Mapangou, a closet poet who prided himself on his imagery, but kept his efforts locked away in the bottom drawer of the pecan desk.

"The other guy, Benedict. What's he look like?"

Dr. Mapangou's description of Jack Spiceman, the ex-FBI special agent, was equally exact and equally detailed. "He has very still eyes," Dr. Mapangou said. "Very . . . remote, like lost lakes."

"How much money was in the attaché case?"

"One hundred thousand dollars."

"For what?"

"It was a . . . retainer."

"A retainer, huh? They retained you to do what?"

"Furnish information."

"To them?"

"And to others."

Reese rose and moved over to Dr. Mapangou's wet bar. He picked up a bottle of whisky and examined its label. Still examining it, he said, "About three months ago, in the delegates' lounge at the UN, a rumor started. The rumor was about Libyan oil and U.S. arms. A trade. Maybe you heard it?"

Dr. Mapangou cleared his throat. "I may have done."

Reese walked back to the pecan desk and planted the whisky bottle squarely in the center of the blotter. "Maybe," he said, "maybe you even started it."

Dr. Mapangou said nothing.

"Well?"

"They . . . supplied me with the information."

"Arnold and Benedict?"

Dr. Mapangou nodded.

"And you just dropped a hint here and there."

Again Dr. Mapangou nodded.

"Maybe to the Nigerians, huh?"

Another nod from Dr. Mapangou—a wretched nod.

"Nothing wrong with that," Reese said, sitting back down in the chair behind the pecan desk. "You're a diplomat. You heard some information. You passed it on. That's what diplomats do, right?"

"Yes," Dr. Mapangou murmured. "That's what they do."

Reese poured two more inches of whisky into his glass. "You mentioned back there a ways that you furnished Arnold and Benedict with information. Was that on a regular basis?"

"Fairly regular, yes."

"What's fairly regular?"

"Once a week."

"Written reports?"

"Yes."

"You keep copies?"

Dr. Mapangou didn't answer.

Reese let his eyes wander around the room. "I could rip this place inside out in twenty minutes—or have it done."

"Yes, I kept copies."

"What was in the reports—just general gossip?"

"Mostly."

"And I suppose they sweetened the pot a little."

"I beg your pardon?"

Reese rubbed his thumb against the insides of his fingers in the ancient gesture signifying money.

"Yes . . . yes, they did compensate me with a little extra."

"How much is a little extra?"

Dr. Mapangou closed his eyes because he didn't want to see the expression on Reese's face when he answered. He whispered the reply. "Five thousand dollars."

Reese's tone was incredulous. "A *month!*"

Dr. Mapangou nodded, his eyes still tightly closed. "A month."

"Jesus Christ. How'd you work it?"

"There is a candy store in Twelfth Street in the Village. The proprietor is blind. I dropped my reports off there every Friday. On the first Friday of every month he would give me my compensation."

"How'd he know it was you if he was blind?"

"A simple code. I would always ask him if he carried Fatimas, a cigarette, I believe, that is no longer manufactured. If he had no instructions for me, he would simply say no. But if he had a message from Mr. Arnold or Mr. Benedict, he would say no, he had no Fatimas, but he did have Murads. Then I would go to a certain phone booth at a certain time and receive my instructions verbally."

Reese nodded slowly with either approval or understanding, or perhaps both. "So what did you do to earn your five thousand a month, Doc?"

"I've just told you."

"No," Reese said, shaking his head. "That might be worth, say, maybe five hundred bucks a month, but not five thousand. What was the big ticket item they had you working on?"

I will not answer, Dr. Mapangou thought, closing his eyes again. Tomorrow I will go to the airport and get on the plane and fly to Dakar and take the bus down to Banjul and then go for bush and never come out. They cannot find me there. Never.

He opened his eyes, and Reese's cold stare hit him like a hard slap. "Felix," Dr. Mapangou said. "They wanted me to locate the man Felix for them."

A big smile spread itself across Reese's face. "Well, now," he said and grabbed his drink and drained it. "Well, now, by God." He wiped the back of his hand across his mouth, but the smile refused to go away. "You fingered him. *You* fingered Felix."

Dr. Mapangou closed his eyes again and thought about Banjul.

"How'd you do it?" Reese said, and for the first time there was nothing but admiration in his tone.

Something flickered in Dr. Mapangou's thoughts, then died, and flickered again. He tried to smother it, but it refused to die. It does, he thought, after all, spring eternal.

"It was complicated," he said, the pride creeping into his voice.

"I bet."

"I have many friends at the UN. They tell me things. Sometimes they don't quite know what they're really telling me. I mean by that that one friend will tell me one thing, and I will tell him something, then another friend will tell me something, and then I put it all together—like a puzzle. In this instance, a PLO friend mentioned something, and a member of the Irish delegation said something else, and then one of my colleagues from Libya let drop a rather careless remark, and the Israelis, of course, are really terrible gossips, and one of them—I won't say

147

which one—gave me, unknowingly, of course, the last item I needed."

"What was the key piece?" Reese asked with naked curiosity.

"It was the name of a doctor—an Indian doctor in London. He was not licensed to practice, but still he did. Or does. He was treating a woman and her child. The woman had tuberculosis. The woman had been sent to him by someone in the IRA. He was, or is, I suppose, the unofficial IRA doctor. Perhaps a specialist in gunshot wounds?"

"Yeah, maybe."

"Well, I heard about the doctor from one person and about the woman and her child from another, and from yet another source I heard that Felix was worried about a woman member of his organization who had tuberculosis. So you see I simply put the various pieces together and then reported my findings to Mr. Arnold and Mr. Benedict."

Reese leaned back in the chair and stared thoughtfully at Dr. Mapangou. For the first time, there was a measure of respect in the look that he gave the small neat man with the graying hair.

"Mr. Benedict and Mr. Arnold," Reese said finally in a musing voice.

"Yes."

"They want to sell Felix to both the Libyans and the Israelis for ten million bucks, right?"

"Yes."

"But there can't be two Felixes, can there?"

"No."

"So what they really plan to do, Mr. Benedict and Mr. Arnold, is run a shitty, right?"

"A shitty? Yes, a shitty, as you say."

Reese leaned forward across the desk and dropped his voice back down to the register where it turned into a confidential rumble. "What was your cut gonna be, Doc—out of the twenty million?"

Dr. Mapangou licked his lips. "Five hundred thousand?" He made it a tentative question.

Reese nodded his big head as if the amount were reasonable, but not overly so. He paused and chose his next words carefully. "How would you like to make, say . . . two million instead?"

The hope that had been flickering somewhere down in Dr. Mapangou's breast burst into a roaring blast. But he kept his voice calm and casual, except for a small squeak at the very end.

"I would like that very much," he said. "Very much indeed."

18

There was some discussion, not quite an argument, about who would get the window seat. It was finally decided that the sad-eyed Englishman would sit there because he liked to look out. After more discussion, with the American growing just a trifle exasperated, it was also decided that the woman, who may have been either British or American—it was hard to tell— would sit next to the Englishman, while the American with the skewed left cheekbone that made him look a bit cockeyed would sit across the aisle from her in seat 3-B next to first-class window seat 3-A, which was already occupied by Faraj Abedsaid, Attaché (Cultural Section), of the Libyan Arab Republic's Embassy in London.

At 8:45 A.M. Dunjee buckled his seat belt just as a flight attendant announced in Italian, English, and French that this was Alitalia flight 317 from London to Rome and flying time would be approximately two hours and fifteen minutes. Dunjee turned to glance at his seat companion and give him what he knew to be his politician's nod, not too friendly, but not too distant either, a nod that in effect said, Even if you can't vote for me, pal, maybe you know somebody who can. Abedsaid gave him a slight nod back.

Once the plane had reached cruising altitude, Delft Csider raised the lid on the large attaché case that rested on her lap and, in a clear, penetrating voice, said, "Congressman, do you want to do the mail first, or do you want that spud-in report from Denver?"

"Let's get the mail over with," Dunjee said, speaking just slightly louder than he normally would.

Delft Csider handed him a sheaf of letters and a clipboard to write on. Dunjee fumbled for a pen, giving Abedsaid sufficient time to glance at the top letterhead which read, "Anadarko Explorations, Inc.," and underneath in somewhat smaller letters, "Tulsa, Oklahoma." There was also an address, a phone number, a telex number, and a cable acronym, ANADEX; but they were all in eight-point type and too small to be read from any distance.

Dunjee started signing the letters with his own name, carefully reading each one first. After signing his name, he passed each letter across the aisle to Delft Csider. Next to her, Harold Hopkins stared out the window at the clouds below. After a few minutes of cloud-staring he leaned back in his seat and went to sleep.

When he reached the last letter in the pile, Dunjee said, "What happened to the one to Minister Obalana in Lagos?"

"You decided it would be better to call him from Rome, Congressman."

"That's right. I forgot. Let's have that Denver report. Never mind, I see it." Dunjee reached across the aisle toward the open attaché case. The clipboard with the last letter still on it slipped from his lap and fell at Abedsaid's feet. The Libyan reached down and picked them up, noting that the letter was addressed to The Hon. Salim Abdulrazzak, who happened to be the Minister of Resources for the State of Kuwait.

"Sorry," Dunjee said.

"Not at all," Abedsaid said, handing him the letter and the clipboard. Dunjee signed the final letter and passed both it and the clipboard over to Delft Csider.

When he was through, Abedsaid said, "You are a United States Congressman?"

Dunjee turned slightly and gave him his best smile—very white, very warm, very wide. "Not any more. My associates just call me that out of habit. It sometimes helps when it comes to making reservations."

"But you formerly were a Congressman?"

"That's right. 'Sixty-nine to 'seventy-one. My name's Dunjee. Chubb Dunjee." He held out his hand.

After less than a second, Abedsaid accepted it, shook it, and said, "Abedsaid."

"Glad to meet you, Mr. Abedsaid," Dunjee said, mispronouncing the name just slightly.

"I noticed that the name of your company was Anadarko."

"Anadarko Explorations, Inc. But we operate out of Tulsa. That's in Oklahoma."

"Really," Abedsaid said. "And you were a Congressman from Oklahoma?"

"No, California. Los Angeles. Where're you from?"

"Tripoli," Abedsaid said, adding dryly, "That's in Libya."

"Libya's a little out of my territory right now," Dunjee said, "but maybe not for long, especially if those Gulf of Sidra finds prove out."

"You're—"

"Offshore specialists," Dunjee supplied him. "Consultants. Started out off Santa Barbara, then did some work up in the North Sea, and after that we got called down to Nigeria."

"The Port Harcourt area?"

"Closer to Bonny, actually," Dunjee said, seeing no reason why he should be tripped up so easily. "Are you in the oil business?"

"Not exactly, although I did take a degree in petroleum engineering from the University of Oklahoma." He smiled slightly. "That's in Norman."

Dunjee appeared to be delighted. So delighted that he reached

152

across the aisle and tapped Delft Csider on the arm. "Hey, Delft. Mr. Abedsaid here went to OU."

Delft Csider smiled coolly. "How nice."

"I found Oklahoma . . . fascinating," Abedsaid said.

"I bet," Dunjee said. "I'm having a little trouble getting used to it myself. Fortunately, we travel a lot."

"Why not locate someplace else?"

"Well, first, because my money men are all in Tulsa, and second, that's where the experts are, there and in Texas. If you want to do any offshore drilling and do it right, you'd better get yourself some good ole boys from Texas and Oklahoma who probably never saw an ocean before they started shaving."

"Yes," Abedsaid said, "I've heard that. Your President, Mr. McKay, is from Oklahoma, isn't he?"

"That's right. Oklahoma City."

"I believe he also served in the House of Representatives."

"Two terms."

"Did you know him there?"

"No, I was there before his time."

"They were also in the oil business, weren't they—the McKay brothers, I mean?"

"Still are—except they've got it all in a blind trust now. From what everybody says, the McKays were both lucky and good, which is usually how you make it in the oil business."

"President McKay's brother. He has a strange nickname, I believe. Strange to me anyway."

"Bingo."

"Do you know him?"

"Everybody knows Bingo. We're not good friends, but we've met a few times."

"In other words you've both howdied *and* shook."

Dunjee grinned. "You might say that."

"How long will you be in Rome, Mr. Dunjee?"

"A few days. I've got some meetings with the ENI people."

"And where will you be staying?"

It was then that Dunjee knew he had him. It was more than the nibble, it was the bite. Dunjee played it cautiously. He leaned across the aisle and said to Delft Csider, "Where're we staying in Rome?"

"The Hassler," she said.

"The Hassler," Dunjee said.

"A very nice hotel," said Abedsaid as he pressed the button that made his chair recline. "I sometimes stay there myself."

Abedsaid closed his eyes and seemed to go to sleep. For the rest of the trip, Dunjee immersed himself in a detailed geological report on a dry hole in west Kansas that had been abandoned at 9,154 feet. Paul Grimes had arranged for the report to be flown in from Denver. It had arrived that morning on the Pan Am flight from Washington. Dunjee read it carefully, turning a page every three or four minutes. Only once did he catch Abedsaid peeking to see whether he was actually reading the report, which ran 159 pages.

After his meeting with Chubb Dunjee the afternoon before, Paul Grimes had gone directly to Heathrow and boarded British Airways flight 189 to Dulles. Flight 189 was the Concorde, which Grimes always took when someone else was paying the $1,508 fare. In this instance the someone else was the President of the United States.

The flight left London at 6:30 P.M. and arrived at Dulles at 5:55 P.M. Grimes's seatmate was a garrulous eighty-year-old retired firetruck salesman whose territory had once been "every state west of the Mississippi." The old gentleman said he had flown in everything from Ford trimotors to 747s, but this was his first time up in the Concorde.

"The way I figure it," he said, "if you could stand in Heathrow and holler loud enough to be heard at Dulles, why, we'd get there before the holler did. Now that's fast."

At Dulles there had been a White House car to meet Grimes, a black Mercury sedan whose uncommunicative driver, Grimes de-

154

cided, was probably a member of the Secret Service detail. The driver kept murmuring into a microphone about Firefly and Ginger, and Grimes decided he would rather be Ginger than Firefly if, in fact, the driver was even talking about him.

The car pulled up in front of the old White House Office Building on Pennsylvania Avenue. The driver and Grimes got out and another six-footer, also neatly dressed, slipped wordlessly behind the wheel and drove off. Grimes's driver said, "This way, Mr. Grimes."

He escorted Grimes into the building, past the guards, and up to the same denlike room on the third floor where Grimes and the President had met before. The driver produced a walkie-talkie from somewhere, probably his hip pocket, Grimes decided, pulled the aerial up, and murmured something else into it about Firefly and Ginger. The walkie-talkie spluttered a reply, but the driver had the volume down so low that Grimes couldn't hear what it said.

"The President will be here in a few minutes, Mr. Grimes," the driver said and then left the room, closing the door behind him.

Actually, it was five minutes before President McKay, dressed in black tie, entered the room and shook hands with Grimes.

McKay slumped down into a chair and put one leg up on the desk. "In twenty-five minutes, I'm having dinner with the mayors of twenty-two big cities and their assorted wives. The mayors all want money. After dinner, entertainment will be provided by a band of Hopi Indian dancers followed by a twenty-two-year-old rock star who's going to sing some songs whose words I probably won't be able to understand. You wouldn't be here unless you had news. If it's bad, I don't think I want to hear it."

"It's news anyway," Grimes said and took an envelope from his breast pocket. From the envelope he removed the Polaroid pictures that Dunjee had given him and dealt them onto the desk one by one. "Their names are all on the back."

McKay turned each picture over. "So that's what he looks like. Felix, I mean."

"That's what he looks like."

"And the blond guy on the bed with the hard-on. He took the pictures, right?"

"Right."

"What else?"

"There's a connection between the blond guy—his name's Diringshoffen—and a Libyan called Abedsaid who works out of their London Embassy. The Libyan's flying down to Rome tomorrow. My guy—the guy whose name you don't want to know—is going to make a move on him."

McKay leaned back in his chair and stared at Grimes for several moments. Finally he said, "What kind of move?"

Grimes shrugged. "I don't know. The way he normally works is to make them approach him."

"And he turned these pictures up?"

Grimes nodded.

"How'd he do it?"

"He spent some money and cut a few corners here and there that you don't want to know about."

"The CIA spends money—boxcars full of it—but the only picture it's got of Felix is the one of him coming out of that French bank with his mouth open. And in—what is it—three days, four? —your guy comes up with a family portrait of the whole fucking bunch. I can have these, can't I?" McKay waved a hand at the photographs.

"You paid for them. They're yours. There's only one hitch."

"What?"

"You're going to turn them over to the CIA, right?"

"Right."

"They'll want to know where you got them."

"I'll give them your name."

Grimes shook his head. "You're going to have to give them my guy's name."

156

Again McKay stared at Grimes for several moments. "Then I'll know it, won't I?" he said softly.

"There's no other way."

"Why?"

"Because he—my guy—wants you to keep the CIA off his back."

"Are they on it?"

"He didn't say."

"He doesn't tell you much, does he?"

Grimes smiled. "He only tells me what he thinks I should know. Then if something happens—something nasty, say—I won't know a whole hell of a lot about it. And neither will you. But you *are* going to have to know his name."

"All right. What is it?"

"Chubb Dunjee."

For a long moment the President said nothing. Then he said, "Well, shit. A Congressman."

"One term."

"Then what?"

"He was in the oil business."

"After that."

"After that he went with the UN."

"Let's skip a few years."

Grimes smiled again. "You must be thinking of Mexico."

"Mexico. The Mordida Man."

Grimes kept smiling. "Newspaper stuff."

"Yeah, I can see it now. 'President Hires Mordida Man.' Not too many votes in that."

"He's good."

"He'd better be."

"There's only one other thing."

"What?"

"He's got this little problem with the IRS."

"How little?"

"They're talking about extradition."

The President rose. "He hasn't got any problem. Not if he helps get Bingo back."

"And if he doesn't?"

McKay shrugged. "I never heard of him."

19

On the same day that Chubb Dunjee flew into Rome, the Minister of Youth and Sport paid his regular monthly visit to the old Mecarro coffee plantation on the northern tip of the island Democratic People's Republic. The Minister of Youth and Sport was also the republic's bag man.

The twenty-nine-year-old Minister had risen to his present post because (1) he was an avid soccer fan and (2) he was the youngest of the Prime Minister's six light-skinned brothers. He was also the biggest brother, standing six-foot-six and weighing nearly 250 pounds. The Minister had once been a beach boy in Miami for nearly three years, and it was whispered that he had killed a man and a woman there because they had wanted him to do something unspeakable. Just what unspeakable act the couple had wanted the Minister to perform provided the republic's citizens with a topic for endless gossip and prurient speculation, fueled by their certain knowledge that there was little, if anything, the Minister wouldn't do for a flat fee of a hundred dollars. The citizens' nickname for the Minister was the Axe.

The Minister had made the twenty-seven-mile drive from the

island's capital by himself in his brother the Prime Minister's Cadillac El Dorado convertible. For company and security he had brought along tapes of Carly Simon, a bottle of fiery 190-proof rum, and a sawed-off shotgun that rested across his lap.

At the entrance to the plantation's drive he honked his horn to wake up two of the republic's soldiers, who composed 20 percent of the force that had been assigned to guard the plantation's distinguished foreign residents. The soldiers rose, yawned, stretched, accepted a drink of rum, gave the Minister their thoughts on the approaching cup final, and when he was gone, settled back down in the shade to finish their morning nap.

Standing on the veranda of the plantation house waiting to greet the Minister was Jack Spiceman, the ex-FBI agent.

"Hello, Jojo," Spiceman said.

The Minister sat motionless in the car waiting for the Simon song to end. "Sings pretty, don't she?" he said.

"Very pretty," Spiceman said, turned, and headed into the house. The Minister got out of the car and followed him, the shotgun in the crook of his left arm.

The meeting was held, as always, in the main drawing room, which was still furnished with chairs and sofas and tables from the 1930s that Leland Timble, the bank robber, had had beautifully refinished and reupholstered by skilled craftsmen in the republic's capital. Timble was sitting in a wingbacked chair when Spiceman entered followed by the Minister. On a nearby couch sat the ex-CIA man, Franklin Keeling. As was his usual custom during the monthly visit from the Minister, Keeling occupied himself by carefully wiping away at a loaded .45-caliber automatic with a lightly oiled rag.

The Minister nodded at both Timble and Keeling, picked out a comfortable chair, sat down, rested the shotgun across his knees, and said, "Got any bourbon?"

Spiceman went to a sideboard, poured a tumbler half full of Jack Daniel's, and handed it to the Minister, who drank it down, wiped his mouth with the palm of his hand, and said, "A couple of guys pulled in last night. From Miami. A forty-two-foot Chris Craft. Claimed they had engine trouble. We let 'em dock. Found 'em a mechanic. Fuel line was all fucked up. No big problem. Okay?"

He held out his glass and waited for Spiceman to refill it. This time the Minister took only a modest swallow.

"So they start moving around town, you know, asking questions. We let 'em ask, just making sure who they talked to—okay?" When no one said anything, he continued. "Pretty good operators. Smooth, you know, not too pushy, just a question here, a question there. You know. Then they somehow got hold of that fuckin' Cornelius."

Timble was the first one to speak. He said, "Ah," and looked interested.

"We're gonna have to do something about that fuckin' Cornelius," the Minister said.

"No," Timble said. "Every community needs its dissidents. Especially its tame ones; and you'll have to agree, Jojo, that Cornelius is exceedingly tame. Besides, he puts out a lively little newspaper that I quite enjoy. A decided community asset."

"He talks too much," the Minister said.

"So they talked to him," Keeling said. "Then what?"

"Well, then they got into a fight with a buncha guys."

"And?"

"One of 'em got his arm busted—the left one. The other one got banged up pretty good around the head. Maybe a concussion. So we took 'em to the hospital, you know, and set the one guy's busted arm without any painkiller, and that made him yell a lot, and we gave the other guy a couple of aspirin—for his concussion, you know—and then asked if they wanted to stay in the hospital a few days, and if they did, how were they gonna pay for it, since somebody had lifted their wallets during that fight they got themselves into. Here."

The Minister took two wallets from a pocket and tossed them to Spiceman, who began examining their contents.

"They decided they'd better go back to Miami," the Minister said and drank some more of his bourbon. "They left early this morning."

"What kind of questions were they asking?" Timble said.

"The usual shit. How much you paid and who got it and if there'd been any strangers up around here. And, oh yeah, they wanted to know all about your security setup. How many and where and had it been beefed up lately. That kinda shit."

Timble nodded. "I see."

"Nice names," Spiceman said and passed the two wallets over to Keeling. "Roger Sawyer and Daryl-with-a-'y' Nicety. I wonder who dreamed Nicety up?"

"From Miami and Omaha," Keeling said, examining the wallets' contents. "Sawyer's a lawyer and Nicety, who's from Miami and owns the boat, is an investment counselor. Not bad."

The Minister rose. "Anything else?"

Timble looked at his two associates, who shook their heads. "I don't think so, Jojo," Timble said. "Thanks for coming by."

"No problem," the Minister said.

He turned to go, and the small game began, the game they played every month. "I think you forgot your case," Timble said.

"Oh, yeah," the Minister said, turning and accepting the tan plastic attaché case that Keeling held out to him. "Thanks."

Keeling went with the Minister as far as the veranda, the .45 automatic still dangling in Keeling's left hand. "Say hello to the Prime Minister for us," Keeling said.

"Yeah, I'll do that," said the Minister of Youth and Sport. He locked the attaché case away in the Cadillac's trunk, climbed into the front seat, laid the shotgun across his lap, stuck another Carly Simon into the tape deck, and drove off into the soft morning air, humming along with her.

When Keeling came back into the drawing room, he put the automatic away in a drawer, poured himself a tall glass of Perrier over ice, squeezed a lime into it, added a whisper of gin for taste, and said, "Well, who were they?"

"Let me show you something," Spiceman said and handed Keeling two blue and white Social Security cards that he had taken from the two wallets that the Minister had left behind.

"What about them?"

"Did you ever watch TV?"

Knowing it was a trick question, Keeling nodded cautiously.

"Ever notice anything about telephone numbers on TV?"

Keeling shook his head, but Timble, smiling his happy-face smile, nodded that he had noticed something. "They all start with 555."

"Right," Spiceman said. "The phone company comes up with them. You want to use a number on TV, that's fine with the phone company as long as it starts with 555."

"But there isn't any 555 exchange, is there?" Timble said.

"None anywhere. The phone company came up with it because if you've got twenty or twenty-five million people watching a TV program, and they hear a phone number, then there're going to be about one or two thousand nuts who're going to dial it just to see who's home."

Keeling looked down at the two Social Security cards he was holding. "These both begin with 999."

"It was the old man's idea," Spiceman said.

"Hoover's?"

Spiceman nodded. "It happened about thirteen, fourteen years ago. Old J. Edgar heard through that grapevine of his that the Agency wanted a new batch of fake Social Security cards. So he passed the word to someone in Social Security that the Director would deem it a personal favor if all of the CIA's fake Social Security cards could be easily identified—in the interest of national security, of course. So the Social Security people came up with the 999 number. They forgot to mention it to anybody out at the Agency, though, and it gave us a nice little handle on you guys."

"Then it would seem," Timble said, "that the two gentlemen in the Chris Craft from Miami were CIA."

"Looks that way," Spiceman said.

Timble leaned his head back against the chair and closed his eyes. "I wonder," he said dreamily, "what Dr. Mapangou is doing?"

Keeling looked at his watch. "You mean right about now?"

Timble nodded slightly, his eyes still closed.

"Well, right about now," Keeling said, "Old Black Joe should be talking to the Libyans."

Dr. Joseph Mapangou had been waiting for forty-three minutes in the sparsely furnished reception room on the twenty-first floor of Libya House, the twenty-three-story building on East 48th Street just west of First Avenue that the Libyans had recently built at a cost of seventeen million dollars to house and office its United Nations delegation and consulate staff, although there was now no consulate staff to speak of because of the rupture in relations between Libya and the United States.

Dr. Mapangou was wearing what he sometimes thought of as his diplomatic uniform—a dark gray, almost black, suit with a pearl-gray vest, a very conservative dark blue tie, white shirt, and a gray Borsalino fedora, which he balanced on his right knee. On his left knee was a chocolate-colored ice cream bag from Rumpelmayer's. For the past fifteen minutes Dr. Mapangou had been wondering how long the insulated bag would keep something from melting. Or thawing.

Just as Dr. Mapangou's wait reached its fiftieth minute, a slim young Libyan dressed in tailored jeans and a gray cashmere jacket came through a set of double doors, closed them behind him, and glided over to his desk. He stood there for several moments, staring down at a sheet of paper and tapping a pencil absently against the desk, obviously lost in deep thought, presumably about world problems.

After fifteen or twenty seconds of table tapping, he glanced up and seemed to notice Dr. Mapangou for the first time.

"Oh. Dr. Mapangou," he said in a practiced you-still-there tone. "Yes, I do believe he's free now."

Dr. Mapangou rose, clutching his hat and his ice cream bag and smiling just a little to demonstrate that he hadn't even noticed the fifty-minute wait. Let the clerks and the small boys have their little victories, he thought. Those are the only ones they will ever win. Thus both cheered and bolstered by his comforting platitude, he followed the young Libyan through the twin doors into a huge corner office. There was no carpet on its cement floor or pictures on its walls or drapes for its immense windows that looked across the street into the windows of another building.

But there was a beautiful partner's desk that may have been three hundred years old. Behind it was a man in his forties who seemed to be examining some swatches of color. In front of the desk for visitors were two canvas camp chairs.

The man behind the desk was Fathi Ashour, Libya's principal delegate to the United Nations. He looked up from the swatches of color and smiled when Dr. Mapangou entered. The smile was wide, white, practiced, and meaningless. A diplomat's smile.

"Joseph!" Ashour said in a clear tenor that went with his five-nine height, 126-pound weight, and busy movements. "How good to see you. Do sit, but I must apologize for—" He completed the sentence with a wave of his hand that took in the bare floor and walls.

"Still moving in, I see," Dr. Mapangou said, lowering himself into one of the camp chairs.

"What do you think—green or tan? For the drapes, I mean." He held up first one swatch of material, then another.

"Green," Dr. Mapangou said firmly.

"Green. Yes, well, green is nice. Tea?"

"Yes, thank you, tea would be good."

Ashour poured two cups from the pot on his desk, handing one to Dr. Mapangou. "Do you realize that we Libyans drink more tea per capita than any country on earth?"

"No, I didn't know that," Dr. Mapangou said and sipped his tea. It was tepid and he put the cup back down on the desk.

"So," Ashour said and smiled.

Dr. Mapangou made sure that his own small, pleasant smile was fixed and steady. "I have an extremely delicate problem to discuss with you."

"Delicate?"

"Yes. Delicate."

Ashour nodded. "I see."

"I think," Dr. Mapangou said slowly and modestly, "that over the years I have acquired some small reputation for total discretion."

"Yes. Of course. Total. No question."

"And this reputation has sometimes—How shall I say it? Propelled, I suppose. Yes, propelled me into situations that are not of my choosing."

"And you find yourself in such a situation now?"

"Yes."

"Mmm. More tea?"

"Thank you."

Ashour topped up Dr. Mapangou's nearly full cup. Dr. Mapangou took an obligatory sip. Ashour clasped his hands across his chest, leaned back in his chair, and smiled some more.

"Because of my small reputation for discretion, I was recently approached by certain persons whose names I cannot reveal. They gave me a message to give to you, which you may wish to transmit to your government. If you insist that I reveal the identities of these persons, then I think our conversation should end here and now."

Ashour frowned. The frown made his eyes narrow. The smile had gone. "Continue," he said.

"With the stipulation that—"

"Yes, no names," Ashour said. "Go on."

"Yes, well, I suppose I had best show you something first. Something shocking."

"Shocking?"

Dr. Mapangou nodded. He put his Borsalino hat on the floor, picked up the chocolate-brown ice cream bag, and placed it on the desk. "Shocking," he said. "I must apologize."

Dr. Mapangou opened the ice cream bag. "Do you have a piece of paper?"

"Paper? What kind of paper?"

"Any kind. It's such a beautiful finish, I don't want to—"

Ashour opened a drawer, took out a plain sheet of bond, and placed it in the center of the desk.

Dr. Mapangou reached into the paper bag, took out a metal cylinder, and twisted off its cap. He glanced at Ashour, whose dark eyes were now wide and staring.

Dr. Mapangou closed his own eyes and shook the severed finger out onto the sheet of bond. He heard Ashour say several words in Arabic which sounded like exclamations. Dr. Mapangou opened his eyes and was relieved to see that the severed finger was pointing toward Ashour. Not that it meant anything, of course, but still . . .

Ashour rose and backed away from his desk, still staring down at the finger. Finally he looked up at Dr. Mapangou. "What have you brought me?"

"A finger."

"I see what it is. Why have you brought it to me? I demand to know why you have done this?"

"I was instructed to. I was also instructed to tell you that the finger comes from the hand of Gustavo Berrio-Brito."

"Felix," Ashour whispered.

"The freedom fighter," Dr. Mapangou said diplomatically.

"Who told you— Who gave you this thing?"

Dr. Mapangou shrugged helplessly. "I cannot tell you."

The flush started then. It began at the neck and spread up Ashour's face until it reached his cheeks. It was a dark red flush, quite dangerous-looking. *"Tell me!"* he yelled.

"I cannot."

Ashour stared at the finger for several moments. Then he reached out and touched it gingerly, jerking his own finger back. "It's cold."

"Frozen."

Ashour stared at Dr. Mapangou. "What do they want?" His voice was a whisper now. "Money?"

"I am to give you a message. I have no authority to negotiate. I can only tell you what I was told to tell you. Do you understand?"

Ashour nodded.

"This is the message: 'If you want the rest of the merchandise, the price will be ten million dollars. Upon receipt of the money, the merchandise will be returned undamaged within twenty-four hours. Dr. Mapangou will serve as intermediary.' That is the end of the message. If you have any questions, I will try to answer them."

"Ten million dollars?"

Dr. Mapangou nodded.

"And you will serve as intermediary?"

Again Dr. Mapangou nodded.

"How do we know this—this thing is Felix's?"

"Fingerprints," Dr. Mapangou said. "I was told the Paris police—or perhaps Interpol—could furnish the proof."

Ashour nodded. "There is a time limit, of course."

"Forty-eight hours."

"I must consult with my goverment."

"I understand."

Ashour nodded coldly. "We will be in touch with you."

Dr. Mapangou picked up his hat from the floor and rose. He

turned to go, but turned back. "I suggest that you wrap that up in aluminum foil and pop it into the freezer."

"Get out!" Ashour screamed in his clear tenor voice.

In the elevator on the way down, Dr. Mapangou smiled to himself. On the whole it had gone quite well. The Libyans had turned out to be tabby cats compared to the Israelis. The Israelis earlier that day had been awful. Simply awful.

20

Later that same day, the day that Chubb Dunjee flew into Rome, the Director of Central Intelligence slowly dealt the Polaroid photographs onto his desk one by one, face up, much in the way that a prescient blackjack dealer will deal out the cards in a hand that he knows is going bust.

Once again Alex Reese forgot and tried to hitch one of the bolted-down chairs closer to the desk so he could study the photographs that Thane Coombs had now dealt out in a neat row. When the chair refused to budge, Reese murmured, "Shit," rose, and leaned down over the desk to give the photographs a careful inspection. Coombs could smell the bourbon on Reese's breath.

Coombs leaned back in his chair as far away as possible from Reese's breath and said, "He wanted to know, in essence, how one man without resources or training could do in a few days what we have been unable to do in—what is it now—five years?"

"You mean these?" Reese said, nodding his big bald head at the photographs.

"Yes. Those."

"The Kraut," Reese said, flicking the picture of the nude Diringshoffen with the nail of his middle finger. "He ain't too well hung, is he?"

"The President was amazed, and a little alarmed, that one man, working alone, could—"

Reese interrupted. "Dunjee got lucky. That's all."

"Lucky," Coombs said, as though it were a foreign word whose pronunciation was in some doubt.

"What else would you call it?"

"Intelligence," Coombs suggested. "Resourcefulness. Imagination. All combined with a certain element of ruthlessness perhaps? That's what I might call it."

"We had a couple of guys on him in London yesterday," Reese said. "He made them pretty quick."

"The President wants them called off."

"That's what Dunjee told them. He said unless we pull them off, he pulls out. They stuck with him anyhow—until I got word back to them to leave him alone. He flew out of Heathrow this morning to Rome. With him was that what's-her-name—Csider, that blonde who works for Paul Grimes—and another guy called Harold Hopkins. British."

"Hopkins?"

"Yeah. Hopkins."

"And what does he do?"

"Well, he did fifteen months not too long back. He's a thief."

"I see. A thief. That might explain these." Coombs indicated the photographs.

"Maybe."

"And this Hopkins is now in Dunjee's employ?"

"It looks that way."

"Where did Dunjee find him?"

"How the fuck should I know? In a bar maybe, or a pool hall, or maybe down at the labor exchange. He needed some pickup help and he went out and found him. Who cares where?"

"It might be useful."

"Then again it might not, and we could've had our guys running all over London trying to get a line on Dunjee's thief instead of doing what they were supposed to do, which, for once, they actually did."

"And that is?"

"Check the passenger roster on Dunjee's flight. The Csider woman made the reservations. She insisted on three particular seats. All first class. She went all the way up to Alitalia's PR office to get them. That's why they remembered it so well."

"Three seats?"

"Three."

"Which means that Dunjee wanted one particular seat, doesn't it? Two on one side of the aisle and one on the other. Who was in the other seat?"

"A Libyan."

"From their London Embassy?"

"Their Cultural Attaché, Faraj Abedsaid. Oklahoma University. PE degree. About thirty-eight or -nine. Single. He runs what passes for their intelligence operation in London. He's also PLO-trained. I'd guess he was the contact."

"Felix's?"

"Right."

"And Dunjee sat next to him for two hours on the plane."

"Two hours and fifteen minutes."

Coombs opened his bottom drawer, took out the pint of California brandy, and pushed it across the desk toward Reese. It was the first time he had ever offered the other man a drink.

By way of thanks, Reese said, "Ashtray," and poured brandy into a water glass. Coombs produced the small ceramic ashtray. Reese lit a cigarette. He then took a large swallow of the brandy. After that he said, "All right. Let's have it."

"I want to do something that we have just been instructed not to do," Coombs said.

"With Dunjee in Rome, you mean."

"Yes."

"But nobody can know about it."

"No."

172

"Which means I'll have to go. To Rome."

"Yes. It would seem so."

They stared at each other. It was a stare full of acknowledged complicity. Finally Reese said, "But I get London."

"Yes. You get London."

"I'll fly out of New York tomorrow."

"Why New York?"

"Here," Reese said and took two sheets of folded paper from his breast pocket. "More midnight musings—all about old Doc Mapangou. He's on the pad. Leland Timble's pad. You remember Leland."

"The computer genius and bank robber. He's keeping well, I trust, on his island paradise."

"He got Dr. Mapangou to plant the rumor."

"About the Libyan shopping expedition?"

"Right. I think Timble got to the Libyans somehow and convinced them that for a price he could set the whole deal up."

"Is that what Dr. Mapangou says?"

"No. He just admits starting the rumor."

"Then he brought it off, didn't he? Timble, I mean."

"But Felix getting snatched soured it."

Coombs leaned back in his chair and tapped his teeth with the folded sheets of paper that Reese had given him. "I wonder what was in it for Timble?"

"Money."

"He has enough. More than enough."

"What's enough?"

Coombs shrugged and said, "Our two apostates are still with Timble, I take it?"

"You mean that fucking Keeling and that fucking Spiceman?"

"Yes. You know, I never believed that about Keeling. That he stole all that gold in Angola."

"He stole it," Reese said. "He stole it and spent it."

"I never believed it. I'm still not sure that I do. He was one of the best—".

Again Reese interrupted. "I sent two of our people out of Miami yesterday to see what they could find out about Timble and his setup. They got the shit beat out of them."

"Whom did you send?"

"Harry Milker and Presse Poole. They broke Harry's arm, and Poole's maybe got a concussion."

"Pity. Who did it to them?"

"The Prime Minister's goons. They staged it pretty good though—made it look like a waterfront brawl. They even set Harry's arm."

"Did they find out anything useful?"

"Nothing—except they made contact with a guy called Cornelius. Peter Cornelius. He's sort of the local Solzhenitsyn. Probably the resident crybaby. But the Prime Minister's bunch tolerates him because he puts out a pretty nifty little tabloid—all tits and ass—and who the fuck reads the editorials? Besides, when the Prime Minister wants to brag about freedom of the press, he can always point to Cornelius. Well, anyway, Cornelius is willing to do a little work for us."

"How will he get it out?"

Reese shook his head. "That's the problem. We'll have to send somebody in."

"I'll take care of it," Coombs said and made a note. "Now, about Mapangou?"

"I want to go up to New York and milk him again before I go to Rome. I want to—" He stopped when a middle-aged woman came into the office and silently laid a half sheet of paper on Coombs's desk. The woman waited while Coombs read and then reread the four typed lines. Coombs thought a moment, then looked up at the woman, and said, "Tell them yes."

The woman nodded and left.

Coombs again reread the four typed lines on the half sheet of paper. He looked up at Reese. "The Israelis," he said. "They've been offered Felix for ten million dollars. Dr. Mapangou is to be

174

the go-between. The Israelis want to know if we'd like to go half. I said yes."

"Yeah, I heard you," Alex Reese said, realizing for the first time that he was perhaps destined to become extremely rich after all.

21

Dunjee found Harold Hopkins where Hopkins had said he would be—in the bar of the Hassler. Hopkins had a drink before him and in his hand a brochure that advertised bus tours of Rome.

"They've got a nice one here that leaves at noon and gets back around four," Hopkins said. "But I'm thinking that today might not be the day for it."

"No," Dunjee said. "It won't be." He ordered a whisky and water.

"You know how much my room is?" Hopkins said.

"How much?"

"Seventy quid, that's how much."

"Nice room?"

"The price ruins it." He moved his drink around in small circles on the bar as though it helped him think about what he planned to say next. Finally he said, "So far the money's been right."

Dunjee waited. When Hopkins remained silent, Dunjee said, "But?"

Hopkins turned to look at Dunjee. The look was cold and speculative. "But I don't know what it's all about, do I?"

"It's simple," Dunjee said. "We're looking for someone."

"And if we find him?"

"Then you'll make a lot more money."

"And if we don't?"

"Then you won't make as much."

"I could ask who we're looking for, but it wouldn't do any good, would it?"

"No. Not yet."

Hopkins nodded thoughtfully. "I'm thinking that if I've got any more questions, I should've asked them before we left London, except for maybe one, that being What's next?"

"That's a good one," Dunjee said, took out his wallet, and removed the small creased piece of ruled paper that he had found in Diringshoffen's effects and seemed to have been torn from a spiral notebook. He handed it to Hopkins. "Remember this?"

Hopkins nodded and read off the initials and the address that were written on the paper. "G. G. Eighteen via Corrado." He handed it back to Dunjee. "You think whoever we're looking for might be there?"

"No."

"I didn't think you thought that. That'd be too simple. Who do you think's going to be there?"

"I don't know," Dunjee said. "Let's go find out."

The building in the Quarticciolo section of Rome at 18 via Corrado might have been a gray slum for a hundred years or even a hundred and fifty, it was hard to tell. The cab driver had shaken his head dolefully and said something disparaging in Italian when Dunjee had given him the address.

He was still shaking his head when he let Dunjee and Hopkins out in front of the six-story building and sped off down the narrow twisting street that was choked with aged cars.

Hopkins looked up at the building and then over at Dunjee. "You've got the address, but no flat number."

"No flat number."

"And no name either."

"No name."

"Then let's go home."

"Not yet," Dunjee said. Near the building entrance, which seemed to lead into a kind of courtyard, stood a group of young Italians, most of them in their late teens. Dunjee moved over to them and said in slow English, "I am looking for someone." As he said it, he took out a twenty-dollar bill, folded it lengthwise, folded it again, and then snapped it a couple of times.

One of the youths detached himself from the group, studied the bill for a moment, and then examined Dunjee. After he was through with Dunjee he inspected Hopkins. "American?" he said finally.

"American," Dunjee agreed.

"You look for the American?"

Dunjee nodded.

The youth turned back to his peer group and said something in Italian that Dunjee didn't understand. The oldest member of the group said something in reply and shrugged.

The youth turned back to Dunjee and stared pointedly at the twenty-dollar bill. Dunjee handed it to him. The youth wrinkled his forehead as he translated what he was about to say from Italian into English.

"Fifty-three," the youth said.

"The American," Dunjee said. "Apartment fifty-three?"

The youth nodded and grinned. He held out his left arm and pantomimed injecting it with a hypodermic needle. His peer group laughed. Dunjee smiled. The youth let his head drop forward suddenly, as if he had just gone to sleep, then slyly peered up at Dunjee and said two words in Italian, which Dunjee took to mean dope fiend. Dunjee nodded knowingly and turned toward the entrance. "Fifty-three," the youth called after him, as if proud of his English. "Fifty-three."

Apartment 53 was five flights up and toward the rear of the

building. The hallway was dark, narrow, and smelled of urine. They stopped at each door and used Hopkins's cigarette lighter to read its number. When they finally reached number 53, Hopkins said, "How do we play this one?"

Dunjee shrugged. "By ear," he said and knocked on the door four times.

Nothing happened. No sounds of dragging footsteps. Nothing scurried about inside. No coughs. No whispers. Only silence. Dunjee raised his hand to knock again when the door opened and the Wreck stood there.

Chronologically, the Wreck may have been forty. The hair that fell to its shoulders was just beginning to turn gray. The hair needed a wash. So did the rest of the Wreck. The rest of it was male, whitish gray, gaunt, a stooped six feet, and not quite unshaved enough to be called bearded.

"Who're you?" the Wreck said through a gray-lipped mouth that had sores on it. Above the mouth was a runny nose that divided the hundred-year-old blue eyes. The eyes looked tired and defeated—as if they had sued for peace in 1916 and lost. For clothing the Wreck wore a snot-smeared Yale sweat shirt with holes in it and below that some jeans. On the bare feet were sandals. The nails on the big toes were thick and yellow and long enough to curl over and down.

The Wreck's question had been asked in a kind of Italian. He tried it again in English. "Who're you?"

"American Express," Dunjee said. "We brought you the money."

Something flickered in the Wreck's eyes. Hope perhaps. It died quickly. "Like hell."

"Let's talk about it," Dunjee said, giving the door a firm, steady push. The Wreck pushed back. Hopkins moved over and leaned his weight against the door.

"How much money?" the Wreck said.

"That's what we'd like to talk about."

The Wreck moved back from the door. Dunjee went in, followed by Hopkins. There was only the one room—a big room, high-ceilinged. It had three windows. The windows were dirty. On the floor in one corner was a mattress. On the mattress a thin female cat nursed four kittens. The kittens appeared to be about five weeks old.

The Wreck went over to the mattress and sat down on it. He petted the mother cat on the head. The cat closed its eyes and purred. "All right," the Wreck said, "talk."

Dunjee looked around the room first. There were no closets, no other doors. A zinc sink with a single tap decorated one corner. The tap dripped and made a steady sharp clinking sound as the water struck something in the bottom of the sink. Hopkins went over and turned the tap off.

There were also three shelves that held some canned goods—sweet stuff mostly—and a wooden table and two chairs that didn't match, and a hotplate, and that was the furniture. All of it. Dunjee decided that if there were any pans and plates, they were in the bottom of the sink.

He moved to the table and sat down. Hopkins took the other chair. Dunjee took out a notebook and a ball-point pen. He leafed through the notebook until he seemed to find the page he wanted. He clicked the pen into writing position, looked over at the Wreck, smiled slightly, and said, "Name?"

"What the fuck is this?"

Dunjee turned to Hopkins. "I thought you said we had him down for five hundred dollars."

"Providing he can come up with a few facts," Hopkins said, "five hundred it is."

"Five hundred?" the Wreck said.

"I'm thinking you could use it, mate," Hopkins said.

"Who the fuck's he?" the Wreck said.

Dunjee smiled at Hopkins. "My associate, Mr. Ralph."

"I know you, don't I?" the Wreck said.

Dunjee shook his head. "I don't think so."

"Yeah, I know you from somewhere. From way back."

"Name?" Dunjee said.

"Five hundred, you said."

Dunjee sighed, took out his wallet, and handed it to Hopkins. "Prime the pump a little, Mr. Ralph."

"Right," Hopkins said, rose, moved over to the mattress, and squatted down by the Wreck. He opened the wallet so that the Wreck could see all the hundred-dollar bills it contained. Hopkins took one out. The Wreck reached for it. Hopkins drew it back. "Name?" Hopkins said.

The Wreck wiped his nose on the sleeve of his Yale sweat shirt. "You know my name," he said. "Goucher. Giles Goucher." Hopkins handed him the hundred-dollar bill.

The Wreck brought it up close to his eyes. Hopkins reached over and patted the mother cat on the head. The cat smiled—or seemed to. "Nice cat you've got here, Mr. Goucher," Hopkins said, rose, and went back to the table.

Dunjee was staring at Goucher. Then he smiled slightly, shook his head, and wrote something down in the notebook. "Age?" Dunjee said.

"Forty-one."

"Looks a hundred, don't he?" Hopkins said.

"With reason," Dunjee said. He looked over at Goucher again. "It might be simpler if you just told us about it."

"About what?"

"Anvil Five—that bunch. You can begin with the German— the blond guy with all the muscles."

"Who are you guys?"

"Foreign correspondents," Dunjee said. "I'm with the New York *Times*. Mr. Ralph's with the *Times* of London."

"Like hell."

"You want the other four hundred, Giles?" Dunjee said.

Goucher drew the other sleeve of his Yale sweat shirt across his nose, looked around the apartment, and then back at Dunjee. "What do you think?"

"Then tell us about it."

Goucher sniffed. "Where do you want me to start?"

"When you left the States."

"That was seven years ago."

"Is that all? I thought it was longer. Where did you go after you left the States—Beirut?"

Goucher stared at Dunjee suspiciously. "I know you from somewhere. From somewhere way back."

"I don't think so."

"Yeah, I know you. I'll get it in a minute. How'd you know about Beirut?"

"I'm just guessing."

"Sure, I went to Beirut. I was there awhile."

"How long?"

"Maybe a year. Maybe longer. Then Damascus for a while. Then Baghdad. I was on the circuit."

"What circuit?"

"The PLO circuit. I gave talks, you know, about how we did things in the States."

"How long've you been in Rome, Giles?" Dunjee said.

"A couple of years."

"No more talks?"

"I got sick."

"Did they come to you—or did you go to them?"

"Who?"

"You want the money?"

"Yeah, I want it. I went to them."

"Three of them, weren't there?"

"I just saw the German. Frank."

"Is that what they call him—Frank?"

"Yeah. Frank."

"What's his real name?"

"I don't know. Something German."

"Try."

"Diringshoffen. Bernt Diringshoffen."

"How'd you know they were in Rome?"

Goucher shrugged. "I heard. I heard they were looking for—" He didn't finish the sentence.

"Recruits?"

"They don't call 'em that."

"But you volunteered."

"We just talked. It was all exploratory."

"But they turned you down."

Goucher looked around the room again. He shook his head sadly at what he saw, sighed, and said, "Well, what the fuck. Can you blame them?"

"What'd they say about Felix?"

"I only talked to Frank."

"What'd Frank say about Felix?"

"He just hinted."

"Hinted at what?"

"Well, he hinted that Felix was having a rough time. That's why they were looking for—for new people."

"But not you?"

"No, I guess not."

"They still in Rome?" Dunjee made the question as casual as he could.

"No. I don't think so anyway."

"Where'd they go?"

"How should I know?"

"For four hundred dollars, Giles—where'd they go?"

"Who the fuck are you guys?"

"I'm with the CIA. Mr. Ralph's with MI 6."

"Like hell."

"You asked," Dunjee said, and then put a hard cutting edge on his voice. "For four hundred bucks, Giles—where'd they go?"

"I met Frank in a hotel, a cheap one down near the Piazza del Popolo. That's where we talked. Somebody came up to the room. A woman. They talked in German—except she had a French accent. They only said a few words, but they were talking about what time a plane left. I had four years of German at Oberlin. I don't guess Frank knew that. So they talked about the plane and when it left."

"A plane to where?"

"Malta."

Dunjee sighed. "Pay him, Mr. Ralph."

Hopkins again rose and went over to the mattress, where he slowly counted out four hundred-dollar bills into Goucher's palm. "Makes you feel just a bit like Judas, don't it, lad?" Hopkins said.

"Fuck off."

Dunjee took out a cigarette and lit it. "Miss the Weathermen, Giles?"

Goucher looked up at Dunjee, then down at the money in his hand, then up at Dunjee again. There was recognition in his eyes. "Yeah," he said, "I know you. You're Dunjee. I remember you now. You were a fucking Congressman."

Dunjee rose. "Let's go, Mr. Ralph."

"Suits me," Hopkins said.

They started for the door, but stopped when Goucher called after them, "Hey, Dunjee."

Dunjee turned.

"I fucked your wife, man!" Goucher yelled. He looked at the money in his hand. "Did you know that, man? I fucked your wife!" He threw the four hundred-dollar bills at Dunjee. They didn't go far. They fluttered down, one of them settling slowly on the mother cat.

"You want me to go pop him one?" Hopkins said.

Dunjee shook his head and opened the door. "For what?" he said. "Telling the truth?"

22

The Polaroid snapshot showed Bingo McKay, left ear neatly bandaged, sitting in a chair, actually smiling as he held the front page of the *International Herald Tribune* up under his chin. There was nothing in the photograph's background—nothing useful anyway—only a white blur, and the Ambassador decided that they probably had used a bedsheet to block out anything that might have hinted at the location.

"He looks . . . fit enough, don't you think?" Faraj Abedsaid remarked as the big man with the round chocolate-colored face and the scarred cheeks produced a small magnifying glass. The big man was His Excellency Olufemi Dokubo, Nigeria's Ambassador to the United States. Dokubo used the magnifying glass to examine the headlines on the *Herald Tribune*'s front page.

Dokubo had flown into Rome that morning from Washington and waited at the Nigerian Embassy for the Libyans to call. He had waited all morning. When the call finally came, just after noon, there had been fifteen minutes of silly palaver over where the meeting should take place. The Libyans had insisted on a neutral site. Ambassador Dokubo had suggested several, including the Swiss Embassy, pointing out that nothing could be more

185

neutral than that. But the Libyans—on one pretext or another—had turned down each of his suggestions until Dokubo finally had suggested the place where they were now meeting.

It was an immense conference room—more hall than room—in the UN's Food and Agriculture Organization complex. Dokubo and Abedsaid sat at the head of a sixty-two-foot-long conference table around which selected food and agricultural experts sometimes gathered to muse about the three billion or so persons in the world who went to bed hungry every night.

The room was high-ceilinged and chandeliered and draped and carpeted. It had a hushed air, as if something monumental was about to be said. Alone in the room, Abedsaid and Dokubo found themselves whispering to each other.

The night before, just prior to catching his flight to Rome, Ambassador Dokubo had had his second meeting with President Jerome McKay. They again had met in the Oval Office. The President looked tired. He had put one foot up on his desk, locked his hands behind his head, and stared at Dokubo.

"We haven't got him," the President said.

Because of his quick mind, it had taken Dokubo only a second to realize what McKay was talking about. "Felix, you mean," Dokubo said, trying to disguise his shock.

"That's right. We haven't got him. We never did. We don't know who has."

"But they still *think* you do. The Libyans."

"Yes."

"I see." Dokubo paused as he decided on the phrasing of his question. "Is there any possibility that he may have been—uh—mislaid?"

The President grinned. It was a sour, even bitter grin. "You mean am I sure the CIA hasn't got him locked up out in a toolshed somewhere? I thought of that myself. They haven't got him. I made sure. Damn sure." He looked at Dokubo sympathetically. "Puts you in a hell of a bind, doesn't it?"

"It reduces my effectiveness as a negotiator."

"There won't be any negotiations."

"You wish me to withdraw?" Dokubo said, not quite sure whether he wanted the answer to be yes or no.

"No, sir, I want you to do me a favor." The President took his foot down from the desk, unlocked his hands, and leaned forward in his chair. His expression was both grave and candid.

He's preparing to sell me something, Dokubo thought.

"Around this town you have a certain reputation, Mr. Ambassador," the President said.

First the flattery, thought Dokubo, nonetheless eager to hear what form it would take.

"The consensus among your peers is this: If their own lives depended upon the services of a skilled diplomat, then ninety-five percent of them would vote for you. I don't know who the other five percent would vote for. Probably themselves."

Dokubo could feel the flush of pleasure rising up his neck until it reached his ears. There was also a very pleasant tingling sensation. He kept his face impassive, and his deep voice rich, but modest. "That is very flattering, Mr. President."

The President shook his head. "I wouldn't call it flattery. I'd call it a pretty realistic assessment. And that's why I'm going to ask you for this favor. I'm going to ask you to save my brother's life."

Dokubo started to speak, but the President held up a hand. "Hear me out. We're trying to get Felix back from whoever's got him. It's being approached from several angles. If we do get him back, then we'll ship him out to the Libyans before he even has time to change his shirt. But I'd be a fool to predict anything at this juncture. So I'm asking you—humbly asking you—to do me this favor. I'm asking you to save my brother's life. If you agree, you'll need all your considerable experience and skill to do the only thing that *will* save it."

"And that one thing is what?"

"Stall."

Dokubo nodded slowly. "For how long?"

"I don't know. Days—perhaps even weeks. It's an art, of course —stalling. I needn't tell you what the tricks are. From what I hear, it would be like telling my grandmother how to suck eggs."

Dokubo smiled and tried not to preen. "I have had some small experience," he said. "At stalling."

In the FAO conference room, Dokubo put down the magnifying glass and looked up at Abedsaid. "He would seem to be still alive—as of yesterday."

"He's quite alive," Abedsaid said. "I trust you have brought similar proof of Berrio-Brito's well-being."

"Felix, you mean?"

"You prefer to call him that?"

"Simpler, don't you think?"

"All right," said Abedsaid. "Felix. Have you brought evidence of his well-being?"

"Before we touch on that, I think we should deal with another pressing matter. And that is, When will the President be allowed to talk with his brother by telephone?"

Abedsaid shook his head. "There will be no telephoning."

Dokubo looked surprised. He did it quite well, even managing to put a measure of shock into his expression. "But it was my understanding that at least one telephone call would be permitted."

"I'm afraid you were misinformed, Mr. Ambassador. There will be no telephoning."

Dokubo sighed. "I will have to report this new development to my principals, of course."

"In the meantime, you can furnish me with the evidence of Felix's safety and well-being."

"I'm afraid that will have to be tabled until our next meeting. My instructions are quite explicit. If we could have begun the negotiations for the telephone call, then the evidence you request could have been discussed. Now, however, our discussions must be held in abeyance until new consultations with my principals have been concluded."

What a slick, smooth son of a bitch, Abedsaid thought. He made his face wrinkle itself into a frown which he hoped was full of foreboding. "I deeply regret the hesitancy that has already crept into our negotiations. My superiors in Tripoli are not men of endless patience. I'm afraid they might even suspect that you could be engaged in delaying tactics."

"Delaying tactics?" Dokubo said, his deep voice full of surprise and resentment. "These are delicate negotiations, Mr. Abedsaid. It was Colonel Mourabet himself who at the outset stated that the fate of civilization may well hang in the balance. I came to this meeting fully expecting to discuss the arrangements whereby the President could talk by telephone to his brother. But there has been no discussion. No give and take. Only a peremptory rejection of what I think is a most reasonable request. Now I must go back to my principals empty-handed. Unless, of course . . ."

Here it comes, Abedsaid thought. "Unless what, Mr. Ambassador?"

"You are quite certain that there can be no telephone call?"

"Quite certain."

"Then what would you say to a tape recording? A brief message from the brother to the President. Perhaps he could read a few of that day's headlines in the *Herald Tribune*—and then, say, two minutes of reassuring chat. It would not be nearly as responsive as a telephone call, of course, but I just might be able to convince my principals to accept it as a reasonable alternative."

"In essence, you're refusing to give me any evidence whatsoever of Felix's well-being?"

Dokubo sighed. "I am afraid we cannot begin to touch on that until the President has heard his brother's voice. About that he was adamant. Now that it is for the first time clear that there can be no telephone call, I think the President might be persuaded to

189

settle for a tape recording along the lines I have suggested. I cannot, unfortunately, guarantee that."

Abedsaid rose. "I will have to consult with Tripoli."

"And I with Washington." Dokubo rose, smiling. "Do you find this place . . . comfortable?" He made a vague gesture that encompassed the enormous room.

"It will do."

"Then to allow ourselves plenty of time to make sure that our next session will prove more productive, shall we meet here at this same time— Let's see, what would you say to forty-eight hours from now?"

Abedsaid smiled coldly. "I'd say you were stalling."

Dokubo shot up his eyebrows. "Stalling?"

Abedsaid nodded, staring thoughtfully at the Nigerian. "Although I'm not yet sure why."

"Forty-eight hours then?" Dokubo said with his best smile.

"Twenty-four," Abedsaid said, turned, and left.

The call from Tripoli had the Libyan Embassy in an uproar. It was Colonel Mourabet himself on the line, demanding to speak to Faraj Abedsaid. When told that Abedsaid was unavailable, the Colonel started sacking Embassy personnel, beginning with the Ambassador himself. By the time the Colonel reached the Third Secretary, Abedsaid returned from his meeting with Dokubo, was rushed to the phone, and spoke soothingly into it in Maghribi.

It was a long conversation, lasting more than an hour. Abedsaid listened mostly at first and then, toward the end, did most of the talking himself. It was there, toward the end, during the last twelve minutes, that the conversation centered around the American, an ex-Congressman called Chubb Dunjee.

Dunjee awoke hungry. His watch was on the nightstand. He reached out with a bare arm and picked it up. They had left a light on across the room—a small lamp with a weak bulb. But it had been strong enough to let them see what they were doing, and he could read his watch by it. It was 9 P.M., actually a minute or two after.

Dunjee turned to look at Delft Csider. She was asleep, breathing softly, her mouth slightly open. The bed covers had slipped down around her waist, leaving her breasts bare. Breasts like what? Dunjee wondered. Larger than lemons, but smaller than melons. Breasts were always being compared to melons. Cantaloupes? Honeydew? Both rather large. More like oranges, he decided, in the scale of things anyway. He reached over and touched the nipple on her left breast.

She stirred, opened her eyes, and smiled. "Again?" she said. "You'll notice I didn't say, 'Not again.' "

"I was just wondering," he said.

"What?"

"If you're hungry?"

She thought about it. "We didn't eat, did we? Not food anyway."

"Not much nourishment in the other. A trace of protein, I think."

She stretched and yawned, not bothering to cover her mouth. He noticed she had no fillings in her teeth. "What's wrong with your teeth?" he said.

"Wrong?"

"No fillings."

"They don't decay. No matter what I eat, nothing happens to them. I've got good gums, too. See?" She snarled at him.

"You're lucky," Dunjee said and reached for the phone. They were in his bedroom. Two hours earlier, still holding their drinks, they had almost wandered into it from the living room of the $220-a-day suite with its fourth-floor view of the Spanish Steps. The preliminaries had been brief and largely silent. The lovemaking had been both vigorous and a bit noisy. They had discovered that they were both talkers. Delft Csider was also something of a screamer—small joyous screams that she cut off by biting anything handy. But she didn't bite too hard, and after a time Dunjee almost began to enjoy it.

"What would you like?" he said when room service answered the phone.

"Eggs and shrimp," she said. "Something gooey and Italian made out of eggs and shrimp. Lots of shrimp."

Dunjee ordered two scampi omelettes and some wine. After he hung up the phone, he looked at her. "Drink?"

She nodded. "Make it weak."

Dunjee rose and went into the living room, returning with two glasses. He handed her one and sat down on the edge of the bed next to her.

"Were you born cockeyed?" she said, touching him gently just beneath his left eye.

He shook his head. "Bayonet practice. A sergeant was teaching me the vertical butt stroke. It shattered the cheekbone. The bone didn't heal right, and ever since I've looked like something out of Picasso."

"It's nice," she said. "It makes you look a little like a—" The knock at the living-room door kept her from completing her comparison. "That couldn't be room service," she said. "Not this soon."

"Maybe it's the tickets."

"To Malta?"

"You did tell them to send them up, didn't you?"

She nodded. "But they said they'd send them up in the morning."

"Maybe it's Hopkins," Dunjee said, looked for his pants, found them on the floor, and slipped them on. He looked for his shirt, discovered it on the floor on the other side of the bed, and put it on, not bothering to tuck in its tails. He went to the living-room door dressed like that, barefoot, drink still in hand, and opened it.

There were four of them, including Harold Hopkins, who was sandwiched in between two large men with mustaches. The two

192

men were young, in their late twenties. The fourth man had done the knocking. He held a pistol in his right hand. The pistol, an automatic, was down by his side, not pointing at anything. The man with the pistol was Faraj Abedsaid.

Abedsaid smiled. "I think," he said, "that you and I must have a talk, Congressman."

Dunjee backed away from the door. Abedsaid waited until the two large men herded Hopkins into the room. Abedsaid followed them in and closed the door, making sure it was locked. The two men moved over and leaned against it.

Hopkins looked at Dunjee and then let his glance roam around the room. "I didn't have no fucking choice, mate," he said and headed for the Scotch bottle.

"Here," Dunjee said, holding out his own glass. "Add a touch to mine."

Hopkins took the glass and began mixing the drinks. Abedsaid waved his pistol toward the bedroom door. "Miss Csider?"

Dunjee nodded.

"Ask her to come out, please."

Again, Dunjee nodded and moved into the bedroom. Delft Csider was already dressing. "We've got a little trouble," Dunjee said.

"How bad?"

"I don't know yet."

"I'll be right out."

Dunjee went back into the living room and accepted the drink from Hopkins.

Abedsaid smiled pleasantly. "It's been rather a frantic day. Much of it was spent in checking you out, Congressman. Our own facilities are a bit limited, so here and there we had to use our friends. You have quite a reputation—at least in Mexico. The Mordida Man. It means the bribe giver, doesn't it?"

"Something like that," Dunjee said.

Delft Csider came out of the bedroom, nodded coolly at Abedsaid, ignored the two who were leaning against the door, and lowered herself into a chair.

"Would you care for a drink, Miss Csider?" Abedsaid said.

"No thank you."

He nodded, looked around, decided on an armchair, and sat down. He held the pistol loosely in his lap. Dunjee and Hopkins continued to stand.

"It was, of course," Abedsaid continued, "no coincidence that you sat next to me on the plane this morning. Allow me to congratulate you on your performance. It was quite convincing. You succeeded in arousing my curiosity, which, I presume, is exactly what you intended to do." Although Abedsaid hadn't posed it as a question, he waited as though expecting an answer.

After a moment, Dunjee said, "Something like that."

"You were signaling, if I'm not mistaken, your availability."

"Or maybe I was just trying to hustle a rich Arab."

Abedsaid smiled again. "Now Mr. Hopkins here is almost equally interesting. Mr. Hopkins is a thief—and a good one, if my informants in London are correct. My apartment there was burgled a few days ago. Another small coincidence."

"Get on with it, Jack," Hopkins said.

"Yes, I suppose I should. All of this brings us to the topic that concerns us all—Mr. Bingo McKay, your President's brother."

"What the fuck's he talking about?" Hopkins said.

"He's not sure yet," Dunjee said, adding softly, "Are you?"

Abedsaid continued to smile. "We want you to take a trip. All three of you. An airplane trip. The plane is standing by. Now you can either go willingly or you can be smuggled aboard, which would be rather messy—drugs, that sort of thing. I strongly urge you to go willingly."

"Go where?" Dunjee said.

"Tripoli."

"Why Tripoli?"

"Someone there wishes to talk to you. Just outside Tripoli, actually."

194

"In the desert?"

"Yes, in the desert."

"Who wants to talk?"

"Colonel Mourabet."

"Himself?"

"Himself."

"All right," Dunjee said. "We'll go."

23

It was somewhat earlier that same day, around midnight, New York time, that Dr. Joseph Mapangou sat on the bench in Central Park wondering how long it would be before he was mugged. He had been waiting for fifteen minutes on the isolated bench, deep in the park, and already he had turned down the importunings of a sad-faced homosexual who had begged him to let him touch it, just for a second.

Dr. Mapangou, concealing his horror very well, he thought, had politely told the man to go away. The man had offered him eighteen dollars. Dr. Mapangou had started to giggle. It was a high-pitched, almost hysterical giggle. The man had cursed him and gone away. Dr. Mapangou had stopped giggling.

He sat now, legs tightly crossed, his head swiveling at each mysterious sound that came from the night creatures who crept through the jungle that surrounded him. But it is not a jungle, he told himself repeatedly. It is only a well-kept park, and if there are creatures in it, they are probably only lost dogs, small dogs. Tiny poodles, most likely, with rhinestone collars.

Behind Dr. Mapangou, well back in the indigo shadows, the big man eased slowly around an old tree. He stood there staring at Dr. Mapangou's back, which was faintly illuminated by what little light came from the park lamp some forty or fifty feet down the path. The big man stood almost motionless, breathing silently through his mouth, as he watched the homosexual come and go. The big man waited another ten minutes before he began to move, one slow, sure step at a time, toward the fretting man on the park bench.

When he was no more than three feet from Dr. Mapangou, the big man said, "Well?"

Dr. Mapangou jumped from the bench and spun around. He peered into the darkness. "Is it you?"

"Who else?" Alex Reese said, moving into the lamplight so that it made his bald head gleam.

"I do not like this place," Dr. Mapangou said. "It is frightening. I could have been attacked, robbed."

"But you weren't," Reese said as he moved around the bench and sat down. "Well?" he said again.

Dr. Mapangou glanced over his shoulder before he lowered himself gingerly to the bench next to the big man who smelled of whisky.

"The Israelis were difficult," Dr. Mapangou said.

"How?"

"They wanted to ask questions."

"But they transferred the money?"

"At two P.M."

"What about the Libyans?"

"At three-fifteen this afternoon. They asked no questions. They were, well—sullen."

"And the banks?"

"I went to both and made sure that they did exactly as you instructed. The money was transferred to your Mr. Brian Brandon in Montreal. I do not understand who this Brandon is."

"I already explained it."

"But I did not understand it."

"Brian Brandon is no one. But he's left standing orders with the Montreal bank, which has instructions to transfer anything over one thousand dollars in his account to the account of one Arturo Foglio in Panama. There, Señor Foglio has left instructions with the Panama bank that any amount over one thousand dollars deposited to *his* account is to be transferred by wire to the bank account of a casino in the Bahamas. Once the money is transferred, the casino is notified. The casino picks up the money in cash. Seventy-two hours later, the funds, still in cash, but now in different currencies, are picked up at the casino by a messenger. For identification purposes, the messenger—whoever he is—needs only a phrase. That's all. The phrase automatically changes every month. This month's phrase is a quote from James Monroe's first inaugural address: 'National honor is national property of the highest value.' "

Dr. Mapangou nodded thoughtfully. "Who selects the monthly phrases?" he said at last.

"They were all selected years ago. The man who selected them was a trusted employee of the CIA. Dead now. Left a wife and three kids. He called the whole thing the Panama Laundry. It was only used once, but nobody ever canceled it. When he died, I cleaned out his safe. The only records of the transfer route were there, in the safe. Somebody got careless and there just happened to be a small Xerox machine in his office. Afterwards, I turned everything in the safe over to security and made sure it was destroyed. Now nobody knows about the Panama Laundry except you and me."

" 'National honor is national property of the highest value,' " Dr. Mapangou said and sadly shook his head. "This is not an honorable thing we are doing."

"No, but it's profitable. Profit and honor aren't often mentioned in the same breath. If you're not as honorable as you were yesterday, you're two million dollars richer. How does it feel?"

Dr. Mapangou didn't seem to hear the question. Again he shook his head, a sad, doleful expression on his face. "But what can I tell them?"

"Who?"

"The Israelis and the Libyans."

"Tell them the truth. Tell them all about Mr. Arnold and Mr. Benedict. You were just the go-between."

"They will not believe me."

"Sure they will," Reese said and suddenly widened his eyes, as though he had just seen something that startled him. "Don't turn until I tell you to. Then turn very slowly, and look where I say."

Dr. Mapangou licked his lips and nodded. His own eyes were popped and round with terror. "Now?" he whispered.

"Not yet."

The two men waited. They waited almost thirty seconds. "Now," Reese said.

Dr. Mapangou slowly turned. "Where?" he whispered.

"Just a little to your left and forty feet or so ahead. Near the lamp."

Dr. Mapangou stared into the darkness. Reese rose silently behind him. He slipped one big hand under Dr. Mapangou's chin and clasped the other over his forehead. He jerked the head back and to the right and broke the neck. Dr. Mapangou died still peering into the darkness, his eyes wide open.

Reese lowered the body to the sidewalk. He went through the pockets quickly, removing the wallet, and stripping it of its cash. He thrust the cash into his pocket, and smeared the wallet on Dr. Mapangou's blue suit. He also slipped a gold watch from Dr. Mapangou's left wrist. He put the watch in another pocket. After that, he rose, looked around, and melted away into the darkness of the trees.

Reese had gone only about ten feet into the trees when the voice said, "If you don't stop, you're dead."

Reese stopped.

"Very slowly," the voice said. "Hands on top of your head."

Reese slowly put his hands on top of his bald head.

"There're two of us," the voice said. "I'm three feet behind you.

I've got a thirty-eight Smith and Wesson. It has hollow-points. They won't go through you—not all the way. But they'll make a mess."

"All right," Reese said.

"We're going to pat you down," the voice said.

"All right," Reese said.

In front of Reese, no more than two or three feet away, a man stepped out from behind some trees. He was a tall man, a bit gangly. "Mr. Arnold, right?" Reese said.

"Hello, Alex," Franklin Keeling said to his former CIA colleague.

"Who's behind me," Reese said, "that fucking Spiceman?"

"Uh-huh," Keeling said and ran his hands over Reese, not forgetting his ankles, his crotch, and the small of his back.

Keeling stepped back. "The way you broke the nigger's neck," he said. "That was kinda neat."

It was the same rented limousine that they always used, the stretched Cadillac with the driver called Henry. The dividing window was rolled up. Spiceman sat in one of the jump seats, both hands around the .38-caliber revolver that was pointed directly at Reese's stomach. Keeling sat next to Reese on the rear seat.

Reese looked out the window. "I suppose you want it back," he said.

"What?" Keeling said.

"The money."

"What money?"

Reese turned to look at him. The expression on Reese's face was one of surprise, which quickly dissolved into deep suspicion. "The twenty million. That money. The money I took off the Libyans and the Israelis, except Langley went halfeys with the Israelis."

"No kidding," Keeling said, his voice totally devoid of surprise. "What'd you use to move it, the Panama Laundry?"

The look on Reese's face quickly rearranged itself back into one of total surprise. "Nobody knew about that. Nobody except Eubanks—and he's dead."

"Eubanks didn't think it up," Keeling said. "I thought it up and handed it to him." Keeling reached into a pocket and brought out a small blue notebook with a leather cover. He thumbed through it. "You wanta hear this month's code phrase? Listen to this: 'National honor is national property of the highest value.' Right?"

Reese nodded slowly, then turned his head to stare out the car's window. "All right. You win. I lose. Now what?"

"You don't lose," Spiceman said. "Not if you work it right."

Reese turned back. "Okay," he said. "How?"

"You know something, Brother Reese," Keeling said, "we're sure glad it's you. Christ, when I think of some of the guys it could've been. You know, real dummies. Or tightasses. That'd've been even worse. But you, you've always been kinda flexible."

Reese nodded slowly. "Flexible," he said. "How flexible?"

Keeling waved one of his big thick hands back and forth. He did it with curious grace. "You're gonna have to bend with the breeze. First one way, then the other."

"I don't think he wants to talk about the breeze," Spiceman said. "I think he wants to talk about the money. The twenty million."

"Well, shit, he can have that. I thought that was all cleared up."

Reese licked a dry tongue over dry lips. "You got anything to drink?"

"Drink? Sure. What're you drinking nowadays, bourbon?"

"Bourbon."

Keeling leaned forward and pulled out a miniature bar. He filled two small glasses with bourbon from a decanter and handed one to Reese, keeping the other for himself. He didn't offer any to Spiceman, who kept his hands wrapped around the revolver that was still aimed at Reese's stomach.

"I can keep the money?" Reese said slowly, as if asking the question of some foreigner whose English depended on the two dimly remembered sessions at Berlitz long ago.

"Sure," Keeling said. "Hell, Spiceman and I don't need it. We've got plenty. Right, Jack?"

"After the first five million, who counts?" Spiceman said, but smiled in a way that kept Reese from believing him.

"What about your boss?" Reese said.

"He's going to be happy it's you," Keeling said.

Again Reese nodded thoughtfully and finished his whisky. "All this started with Felix, didn't it?"

"Felix was just a tool," Keeling said.

"A tool to do what with?"

"To give us a handle."

"On me."

"Or somebody like you."

"What happens to Felix now?" Reese said. "You going to hand him back?"

Keeling looked questioningly at Spiceman. After a moment, Spiceman shrugged. Keeling turned back toward Reese. "Well, poor old Felix, he sort of had an accident."

"An accident?"

"Uh-huh."

"Bad?"

"Pretty bad. Fatal."

"No shit?" Reese said.

"No shit."

Reese held out his glass. "How about another little touch, just to ease the sorrow."

As Keeling poured him another drink, Reese said, "The fingers. Was he dead or alive when you cut them off?"

"Dead. He just went to sleep and never woke up. It must've been real peaceful."

"They think it was us."

202

"Who?"

"Felix's bunch, Anvil Five. They think it was Langley. So do the Libyans."

"Is that a fact," Keeling said, not quite succeeding in making it a question.

"But that's all anybody's going to get back—the two fingers?"

"That's all that's left. By now, the fish have had the rest."

"They're going to start wondering what happened to their money."

"Well, I guess they'll just have to ask old Doc Mapangou about that, won't they?"

Reese was silent for a moment. Finally he said, "Mapangou could have told them about you."

"You mean about Mr. Arnold and Mr. Benedict? That's all he ever knew us by."

"Yeah, that was sort of cute. They could backtrack though. Especially the Israelis. They're not bad at it."

Spiceman shook his head, not taking his eyes off Reese's stomach. "They're not all that good either. But let's say they did get a line on us. Guess who we'd lead them to."

Reese's big chin went up and down three times in a trio of slow, thoughtful nods. "What've you got—pictures?"

"Of you and Mapangou?" Keeling said. "Yeah, we've got pictures. Jack here's the camera nut. Fast film, infra-red. Whatever. He's got you coming out of the bushes and sitting down and getting up and breaking Old Black Joe's neck and all that. But look at it this way. If you pick up the money down in the Bahamas, we really won't need the pictures, will we?"

Reese drained his glass of whisky, then tipped it up again to make sure he had got the last drop. He was still looking at the glass when he asked his question. "What do you really want?"

"Really?" Keeling said. "Well, we thought we'd let the boss tell you that."

The limousine took a sudden right turn. Reese looked out the window and realized where they were going. He turned back to Keeling. "In Jersey?"

"In Jersey," Keeling agreed.

There was a uniformed guard on the Newark International gate that led to the area where the 727 was. The guard held up his hand for the Cadillac to stop. He went around to the driver's window. The window went down, and a hand came out. In the hand was a plain white envelope, unsealed. The guard peered into the envelope, looked around quickly, stuffed it away, and moved to the gate, which he slid open. The Cadillac rolled through it onto the field.

Keeling went up the rear steps of the cream-colored 727 first, followed by Reese. Behind Reese came Spiceman, still holding the pistol with both hands. The three men entered the lounge section of the airplane, the same section through which the man called Felix had been carried and then tumbled out and down through the rear entrance a mile into the sea.

Seated in one of the lounge section's armchairs was a young man with a roundish, childlike face. He smiled as the three men entered the lounge section. It was a warm, almost cozy smile that displayed no teeth.

Keeling made the introductions. "I don't think you know the boss. Alex Reese. Leland Timble."

"So happy you were able to join us, Mr. Reese," Timble said, ignoring the pistol that was still aimed at Reese's chest. "Please," Timble continued and waved vaguely. "Let's everyone sit down."

Everyone sat down. No one said anything as the co-pilot came through and saw to the raising of the rear steps. On his way back, the co-pilot pretended not to see the pistol and said, "Fasten your seat belts, folks."

Spiceman waited until Reese fastened his seat belt before he put the pistol down in his lap so he could fasten his own. The pilot started the engines one by one. A few moments later the plane began to taxi toward a runway.

Finally Reese spoke. "Where're we going?"

Timble smiled. "That depends on you, Mr. Reese. We can either go to our place, which is quite nice—or we could go to the Bahamas. I think for you the Bahamas would be far more profitable."

24

No one spoke as the plane taxied onto the runway. There was that familiar pause when the plane seems to gather its strength, as though preparing to lunge. Then the engines screamed, the plane began to move, and Timble's face paled and stayed that way until the plane was up and level. Reese noted the blanching and filed the fact away in his mind. Maybe it would prove useful. But he wasn't too hopeful. Reese decided that he had just about run out of hope.

He leaned forward in his chair toward Timble, his arms and big belly resting on his knees. When he spoke, his deep voice was a confidential rumble. "Let's have it, sonny. The bottom line."

" 'The bottom line,' " Timble said, as if repeating a scrap of half-forgotten poetry. "Do people still say that? They were saying that years ago when I first—well, went abroad. The . . . bottom . . . line. Well, Mr. Reese, the bottom line is simply this: I want to go home."

"Home? Back to the States?"

"Yes."

Reese shook his head. "It's got to be complicated."

"Yes, it is—and it becomes more so."

"Leland's mind," Keeling said, "it doesn't work like yours and mine, Alex."

"I'd sort of like to hear how it does work."

Timble smiled his happy-face smile, which he almost always did when given a chance to show off. "I think I shall start at the very beginning. Not too far back, of course. Only about six months ago when I awoke one morning and decided that I was, well, homesick." He smiled again, shyly this time, as if admitting to some minor but forgivable vice. Thumbsucking, perhaps.

"Homesick," Reese said.

"Yes."

Reese nodded, trying hard to believe. "Okay."

"Well, after deciding that there was really only one cure, I also decided that one simply couldn't return empty-handed. I mean, who knows how long it would be before I again had the opportunity to develop a project that was—well, let's say, beyond the pale. Do you follow me?"

Reese nodded again. "So far. You wanted to make one last big score, right?"

"Exactly. So I decided to become an honest broker. I decided to patch up relations between the U.S. and Libya."

"You decided?" Reese said.

"Yes."

"Just like that?"

"Leland's got just an awful lot of confidence," Spiceman said, his face perfectly straight.

"It wasn't really all that difficult. First of all, we made a discreet approach to the Libyans to see how much they would be willing to pay to repair their ruptured relations with Washington. Eventually we negotiated a most reasonable flat fee, one that included all expenses."

"How much?" Reese asked, fascinated.

"Twenty million."

"Dollars?"

"Dollars. That would, of course, include all"—Timble paused

to smile—"bribes. Naturally, we told them that the bribes would be simply enormous. They accepted that as a matter of course, and we requested and received an initial payment of five million. Then we went to work."

"Rumors," Reese said.

"Yes, rumors and hints. A little cash here and there—not too much—helped things along, and before you could say Jack Robinson the window-shopping trip was on. For arranging that we asked for another five million, and things were going quite nicely until something happened out there in California, which I still can't understand, and the trip was canceled."

"That was about the time you were putting the grab on Felix in London," Reese said.

"Do you think the two might be connected?" Timble said.

Reese shrugged. "Who knows? Tell me about Felix."

"Yes, well, Felix was to be my ticket home, providing everything worked out according to plan, which it seldom does. But you allow for that. You prepare fall-back positions, contingency arrangements. There is no such thing as too much planning."

"I'm a little slow," Reese said. "You've got to sort of spell it out for me—I mean, how Felix was going to be your ticket home and all."

"Public service," Timble said. "Felix was a simply dreadful man. No conscience whatsoever. Bringing him to justice would be a tremendous public service, don't you agree? And there would have to be some reciprocation. A quid pro quo—that sort of thing. The Israelis would've been most grateful. I'm sure that with their intercession I very quietly would have been granted a pardon, or perhaps even a light suspended sentence, which I was quite willing to settle for."

"Felix for a pardon," Reese said. "A trade-off."

"You got it, pal," Keeling said.

Reese nodded thoughtfully. "It might've worked. Maybe."

"Except for the fact that poor Felix passed away on us," Timble said. "We then had no recourse but to fall back on our contingency plan."

208

"You sliced off his fingers."

"Well, we did have to have some evidence that he was, in fact, in our possession. The forefingers served quite nicely. You know the rest, about our use of Dr. Mapangou to serve as our intermediary with the Israelis and the Libyans."

"Yeah, I know about all that," Reese said.

Timble smiled and wiggled in his chair. He seemed to be filled with an almost unbearable anticipation. "Don't you think our operation was just a teeny bit sloppy?"

Reese stared at him. It took him only seconds to run the past week or so through his mind, and after he did he sighed, a long, heavy sigh that seemed to drain him of all vitality. "A setup," he said hoarsely. "From the first, it was a setup."

"You see," Timble said, leaning forward, anxious to explain, "when Felix died on us we had to create an *unbearable* scandal. I purposely stress the word unbearable. What better scandal, especially at this particular juncture and with this particular administration, than a high-ranking CIA official involved in bribery, perhaps treason, and murder—" Timble broke off, his face suddenly coated with alarm. "There was murder, wasn't there?"

"He broke Mapangou's neck," Keeling said.

Timble relaxed and the alarm dropped away from his face to be replaced with a look of sadness, which stayed only for a second, the length of his mourning for the late Dr. Mapangou. Then the sadness went away and its place was taken by a look of curiosity which seemed to be directed toward what Reese would say next.

It was thirty seconds before Reese spoke. "You didn't know it was going to be me."

"We really didn't care, but we are delighted that it is you. All we did was create simply irresistible opportunity. We worked on it—all of us—quite diligently."

"So what do you do now—turn me over?"

"Certainly not. You take the money—all twenty million. Then you run. We then inform Washington. We offer our silence in exchange for immunity. Or even a light suspended sentence in my case. Otherwise we deliver the photographs—" Again he stopped. "There *are* photographs?"

"I got it all," Spiceman said.

"Yes, well, otherwise we deliver to the media our photographs of a high-ranking CIA officer in the very act of murdering a foreign diplomat, along with the rest of our rather sordid evidence, and the administration suffers a crippling international and domestic blow. I don't quite think they will choose to do so."

For almost a full minute Alex Reese sat quite still, his belly and his elbows still resting on his knees, his eyes fixed on Timble's face. It was a hard stare, seemingly endless, full of cold appraisal. Then it went away. The eyes either sparkled or twinkled. Reese sat up. A smile split his face. A harsh chuckle came out of his mouth. He slapped his hands on his knees, then he unbuckled his seat belt and rose. Spiceman was immediately up, the pistol aimed, two-handed, at Reese's chest.

"You can put it away, Spiceman," Reese said, still smiling. "You can put it away and break out the booze, because the kid here and I are fixing to cut a deal." Reese leaned down until his face was no more than a few inches from Timble's. "California, sonny. You don't really know what happened in California, do you?"

Spiceman jammed the pistol into Reese's side. "Sit down."

"Wait," Timble commanded. "What happened, Mr. Reese, in California?"

"Bingo McKay."

"He was on the tour."

"They sliced off his ear. The Libyans. They sliced it off and sent it to the White House because they think Langley snatched Felix. The Libyans have got Bingo, kid, and it's all your fault. There ain't gonna be any pardon. There ain't even gonna be any light suspended sentence."

The color drained from Timble's face, and it became very still.

There was no movement in it. None at all. Keeling watched it closely, curious about what the mind behind the face was doing. Nothing happened for nearly thirty seconds. Timble's face remained perfectly still. Then the lips moved. "Give Mr. Reese a drink," the lips said. After that the face resumed its remote stillness while Keeling, still fascinated, still watching closely, prepared three drinks and served them.

It was then that Timble smiled. His lips, pressed tightly together, curved up and his eyes narrowed and seemed to form two happy half circles. "Bingo McKay," he said. "The Libyans have him, you say."

"That's right, kid," Reese said with a savage grin. "The Libyans."

"Well," Timble said, "we'll simply have to get him back, won't we?"

25

Ko Yoshikawa watched the black queen slash diagonally across the board until it reached the white knight. The queen knocked the knight over none too gently. Bingo McKay picked up the knight and said, "Check—and mate in two. Three if you try and get cute."

Ko studied the board. At last he nodded. "Yes, two—unless I try to get cute." He leaned back in the chair and stretched. "What time is it?"

McKay looked at his watch. "A couple of minutes past three."

"And the score?"

McKay picked up an envelope. On its back were three vertical rows of score-keeping figures that looked something like Roman numerals. He counted them up and added a vertical line. "So far, thirty-nine for you, forty-one for me, and six draws. You want to play another?"

"Don't you ever sleep?"

"Do you?"

Ko smiled slightly. "Not a great deal."

McKay took a cigarette from a half-empty packet of Gauloises and lit it. He inhaled the smoke, blew it out, and said, "Strong fuckers." He peered through the smoke at Ko. "It's getting to you, isn't it?"

"How long has it been now—ten days?"

McKay looked at his watch again. "Nine days, fourteen hours, and thirty-two minutes—by west coast time. I don't count the seconds any more."

They were seated at a table in the main stateroom of the yacht that had been built for King Idris I. In a chair near the door a young Libyan guard sat sleeping and snoring gently, an Israeli-made submachinegun across his lap.

"Why don't you wake up the Moose over there and send him out for some coffee," McKay said.

"All right." Ko turned in his chair. "Hey, Moussef!"

The young soldier awoke instantly, a sheepish smile on his face.

"Coffee," said Ko in English and again in Italian.

The young soldier nodded and rose. He opened the door and said something in Arabic. Another Libyan guard came in and took Moussef's place. The new guard was older and didn't look at all sleepy. He kept his submachinegun cradled under an arm.

"Tell me something," McKay said.

"What?"

"If push comes to shove, who'll do it—him?" He nodded toward the new guard. "Or you, or old Frank?"

"What do you want to know for?"

"Just curious."

"It's morbid."

"Well, hell, if you were in my fix, wouldn't you be curious?"

"It won't come to that."

"Suppose it does?"

Ko sighed. "Frank. Frank would do it."

"Fast?"

"So fast you'll never even know it."

McKay snorted. "I'll know it. But I figured it'd be old Frank. Trouble with him, he was born too late. He should've been born

213

around 'twenty-two or 'twenty-three. Could've gone into the SS and made something out of himself."

"You're typecasting again."

"Well, you gotta admit, old Frank sure *looks* like an SS recruiting poster."

"What if you were typecasting me? You don't even know where I was born."

"Where?"

"Utah. In a concentration camp. An American concentration camp, except they didn't call them that. They called them relocation centers, or some such shit. My old man died of pleurisy in the spring of 'forty-five, just before the war ended. After it was over, the war, she took me back to Japan. Tokyo. And we lived with her folks. She finally got a job. My mother. Guess what she did?"

"What?"

"She sold cigarettes in the PX. She worked in that PX for sixteen years and the four of us lived in one room and she saved her money for just one thing—to send me to Stanford. Well, I went to Stanford."

"When was that—'sixty-one, 'sixty-two?"

" 'Sixty-two."

"Sort of quiet on campus back around then, as I recollect."

"Not necessarily. Not if you're seventeen and dirt poor and in a foreign country and your nickname's Tojo. It's not exactly quiet. Your rage keeps it from being quiet."

"Yeah," McKay said after a while. "I imagine."

"Imagine this, Bingo. Imagine that sheer loneliness drove you to the books. And because you read the books so diligently, and remembered what you read, they started giving you rewards. Scholarships. Prizes. Liberals like that—giving prizes to Jap kids and nigger kids and spic kids. Goddamn, it made them feel good! Well, I took their bloody prizes and scholarships and kept on reading, and the more I read the simpler it got. You have to go way past Marx to get where I got. Marx still had doubts—little niggling doubts—so you have to go past him and the others into a kind of place where there aren't any doubts. You just know. It was a kind of metamorphosis."

Bingo McKay nodded thoughtfully. "Yeah, I think I know what you mean. Something like that happened to me back in 'forty-six, right after the war."

"What?"

"I went back to school—to OU. And hell, I was poor. I was living on the GI bill and wearing suntans to class and eating quarter hamburgers and then one day, sitting there in a Government 101 class, it just came to me. So I got up in the middle of that class and walked out and never went back. Like you said, I just all of a sudden *knew*."

"Knew what?"

McKay grinned. "That I was gonna be rich."

There was a knock at the door. The guard rose and opened it. Standing there holding a tray with a Pyrex carafe of coffee and three cups on it was Bingo McKay's executive assistant, Eleanor Rhodes. Behind her was the guard Moussef, his submachinegun tucked under an arm.

"That woman needs help," Rhodes said as she entered the stateroom and put the tray down on the table next to the chessboard. Moussef nodded at the older guard, who turned and left, closing the door behind him. Moussef resumed his seat.

"What now?" Ko said as he watched Rhodes pour the coffee. She handed cups to McKay and Ko. Pouring one for herself, she sat down next to McKay. "She won't let me sleep," Rhodes said. "She talked until two yesterday and until—what, three this morning? I know all about her childhood in Algiers. I know all about her father, the paratroop colonel, and her mother and her mother's lovers, all of them, each one dissected and analyzed down to his socks. And Paris in 'sixty-eight; I know all about Paris then, too. That woman needs help."

"Or a sympathetic ear," Ko said.

"She asleep now?" McKay said.

215

Rhodes shrugged. "If you can call it that. When I saw Moussef go by heading for the galley, I escaped. When he said you were still up, I offered to carry the coffee." She looked at the chessboard. "Who won?"

"Bingo," Ko said. "Are Françoise's dreams getting worse?"

"They're not dreams, they're nightmares," Rhodes said. "Do nightmares get better? Do you grade them? Hers are all about death. She dies, you die, I die, we all die. And Felix. He keeps dying, too. Over and over. First one way, then another, and all of them horrible. Then she wakes me up and tells me about them, every last detail. Damn it, I'm the hostage, the victim—not her! I'm the one who should be going crackers or sinking into despair or whatever happens. I want somebody to listen to me. I don't like this role. I don't want to be the Female Terrorist's Best Friend. God damn it, I want somebody to—"

Her voice had risen steadily until it cracked. She started sobbing and buried her head in her arms on the table. McKay reached over and put a hand on her shoulder. "Easy, sugar," he said. "Just take it easy." He couldn't think of anything else to say.

The sobbing died away. Rhodes looked up at McKay. Her nose was red, her eyes bloodshot, her cheeks tear-stained. McKay thought she looked beautiful. "That goddamned bandage needs changing again, too," she said.

"Yeah, I know," he said, automatically touching the bandage. "Old Doc Souri said he'd tend to it tomorrow."

"I'll talk to him about Françoise, too," Ko said. "Maybe he can give her something that will calm her down and help her to sleep."

"You'd better—" A new knock at the stateroom's door interrupted Eleanor Rhodes's admonishment. Moussef rose and opened the door. The yacht's Libyan radio officer stepped into the room. "It's from Rome," he said in Italian and handed a folded sheet of paper to Ko.

When the officer had gone, Ko unfolded the sheet of paper and read it slowly. He looked up first at McKay, then at Rhodes.

"Hostages should be kept in the dark," he said. "It destroys their morale. I think it's in the book."

"But you ain't gonna go by the book, are you, old buddy?" McKay said.

Ko smiled. It was a sad philosopher's tired smile. "The news is not good."

"But it's news."

"The Nigerian Ambassador to the States met yesterday afternoon in Rome with a representative from Libya. They got nowhere. The Nigerian seems to be stalling."

"Well, shit, they're meeting anyway."

"That's item one. Item two: Do you know an American called Chubb Dunjee?"

McKay commanded his face not to betray him. He frowned slightly as if trying to recall the face that went with the name. But his thoughts raced. Hot damn, the Mordida Man. The kid remembered. He called in Grimes and, god damn, old Paul must've dug up Dunjee somewhere.

"Dunjee," McKay said slowly, but not too slowly. "Used to be a fellow in Congress by that name, why?"

"He served one term," Eleanor Rhodes said. "He—" She broke off abruptly.

Ko looked at her curiously. "He what?"

"He went to the UN after that, I believe."

McKay nodded proudly. "By God, she's got a memory, hasn't she? I believe he was with the UN for a while." Innocence crept across McKay's face. "Why?"

"They're on their way to Tripoli," Ko said. "Not too willingly, it would seem."

"They?" McKay said, as indifferently as he could.

"Dunjee and his associates, who seem to be an English thief and a woman of uncertain nationality."

God damn, but don't that sound just like Dunjee, McKay thought. Got himself a pickup crew somewhere and a hip pocket full of money—from the kid, most likely—and he's wiggling his way right into the henhouse. God bless the kid, God bless Paul

Grimes, and God bless the Mordida Man. It was as close as McKay had come to prayer in forty-one years.

"You don't know this Dunjee, you say?" Ko asked.

"I'm trying to recollect. I believe we did meet once at a convention. 'Sixty-eight in Chicago. I think he was there and we maybe shook hands and said hello. And I think maybe we bumped into each other at a cocktail party in Washington one time. Probably talked a couple of minutes. But that's about it."

"Eleanor?" Ko said.

She shook her head. "I never met him."

"How come Tripoli?" McKay said, putting another cigarette into his mouth to supplement the casualness of his tone.

"How come?" Ko said. "Because he was sent for apparently, that's how come."

"Sent for by who?"

"Mourabet."

"The Colonel?"

Ko nodded. "Himself."

"No kidding?" Bingo McKay said.

26

The plane in which Chubb Dunjee flew across the Mediterranean from Rome to Tripoli was the same Boeing 727 in which Bingo McKay's ear had been removed. Because of some kind of unexplained mechanical difficulties, the plane had not left Rome until nearly five o'clock in the morning. At 5:46 A.M., the plane's passengers could watch dawn break over the sea.

"It's getting light," Delft Csider said. Dunjee and Harold Hopkins turned to look out the window, then turned back.

"You resist, he implores, then you give in," she said and shook her head. "I hope you know what you're doing."

"What's she talking about?" Hopkins said.

"It's how he works," Csider said. "He puts his neck in the noose, then tries to talk his way out of it before they draw it tight and cut off all the air. All the hot air."

Hopkins frowned. "I didn't sign on for this, mate. I signed on for Rome with maybe a quick peek at the Colosseum. I didn't sign on for Libya. What the hell's in Libya?"

"A lot of sand," Dunjee said. "And a lot of oil."

"Before the oil, you know what they used to call it?" Csider asked.

"The poorest country on earth," Dunjee said.

"I forgot," she said. "You were with the UN."

"World War Two scrap and esparto grass. That's about all Libya had to export then. They didn't even want to let them into the UN, because everyone knew they'd be just another LDC with their hand out."

"What's an LDC?" Hopkins said.

"A lesser-developed country," Dunjee said. "They used to call them underdeveloped, but that hurt their feelings, so they started calling them 'developing countries.' But then some sticklers insisted that that wasn't quite accurate either, because a lot of them weren't developing anything except their politics. So about the time I went with the UN they'd started calling them lesser-developed, which seemed to please almost nobody. But that's one of the things the UN is good at—pleasing nobody."

"Fooled 'em though, didn't they?" Hopkins said. "I mean with all that oil they found and the price it's bringing. But I don't blame 'em, the Arabs, I mean. If I'd been poor all me life, which I bloody well have been, and then woke up one morning and found out I had something everybody in the world was dying to get their hands on, you think I wouldn't sell it dear? Not likely, mate. What the traffic would bear, that's what I'd sell it for. What the traffic would bear."

Hopkins nodded as though he found his economic analysis unassailable. They were seated in the lounge section of the plane. The door to the forward section was locked. The forward section was where Bingo McKay's ear had been sliced off. It was now occupied by Faraj Abedsaid and the two tough young Libyan guards. The guards had remained in the lounge section with Dunjee and the others during the long delay on the ground in Rome. But once the plane was airborne, they had gone into the forward section, locking the door behind them.

"When we get to wherever we're going—"

"Tripoli," Dunjee said.

Hopkins nodded. "Right, Tripoli. What then?"

"I see the man."

"The chief panjandrum, huh?"

"Right."

"Then?"

Dunjee sighed. "Then I try to convince him that I'm the sole supplier."

"Of what?"

"Of whatever his heart desires," Dunjee said, and attempted a smile, which turned into a lip-stretching exercise without either humor or confidence.

The three of them turned when they heard the door to the forward compartment being unlocked. Abedsaid came through it. He bent down to peer out a window and then looked at Dunjee.

"We'll be landing in about twenty minutes," he said, straightening up. "The Captain wants you to fasten your seat belts."

"What happens after we land?" Dunjee said, snapping his seat belt together.

Abedsaid frowned, as if weary of answering questions. He apparently had had no sleep in the forward compartment. The lines around his mouth had deepened. His eyes were bloodshot.

"You and I," he said, still frowning at Dunjee. "You and I will take another small journey."

"Where to?"

Abedsaid shook his head. "The name would mean nothing. As for your two colleagues, they will be taken to a hotel. The Inter-Continental, I think. It's quite comfortable."

"You sure it's a hotel?" Dunjee said.

"A prison perhaps?" Abedsaid said. "A dungeon even?"

"All right. It's a hotel."

"You're very suspicious, Mr. Dunjee."

"You're right," Dunjee said. "I am."

From one thousand feet up Dunjee counted six chrome-shiny Airstream trailers. They formed an L. Next to them were parked two flatbed trucks. On the beds of the trucks were diesel generators. Parked near the generators were two tanker trucks containing the oil that ran the generators. Scattered here and there were at least two dozen sedans and heavy-duty pickup trucks. Farther away were two French six-passenger Aérospatiale AS 350 Squirrel helicopters, twins of the one that had flown Dunjee and Abedsaid east and south of Tripoli for a little more than forty-five minutes.

Some one hundred yards away from everything was the black tent. Cables from the generators snaked across the sand to it. Near the tent were some stunted trees of some kind.

"That's the oasis?" Dunjee said as the helicopter wheeled and started down.

"What did you expect?" Abedsaid asked. "Date palms surrounding a small crystal clear pool with cool deep shade and belly dancers?"

"Yeah," Dunjee said. "Something like that."

The helicopter landed on a hundred-foot-square of thick green heavy-duty staked-down plastic, something like that used to make garbage bags, only heavier, thicker. Abedsaid said it was to keep the dust and sand from blowing.

But it wasn't sand that the plastic covered. It was more like a not-quite-formed thin gravel that was mixed together with a gray grit. Nothing grew in it.

Dunjee kicked at it once after they got out of the helicopter and started for the black tent. The blow of his foot made a small plume of gray dust that settled slowly. There was no wind. The dry heat was not quite unbearable. Dunjee guessed that it was just over ninety-five degrees Fahrenheit.

Uniformed soldiers and civilian technicians stared at Dunjee curiously as he followed Abedsaid toward the black tent. Near the generators they passed two inclined banks of round shiny discs.

"Solar?" Dunjee said.

Abedsaid nodded. "Solar."

There were two young uniformed guards armed with rather fancy-looking machine pistols at the entrance to the tent. They stood in the shade cast by a liplike square of the heavy black material made out of goat hair that protruded from the entrance.

Dunjee had to duck only slightly to enter the tent behind Abedsaid. Once inside, the tent soared up. The ground, he noticed, was covered with the same thick green plastic. The plastic was overlaid with rugs. The rugs looked expensive.

The man Dunjee had come to see sat cross-legged on a rug near the center of the tent. Next to him was a Carrier air conditioning unit. On a nearby small low table rested a white telephone. Next to the telephone was a silent teletype. Just behind the man who sat cross-legged was an office-size refrigerator. And next to that was another small low table that held two thermos carafes and some tiny porcelain cups. The man watched Dunjee approach. He wore a loose white slipover shirt and white duck pants. He was barefoot. He looked younger than Dunjee had expected.

Abedsaid and the seated man spoke in Arabic for nearly a minute while Dunjee stood and waited. It was surprisingly cool in the tent, at least ten or fifteen degrees cooler than out in the sun and it wasn't because of the small air conditioning unit, which seemed mostly for show. Dunjee, who was still sweating from his walk from the helicopter, took off his jacket.

Abedsaid turned to him, and made a small gesture. "Colonel Mourabet, Mr. Dunjee," he said.

The seated man stared up at Dunjee. He had a strikingly handsome face, big-nosed and strong-chinned with deepset bitter-brown eyes that managed to look both sad and lively. His hair was black and thick and slightly disarrayed, as if he unconsciously combed it with his fingers. The only evident touch of vanity was the mustache, carefully clipped and tended, that spread across his wide upper lip. It was, Dunjee decided, a smart man's face. Very smart.

"Sit, Mr. Dunjee," Mourabet said with a curiously polite gesture. "Sit and we will talk American. You observe I didn't say English."

"I noticed," Dunjee said as he dropped his jacket to the rug and lowered himself down, imitating Mourabet's cross-legged position.

Mourabet glanced up at Abedsaid. "You may leave us," he said. Abedsaid nodded, turned, and left. Mourabet shifted his gaze to Dunjee and smiled. It was a warm smile, very wide, very friendly. Dunjee automatically discounted its sincerity and smiled back.

"Would you like some tea or coffee?" Mourabet said, gesturing toward the two carafes. "Did you know that we Libyans drink more tea per capita than any other country in the world?"

"I read that somewhere," Dunjee said. "Quite an accomplishment."

"But then for guests, foreign guests, I also have beer. American beer. Schlitz, I think."

"A beer would be nice."

Without getting up, Mourabet turned and opened the small refrigerator. He took out a can of Schlitz, leaned forward, and offered it to Dunjee. "They say it is better drunk from the can. It stays cold longer."

"The can will be fine." Dunjee flipped the top open and then waited for Mourabet to pour himself a cup of tea. Mourabet took a sip of the tea; Dunjee took two long swallows of the beer.

"If you were asked, how would you identify yourself?" Mourabet said.

"Chubb Dunjee."

"And your race?"

"American."

"That's not a race."

"No, but it's handy."

Mourabet nodded. "If I were asked the same question, I would say I am Mourabet, a Moslem, one of the Arabs who happens to be a Libyan."

"A somewhat broader concept," Dunjee said politely, and waited to see what would come next.

"What were you doing in 1969, Mr. Dunjee?"

Dunjee paused, as though to give it some thought. "I was in Congress."

"And your age then?"

"Twenty-nine."

"You are forty-one now?"

"Yes. Almost forty-two."

"I am a year younger. Qaddafi was the youngest of us all. He was only twenty-seven in 'sixty-nine. I suppose you never met him?"

"No."

"He and I went through the academy together. And later, they sent us to England for ten months in 1966. To Beaconsfield. We studied communications. He began planning for the revolution when he was twenty-one—back in 1963. Some of us at first were skeptical. But he overcame our doubts. There are some men who God chooses as leaders. He was one of them."

"He died—rather unexpectedly, I understand."

"A stroke. The entire country was . . . desolated. I comfort myself sometimes with remembering his courage and bravery on the first of September."

"In 'sixty-nine."

"Yes. Idris was in Turkey. We had postponed it twice already. Some of us wanted to postpone again. Qaddafi would not hear of it. He convinced us through his—will, his personality. At two o'clock in the morning we struck. Not one single person died."

"I remember," Dunjee said and drank some more of his beer.

Mourabet waited politely until Dunjee lowered the can. "When I asked you how you would identify yourself, I did so for a reason."

"So I suspected."

"You see, Qaddafi was convinced—and I shared his conviction—that we have a broader responsibility, one that extends beyond the borders of our country. What we have accomplished here in Libya, we feel we must help others to accomplish."

"Revolution," Dunjee said.

"Or justice."

"Through revolution."

"As an American, you must believe in revolution."

"It depends on what comes afterwards."

"Democracy, you mean."

Dunjee shook his head. "Not necessarily. Democracy's never perfect. You can try it, find it doesn't work, discard it, and then go back to it when the time's ripe. Nigeria's an example of that. This time I think it'll work there."

Mourabet smiled. "You mean they can afford it now?"

Dunjee smiled back. "Something like that."

"I think we understand each other. Do you know who my first American was?"

"Who?"

"Captain Eugene Stallings of Memphis, Tennessee, and the United States Air Force. Or rather Madame Stallings. They were my first Americans and I was their first servant. At Wheelus. I was the houseboy. Madame Stallings taught me English—or American, I suppose. I have that accent, I am told."

"Sort of southern," Dunjee said.

"Really?"

"But charming."

"And the grammar?"

"Perfect," Dunjee said.

"She was a former schoolteacher. She really wasn't quite sure whether to order me around or adopt me. Later, an American, a black American, told me I was probably what he called the house nigger. I was only thirteen then. But through the Stallings' efforts, I was later able to enter the academy. Years later, I decided that I quite despised them—especially her."

"Indebtedness is not always a comfortable feeling," Dunjee said and finished his beer.

"Another?" Mourabet said.

Dunjee shook his head. "No thank you."

"These broader responsibilities I spoke of. Several years ago we decided that some of our revenues should be used to finance the efforts of those who were trying to overcome oppression, regardless of its form."

"So you bankrolled freedom fighters."

Mourabet blinked. "I was quite sure you would call them terrorists."

"I am Dunjee, an American. You are Mourabet, a Moslem, one of the Arabs who happens to be a Libyan." Dunjee shrugged. "Labels."

Mourabet nodded slowly. He then reached into a pocket of his loose cotton pullover and took out a folded sheet of paper that seemed to have been ripped from the teletype. He unfolded it carefully. "This is your curriculum vitae, I believe it is called. You have had a strange career."

"Which is probably why I'm here."

"Yes, I reckon so. That's southern, isn't it? Reckon so?"

"That's southern."

"This was supplied us by our friends in the PLO."

"You've patched things up then?"

"With the PLO? Oh, yes. Some time ago." Mourabet looked down at the paper. "The Mordida Man. That means the giver of bribes, I believe. Spanish—or Mexican?"

"Mexican," Dunjee said.

"What did you do exactly in Mexico?"

"I got people out of jail. Rich people. Rich people's kids, to be precise."

"By giving bribes?"

Dunjee shook his head. "Not always. Sometimes those who could arrange the release were more interested in something else."

"More than money?"

"More than money."

"What?"

"Recognition."

"Aaah! I think I understand. And you were able to supply this
. . . recognition?"

"Sometimes."

"And what else would they want, those who could arrange the
prisoners' release? Some of them already must have had all the
money and fame they could use. What else would they want?"

"What else?" Dunjee said. "Usually revenge."

"Aaah! Revenge. Yes. The colder it is the sweeter it tastes.
What form did this revenge take?"

"Political embarrassment mostly."

"You could arrange this?"

"With enough money, you can arrange almost anything."

"How severe was the embarrassment?"

"People went to jail sometimes. Sometimes not."

"So by arranging the imprisonment of one, you secured the
release of another?"

"Sometimes."

"And you did this for a living?"

"That's right."

Mourabet turned and opened the refrigerator again. He removed a can of beer and handed it to Dunjee. "Here," he said.
"You look a bit thirsty."

"Thank you."

From the refrigerator's freezer compartment Mourabet also
removed something small and oblong and carefully wrapped in
heavy aluminum foil. He placed it on the rug in front of him.

"Today—here—you are representing who— Whom, isn't it?"

"Whom," Dunjee said. He took a deep breath. "The President
of the United States."

"Really?" Mourabet said and began peeling back the aluminum foil. When he was done a severed finger lay on foil. The
finger was pointing at Dunjee.

He stared at the finger for a moment, then looked up at
Mourabet. "Felix?"

"Yes. Felix. We paid ten million dollars for it. I'm beginning to suspect that we paid it to the CIA."

Dunjee shook his head. "No."

"Why do you say that?"

"You're sure it's Felix's finger?"

"We're sure. It was flown from New York to Paris. The French have his fingerprints on file. At present, we're rather chummy with the French for a change. Chummy. American or English?"

"Both. But more English than American usually."

"Yes. Well, they identified it. The French."

"How'd you pay out the money?"

"Through a bank transfer to an intermediary in New York. He's Gambia's permanent representative to the UN."

"Dr. Mapangou?"

"Do you know him?"

Dunjee nodded. "I've been to his parties."

"An honest man?"

Dunjee thought about it. "Maybe. Also greedy. Very greedy."

Mourabet shrugged. "Well, no matter. I received a call from New York early this morning. Dr. Mapangou was found dead yesterday in a park. His neck had been broken."

"So you're out ten million dollars."

Mourabet nodded. "Ten million. Mr. Dunjee, we have a country that is two and one half times as large as Texas with a population that barely equals Houston's. Our per-capita income is among the highest in the world. Ten million dollars to us is of no particular consequence. Felix is. He is to my government an important symbol, not an altogether attractive one perhaps, but still of great importance to us in our relations with a large number of dissident groups around the world. We gave Felix sanctuary when no one else would. We personally guaranteed his safety. His kidnapping diminishes us in the eyes of those we support. We will—and I wish to stress this—go to any lengths to get him back."

Dunjee stared at Mourabet for several seconds. Finally, in a clear, firm voice he said, "The Americans don't have Felix. They never had him."

Mourabet stared back. There was a long silence. Mourabet finally broke it. "You could be lying."

"What good would it do?"

Mourabet seemed to consider that. He ran his fingers through his hair. After a moment, he carefully began rewrapping the finger in the aluminum foil. When he was done, he replaced it in the small refrigerator's freezing compartment and turned back to Dunjee.

"Do you think he's alive?"

Dunjee shook his head. "No. Do you?"

Mourabet sighed. "Probably not. You want something, of course."

"Yes."

"President McKay's brother. That is what you want, isn't it?"

"Yes."

Mourabet cocked his head slightly to one side as he studied Dunjee. "And you are prepared to offer me something in exchange. I am trying to decide what it will be. Not money, of course."

Dunjee smiled slightly. "Hardly."

"What then?"

"I'll give you whoever kidnapped Felix."

"Aaah! Revenge!"

"Revenge."

"You are, I'm beginning to think, a very clever man, Mr. Dunjee. You're offering me the one thing you know I cannot resist. But, of course, I first have to give you something in exchange, don't I?"

"Yes."

"Not money."

"No."

"I could make you quite wealthy, you realize."

"It's tempting."

230

Mourabet smiled. "But not tempting enough?"

"No."

"What then?"

"You tell me where Bingo McKay is being held. That's all."

"That is not much of a bargain. If I told you that, then your President could send in a CIA or Army team to try to rescue him."

Dunjee shook his head. "You'd kill him first."

Mourabet nodded thoughtfully. "Yes, we would, I'm afraid."

"And besides, I'm not going to tell the President."

"You distrust his associates?"

"I distrust their ability to keep their mouths shut."

There was another lengthy silence as Mourabet again studied Dunjee, much in the way he might study an interesting but abstract piece of sculpture, which he found himself liking, although he wasn't at all sure why.

At last, he said, "I think I finally have decided what you really are, Mr. Dunjee."

"What?"

"A patriot. A curious one, but a patriot nonetheless."

Dunjee grinned. "Does that mean we have a deal?"

"Yes," Mourabet said. "With a few caveats on my part, I really believe we do."

"Bingo McKay," Dunjee said. "He's in Malta, isn't he?"

For the first time, Mourabet scowled. "I must insist on knowing who told you."

"It was none of your people."

"Who?" Mourabet demanded.

Dunjee tried to decide how best to describe the Wreck in Rome. At last he said, "A family friend."

27

In the small denlike office on the third floor of the Old Executive Office Building, the Director of Central Intelligence, a stiff, stubborn look on his face, said, "For the record, Mr. President, I must object to Mr. Grimes being present at our discussions."

Paul Grimes smiled sleepily, as if trying to fight back a yawn. The President shifted in his chair behind the desk and stared at Thane Coombs with a look that mingled amazement with dislike.

"Let me tell you something, friend," he said. "You're not in any shape to be objecting to anything."

A tide of pink rushed up Coombs's neck and brightened his ears. "For the record, Mr. President," he said stubbornly.

"Noted," the President snapped. "Now tell him what you told me."

"That *is* an order?"

"Tell him, god damn it!"

"Yes. All right." Coombs shifted in his chair so that he could look at Grimes. Actually, he looked at a spot that was an inch to the left of Grimes's right ear. "The Israelis in New York were approached by Gambia's permanent representative to the UN, a

Dr. Mapangou. He claimed to represent the kidnappers of Gustavo Berrio-Brito."

"Felix," Grimes said.

"Yes. Felix. Dr. Mapangou had evidence. The evidence was in the form of Felix's severed right forefinger. Its print matched those on file in Paris. Mapangou said the kidnappers were demanding a ransom of ten million dollars. The Israelis contacted us. We agreed to pay half the ransom. The ransom, the entire ten million, was paid. A few hours later, Dr. Mapangou was murdered in Central Park. Nothing has been heard from the kidnappers."

Grimes nodded. "What about Bingo?"

"His name was never mentioned during the negotiations, according to the Israelis."

"Ten million," Grimes said. "A lot of money. It wasn't cash?"

"No. A bank transfer."

"Can't you trace it?"

Coombs turned back to look at the President. It was an almost beseeching look.

"Tell him," the President said.

"The method used to transfer the money was set up by the CIA several years ago. It is virtually foolproof. The money, changed into several currencies, was picked up yesterday afternoon at a casino in the Bahamas."

"Where in the Bahamas?"

"Nassau."

A wise smile spread across Grimes's face. "Who owns it?"

Coombs opened his mouth, but nothing came out. He closed his mouth, snapped it shut actually, then opened it to try again. He failed.

Grimes looked at him almost sympathetically. "Let me guess," he said. "It's owned by Gogo Consentino and his bunch."

"They are not the owners of record," Coombs said.

"Well, bullshit, mister, you'd better get your head out of the sand. What was their payoff for washing the money?"

"One percent."

"And what did you call it—the system, the route, whatever?"

Coombs shifted in his chair again and resumed his examination of the spot an inch to the left of Grimes's right ear. "The Panama Laundry," he said after clearing his throat.

Grimes nodded. "All right. Now the obvious question. Who thought up the Panama Laundry—invented it?"

"The man is dead. His name was Eubanks."

"Okay. Eubanks is dead. But who else knew about it—other than Eubanks?"

"Only two persons."

"Who?"

Coombs gripped the arms of his chair. He stared at the space on the carpet between his feet. "The former Director . . . and myself."

"Well, hell, he's ambassador to where now—Brazil?"

"Brazil," the President said.

"And you," Grimes said, staring at Coombs, who still sat, head bowed, gazing at the floor. "Well, hell, you don't look hungry enough. So there must've been somebody else."

"There was nobody."

"Nobody you know about anyway."

"Tell him the juicy part," the President instructed Coombs.

Coombs slowly raised his head and turned to stare past Grimes and out the window. The view between the drapes was a small slice of Pennsylvania Avenue that included the top floor of Blair House.

"At two P.M., Nassau time, yesterday afternoon," he began in a dry, distant, precise tone, "a young black man approximately seventeen or eighteen years old drove up in front of the casino in a van. He identified himself to the casino authorities as Samuel—" Coombs stopped and sighed. "Samuel Jones. He then recited the coded phrase."

"The password?" Grimes said.

"Yes, all right, the password. Or words. The money was transferred to the youth's van. It was later found abandoned. The youth has not been located."

"They just gave him the money?" Grimes said, trying to keep the incredulity out of his tone, but failing. "All ten million?"

"It was actually twenty million," Coombs said in a whisper.

"Twenty million! How the fuck could it be twenty million."

"There were two transfers out of New York to the bank in Montreal. One was from the Israelis. The other ten million came from the Libyan Arab Republic's account at Chase Manhattan."

"They sold him twice!" Grimes said, staring at the President. "The fuckers went and sold him twice."

The President nodded wearily.

"And they just gave this kid the money—all twenty million?"

"Less their one percent commission. Their instructions were strict, explicit, and of long standing."

"And Consentino made a nice little profit." Grimes frowned. "Okay. You couldn't find the kid. So you started checking who was in and out of Nassau yesterday. Private planes, boats, yachts, all that. Who?"

"Now comes the real juicy part," the President said.

Coombs's eyes flickered around the room as though seeking sanctuary. They finally lit upon a wastepaper basket in a far corner of the room and stayed there. He said something in a voice so low that it was almost impossible to hear.

Grimes leaned forward. "Sorry."

Coombs repeated the name of the twenty-seven-mile-long, one-mile-wide island Democratic People's Republic in the Caribbean. "They bought a plane some time ago," he said. "They bought it for one dollar and then leased it back for one million a year to the person who sold it to them. The plane, a Boeing 727, landed at Nassau yesterday. Only one person got off. He carried a Canadian passport. The airport officials made no record of his name. They never do. Their description was vague. The man returned in an hour and loaded six crates of bonded rum aboard the plane. The customs officials, of course, did not inspect the rum. The plane then took off after filing a flight plan for Miami. It never landed in Miami."

"The plane," Grimes said. "Who leases the plane?"

With his eyes still locked on the remote and apparently comforting wastepaper basket, Coombs swallowed and said, "Leland Timble."

Grimes blinked and then said totally without inflection, "Well, I'll be goddamned."

There was a silence while Grimes stared first at Coombs, then at the President, then back at Coombs. "Timble. The boy genius bank robber, right?"

"Yes."

"The finger. How'd Timble get hold of Felix's finger?"

"Records at London's Heathrow show that the plane, the same 727, was there for four days prior to and including the day that Felix was kidnapped."

"Timble snatched him, then. By himself?"

"It gets even better," the President said.

Grimes stared at Coombs. "Well?"

Coombs sighed. "Timble has a former FBI special agent and a former CIA employee working for him. Either one—or both—could have engineered the abduction."

Grimes stared up at the ceiling. "You know what?" he said. "I bet they cut off two fingers and sold one to the Israelis and one to the Libyans. I bet that's what they did." He looked at Coombs again. "Okay. The plane. The 727. Where is it?"

"Tell him," the President said.

"It's in Haiti."

"And Timble and his bunch?"

"There is no record of them getting off the plane. However, four men chartered a private plane and flew to Santo Domingo."

"The Dominican Republic?"

Coombs nodded. "There they caught a commercial flight to Caracas."

"And in Caracas?"

"We think they flew commercial to Rome. We're not positive."

Grimes looked at the President. "Dunjee's in Rome. Does he know about Dunjee?"

"Ask him," the President said, nodding at Coombs, who was now giving the small liver spot on the back of his left hand a careful examination.

Without waiting for Grimes's question, Coombs said, "We became aware some time ago, Mr. President, that you retained or employed this man Dunjee in some private capacity whose exact nature you were not willing to share."

"I hired him to get my brother back. Or Felix. Or both."

"I am not sure that you have made a wise choice."

"I'll worry about that," the President said. "What I want to know now is who we've got in Rome. I want that little prick Timble. I want him bad."

"Yes, I quite understand. Well, we have our normal complement in Rome. In addition, I have already sent in several of our best people from both our Paris and Bonn stations."

"Who's going to be in charge?" the President said.

"Alex Reese. He was due there yesterday."

"Reese?" the President said. "Is he that big bald guy with the gut who everybody says drinks like a fish?"

"He's brilliant, Mr. President. Absolutely brilliant."

"And he's the best we've got?"

"The very best."

"God help us. One thing, Coombs."

"Yes, sir?"

"Tell Reese hands off Dunjee. Understand? Absolutely hands off."

"I understand, Mr. President."

The President looked at Grimes. "I've asked Ambassador Dokubo to keep the talks in Rome with the Libyans going—to stall, if he has to. He's good at it." The President paused. "Rome?" he said and looked questioningly at Grimes.

Grimes nodded decisively. Then he pulled his big, heavy body up as he always did, smoothly, easily. "I'm on my way."

28

The day after Dunjee was flown back to Rome from Tripoli, he sat with Faraj Abedsaid at a sidewalk table at Doney's, a brandy and an espresso before him. In front of Abedsaid was a small bottle of San Pellegrino mineral water. It was shortly before two o'clock in the afternoon.

"How many did you say are on you?" Dunjee said.

"When I left my hotel at noon, I think I spotted three. Possibly four. If there is a fourth one, he's very good."

"Any of them around now?"

"One behind you about six tables away. Twenty-nine or thirty. He's found something terribly interesting in the *Daily American*. There's also a woman. Twelve tables up. Fat, frumpish, about forty. She's not bad. Green polyester slacks, orange sweater, mouse hair. She has tourist stamped all over her."

"Just so we've got our audience."

"We have it."

"When's your meeting with Dokubo?"

Abedsaid looked at his watch. "In about thirty minutes."

"Still at the FAO?"

"Yes."

"How is he?"

"Dokubo? Very bright, very smooth, very skillful—and exceedingly adept at scrambling about in quicksand. Using charm alone, I think he could keep these negotiations stalled for another six months. Back in Oklahoma, we'd say he was all hat and no cattle."

Dunjee smiled. "Well, let's do it."

"Would you prefer me to be imperceptible—or obvious?"

"Hell, you're the spy."

"Yes, and I'm violating every precept of my trade. I do think I'll be a wee bit clumsy—just so they don't blink and miss it."

Abedsaid looked at his watch again. "Well, I really must be going," he said. Abedsaid started to rise, seemed to notice a forgotten folded copy of the *Herald Tribune* in his lap, and caught it before it fell. He placed the newspaper on the table as if he had finished reading it. "Keep in touch," he told Dunjee.

"Right."

Dunjee continued to sit at the table, people-watching and slowly sipping his brandy. After fifteen minutes, he glanced around as if trying to find his waiter. He spotted the fortyish woman in the green slacks and orange sweater. She seemed to be devoting all of her attention to a rather large mound of ice cream. Dunjee could not locate any young man with a *Daily American* who fitted Abedsaid's description.

After paying the bill, Dunjee rose, tucked the folded *Herald Tribune* under his arm, and turned right down the Via Veneto in the general direction of the American Embassy. He walked slowly, strolling really, and at the next corner turned right, as though wandering back toward his hotel.

He stopped several times to gaze into shopwindows. He even turned around once to go back and inspect a display of antique jewelry that seemed to fascinate him. As far as he could determine, no one was following.

His casual, almost peripatetic stroll led him past the Eden Hotel. He continued to stop frequently at shopwindows. It was

239

seventy-five yards past the Eden Hotel that the green Peugeot sedan pulled up in a no-parking space and the big man with the bald head and the sloped shoulders opened the rear door and got out. In the front seat, near the curb, was another man with a big jaw and a rubbery face. His eyes never left Dunjee.

The big bald-headed man walked slowly back toward Dunjee. As he came he hitched his pants up over his protruding stomach, but they immediately slid back down.

"You're Chubb Dunjee?"

"That's right."

"We'd like to talk to you."

"Who's we?"

"My name's Reese. Alex Reese. We're with the government."

"Whose government?"

"Your government."

Dunjee stared at Reese. Then he smiled. It was Dunjee's best smile, full of charm and exceedingly white. "See my lawyer," he said and turned away.

The front door of the Peugeot popped open. The man with the big jaw and the rubbery face was now blocking Dunjee's path. It had taken less than a second.

"You with the government, too?" Dunjee said.

The man wiped a hand hard across his mouth. It seemed to be a habit. Perhaps a nervous habit, although Dunjee thought the man looked about as nervous as a rock.

"My name's Arnold," the man said. "I'm with him."

"There're two of you," Dunjee said, as if slightly surprised at how his addition had turned out.

"And one in the car makes three," Reese said.

"Have you got anything that says you're with the government —a piece of paper, a badge maybe?"

Reese reached into a pocket and came out with a plastic sealed card with a photograph on it. "This do?" he said, giving Dunjee a glimpse of it.

"A guy flashed something that looked like that at me in East

240

St. Louis once," Dunjee said. "It wound up costing me about three hundred bucks."

"He'd like a closer look," said Franklin Keeling, who had said his name was Arnold.

"Here," Reese said, and handed Dunjee the ID card.

"Alex Merrifax Reese," Dunjee read. "I used to know some Merrifaxes in Borger, Texas. Any kin?"

Reese shook his head.

Dunjee went back to his reading. "Twenty-two forty-one Bonnie Brae Drive, Bethesda, Maryland. Bonnie Brae. Is that out near Glen Echo along the C and O Canal?"

"Around in there."

"Nice part of town." Dunjee read some more. "United States Department of Agriculture." He looked at Reese. "Chicken inspector?"

"You've got a very quick mouth, Mr. Dunjee," Reese said with a pleasant smile.

"I'm just trying to keep from getting into a car in a strange town with three guys I don't know."

Franklin Keeling wiped a hand across his mouth again. "You haven't got any choice."

Dunjee shrugged. "It's beginning to look that way." He looked around and found what he needed. A trash receptacle. He removed the folded *Herald Tribune* from under his arm and took a step toward the receptacle. "Since I've already done the puzzle, I'll just toss this first."

Reese took the newspaper out of his hand. "I'll take it," he said. "I haven't read the funnies."

"I was afraid of that."

"Yeah," Reese said and smiled. "I thought you might be."

They sandwiched Dunjee in between Reese and Keeling in the back seat. It was a tight fit. Jack Spiceman, the former FBI special agent, drove. The Rome traffic didn't seem to bother him.

Dunjee paid almost no attention to where they were going.

241

Instead, he watched as Alex Reese carefully opened the *Herald Tribune* and then began turning it, page by page.

The envelope was where it was supposed to be, between pages eight and nine. The envelope was sealed. Reese examined its front, then its back, and then the front again, reading aloud the name that was printed on its upper left-hand corner.

"The Grand Hotel," he said. "Nice old place."

"Just off the Baths of Diocletian," Dunjee said. "An easy stroll to the Via Veneto."

Reese put the envelope up to his ear and shook it. "You're staying at the Hassler, right?"

"That's nice, too," Dunjee said. "A little expensive, but what the hell."

"Let me use your knife, Frank," Reese said. Keeling dug around in a pants pocket and produced a a small penknife. Reese opened it and carefully slit the letter. He closed the knife and handed it back to Keeling.

"How'd you run into Abedsaid?" Reese said.

"Accidentally," Dunjee said.

Reese nodded. "I bet." He peered into the envelope. "A piece of paper." He took the paper out carefully. It seemed to be a piece of hotel stationery, folded in the conventional manner. Reese unfolded it. "Well, now," he said. "What do you know—a map."

"Is that what it is?" Dunjee said.

"Sure. Look. Here's a road or something and here's what looks like a house. And here's the scale down here, see? One centimeter equals five meters. Not a very big map though, is it?"

"Not very," Dunjee said.

"You know something?"

"What?"

"I'm not really with the Department of Agriculture."

"You fooled me," Dunjee said and began looking out the window as the car turned left and started up a steep winding street. He had no idea where he was.

242

"You know who I'm really with?" Reese said.

"Who?"

"The CIA."

"That must be interesting."

"No, it's really kind of frustrating sometimes," Reese said. "Take for instance yesterday and today. I flew in here day before yesterday to take charge of a certain operation. We're looking for somebody, somebody important. You follow me?"

Dunjee nodded. "I think so."

"Well, we've had all our people alerted for days. So I check in with our chief of station here in Rome. That's what we call them—chiefs of station. So I say to him, Well, what've you got? And he gets this funny look on his face."

Reese fell silent for several seconds as though haunted by what he had seen on the face of the Rome chief of station.

After another few moments, Dunjee said, "A funny look, you said."

"Yeah, a funny look. Well, it seems that some of our casual help sent in a report. And somehow it dropped between the cracks. Until yesterday. It seems there was this yacht docked in Valletta."

"In Malta," Dunjee said.

"Yeah, Malta. A Libyan yacht. A ninety-two-footer called the *True Oasis*. It was built for King Idris of Libya. Well, to make a long story short this part-time help we've got in Malta reported some funny kind of people going aboard the *True Oasis*."

"What kind of funny-looking people?" Dunjee said.

"According to this report that sort of dropped between the cracks, there was an Oriental—maybe a Japanese—a German—or a Dutchman—and a woman, young, thin, brunette, and possibly French."

"Going aboard a Libyan yacht," Dunjee said.

"Right. Well, I won't go into all the details, but we figured these three funny-looking people maybe could've led us to the guy we're really looking for. You follow me?"

243

"I think so."

"So quick like a snake I send some of our people over to Valletta, and guess what?"

"No yacht."

"No yacht. Well, hell, you can't hide a ninety-two-foot yacht, so we call the Navy. And they send some planes up and guess what?"

"This time I give up."

"Well, out there in the Mediterranean, halfway between Valletta and Tripoli is the *True Oasis,* broken down with engine trouble and radioing for help. And the real funny thing about it is that they're radioing for help when a U.S. destroyer is only about five miles away. Well, this destroyer of ours rushes over and hoves to, or whatever the hell they do in the Navy, and sends a crew aboard. A twelve-man crew. And sure enough those Libyans have got engine trouble, which took our guys about fifteen minutes to fix. Then the Libyans claim that they've got a few other problems they'd like the U.S. Navy to look at while they're there. So our guys are given a tour of the whole fucking yacht, from stem to stern. And you know what? There weren't any funny-looking people aboard any more—not unless you count the Libyans."

"That's quite a story," Dunjee said as the car reached the top of the hill and turned into a short straight drive which led to a garage that occupied half of the ground floor of a four-story cream-colored villa.

In the front seat, Jack Spiceman took out a small metal box and pointed it at the garage. He pressed a button and the overhead door went up. The car drove into the garage. The overhead door came down.

"This is what in our business we call a safe house," Reese said.

"A safe house."

"We're all going to get out of the car and go upstairs and talk to somebody about that little map of yours."

244

"Who're we going to talk to?" Dunjee asked.

"A patriot."

"You know something?" Dunjee said.

"What?"

"That's what somebody accused me of being the other day."

29

They went up three flights of stairs, Alex Reese leading the way, with Dunjee next and Keeling and Spiceman bringing up the rear. They were narrow wooden stairs, located in the rear of the building. Dunjee decided they were the servants' stairs. The building appeared old enough to have been built back when there were still servants to be had.

At the top of the stairs they walked down a short hall and into a large sun-drenched corner room that seemed to be mostly windows and angular furniture made out of chrome and glass and leather. There was also a marble floor. Part of it was covered by a thin worn rug that looked old and expensive.

Seated in one of the chrome and leather chairs was Leland Timble. He wore an Indian-made military style shirt with many busy pockets in the sleeves, tan slacks, and on his face a happy smile that Dunjee thought looked silly. Timble studied Dunjee carefully. Dunjee only glanced at Timble and then looked out the windows at the view of Rome. He decided it was a splendid, probably expensive view, but one that did nothing at all to tell him where he was.

"You are, I expect, Mr. Dunjee," Timble said.

Dunjee looked at Timble again. "I'm Dunjee."

"I am Leland Timble."

Dunjee nodded. "You rob banks."

Timble giggled. "And you are the Mordida Man."

"Newspaper stuff."

"Isn't it dreadful?"

"Terrible," Dunjee said. He turned toward Alex Reese. "This is the patriot you were telling me about?"

Reese smiled and shrugged. "He's working on it."

"Now then, what does Mr. Dunjee have for us?" Timble said.

Reese took the Grand Hotel envelope out of his pocket and handed it to the seated man. Timble slipped out the folded sheet of paper and opened it. He studied it carefully.

"Exceedingly well drawn; quite detailed." He looked up at Dunjee. "The building would appear to be a farmhouse of some kind."

"I didn't get a very good look at it," Dunjee said.

Timble held out the sheet of paper. Dunjee moved over, accepted it, and looked at it carefully. "As you said, a farmhouse."

"It would appear to be near the sea," Timble said.

Dunjee nodded, still examining the map. "Looks that way."

"But what sea?"

"I wouldn't know," Dunjee said and handed the map back to Timble. It took several seconds for Timble to refold the map and slip it back into the envelope. The happy-face smile vanished. He looked up at Franklin Keeling and nodded glumly.

Keeling turned quickly and hit Dunjee hard in the stomach, just below the belt buckle. The air exploded out of Dunjee's mouth. Keeling hit him again, again very hard, in approximately the same place. Dunjee doubled over holding his stomach. He fought for air, but his lungs refused to work properly. He sank to his knees on the marble floor, still doubled over. The nausea came then and Dunjee tried to fight it back, but lost, and vomited on the marble floor.

Jack Spiceman turned and left the room. When he came back,

Dunjee was still bent over on the floor. Spiceman tossed him a rag. "Here," he said. "Clean it up."

Dunjee straightened slowly. He tried a series of quick shallow breaths. They seemed to help. He used the rag to mop up the vomit. Then he rose slowly, took out a handkerchief, and used it to wipe the tears from his eyes and the vomit from his mouth.

"That was to save time, Mr. Dunjee," Timble said. "We're extremely short of time."

"What do you want?" Dunjee said.

"Why don't you sit down—over here by me?" Timble said, patting a chair.

Dunjee moved over and lowered himself into a leather chair whose chrome frame somewhat resembled a Z.

"What we want is quite simple," Timble said. "We want Bingo McKay. The President's brother," he added, as if there might be several of them.

Dunjee nodded.

"Abedsaid knows where he is, doesn't he?" Reese said.

Again, Dunjee nodded and pressed his right hand against his stomach. It did nothing to ease the pain.

"The way I figure it," Reese said, "it's a two-stage deal. That little map. That's the first stage. The second stage is where you get the map coordinates, the latitude and longitude and all that good stuff, which you need to tell what country it's in, right?"

Dunjee cleared his throat. "Something like that."

"Tell me," Reese said. "What're you using on Abedsaid—bribes or blackmail?"

Dunjee stared up at him. "A little of both."

Reese nodded, almost in approval. "How little's a little—the bribe, I mean?"

"A million."

"Where'd you get it?"

"Paul Grimes," Dunjee said. "He transferred it this morning."

"Grimes got it from the President?"

Dunjee nodded.

"And the million paid for our little map, right?" Without waiting for an answer, Reese continued. "What's going to buy the coordinates?"

"Pictures," Dunjee said.

"Dirty pictures?"

"Filthy," Dunjee said. "The Colonel's something of a prude."

"Where'd you get the pictures?" Reese said.

"Abedsaid's apartment. In London."

"What're the pictures of?" Spiceman said.

"Abedsaid and the German—Diringshoffen."

"In the sack together?"

Dunjee nodded.

"No kidding?" Spiceman said. He looked at Reese. "Does Diringshoffen swing that—"

Leland Timble interrupted. "We're at an impasse," he said in a tone that ruled out any further discussion.

Franklin Keeling smiled at Dunjee. "Leland's always a little bit ahead of the rest of us slow thinkers."

"He's right," Dunjee said.

"You do see it, don't you, Mr. Dunjee?" Timble said.

"I see it."

"See what?" Keeling said.

Timble sighed. "We wish to rescue Mr. Bingo McKay from his captors and return him safely to his family. For this patriotic action we, of course, expect to be rewarded. At worst, a light suspended sentence for our past youthful mistakes. Mr. Dunjee's objective is essentially the same as ours—rescuing Mr. McKay. However, Mr. Dunjee is near his objective, while we are as far away as ever."

"We've got Dunjee," Keeling said.

"But only Mr. Dunjee has any rapport with Mr. Abedsaid. We have no leverage. Mr. Dunjee does. However, we cannot let Mr. Dunjee go his own way, can we? At least, not until Mr. McKay is safely on his way home."

Dunjee pressed both hands against his stomach, closed his eyes, and leaned back in the chair. He wondered how long it would be before they arrived at the solution and which one would suggest it first. He decided to place a small private bet on Reese.

He lost. It was Spiceman who said, "We've got half the answer already. All we need is the other half."

Dunjee opened his eyes. Spiceman was staring at him. "What was he going to hand over to you when you gave him the dirty pictures?"

"A map. The real map."

"When?"

"At six this evening."

"Where is he now—Abedsaid?"

"At the FAO—negotiating with Ambassador Dokubo."

"The Nigerian?"

Dunjee nodded.

"The delay in the final transaction," Timble said, "that was to make sure that the money was actually transferred to Abedsaid's account in what—some Swiss bank?"

Again Dunjee nodded and closed his eyes. Now it comes, he thought.

"He's with Ambassador Dokubo now," Timble said. "How long do these negotiating sessions usually go on?"

Dunjee opened his eyes again. "You talking to me?"

"Yes."

"Abedsaid told me a couple of hours. Dokubo is stalling."

"He wouldn't carry the real map around with him, would he?" Timble said. "No, of course not."

"Why not?" Dunjee said.

"The scale," Timble explained, as if to a child. "If the extract you showed us is from the original map, it is an extremely large scale. One centimeter to five meters. It would be most cumbersome."

"His hotel safe, maybe?" Keeling said.

Timble shook his head. "No, I think not. It might draw attention to it. I think . . . yes, I think if I were Mr. Abedsaid, I would

250

keep the map in my hotel room. Tucked away securely, of course." Timble shifted his gaze to Jack Spiceman, the former FBI agent.

"A black bag job," Spiceman said. "Right?"

Timble nodded. "Don't you agree?"

"But not me," Spiceman said. "If I got caught, it would blow everything."

"No, not you, Jack," Timble said. "What we need, it would seem, is a rent-a-thief. A good one." He smiled his happy-face smile and looked around the room.

After a moment, Dunjee said, "I know one. A good one."

30

In his third-floor room in the Hassler Hotel, Harold Hopkins answered his phone on the second ring with a hello.

"This is Dunjee. We've got a small problem."

"A small one, you say? How small?"

"Almost tiny."

"Tell me about it."

"I think," Dunjee said, "that the Arab's going to try a cross."

"Shame on him. What kind of cross?"

"I think he's going to take his money and run."

"What about all those lovely pictures? Of him and the German gent with all the blond hair."

"I think he's decided to bluff it out—if we send them to the Colonel, which he probably doesn't think we will."

"And he's right, isn't he?"

"There wouldn't be much point."

Hopkins was silent for a second or two. Finally he said, "That means no map."

"No map," Dunjee agreed. "Unless you'd like to make an extra—say—ten thousand?"

"Ten thousand. Dollars?"

"Dollars."

"Something to do with the map, most likely."

"Take it out of his hotel room."

"For ten thousand?"

"Ten thousand."

"No thanks," Hopkins said.

"Look, Harold, it's a quick in and out. Abedsaid's not there. He's negotiating with the Nigerian Ambassador. You've got at least an hour—maybe even an hour and a half. Five minutes' work and you're fifteen thousand richer."

"Fifteen now, is it?"

"Fifteen."

There was a long silence. At last Hopkins broke it. "Okay. What do I look for?"

Dunjee told him exactly what to look for, and Abedsaid's room number in the Grand Hotel, and where to bring the map after he had stolen it. Hopkins wrote it all down on a sheet of Hassler stationery.

"I still don't like it," Hopkins said.

Dunjee sighed over the phone. "Fifteen, Harold."

"Not much lolly, is it?—considering the risk and all."

"Fifteen, Harold. Top price."

"Well, I had to try, didn't I?" Hopkins said and hung up.

He turned from the telephone, a smile on his face, and looked at the two persons seated in his room, the man in the chair, the woman on the edge of the bed.

"How was I?" Hopkins said.

"Utterly convincing," Delft Csider said.

Paul Grimes nodded his head and his several chins. "Perfect."

"Now it gets a bit tricky, I imagine," Hopkins said.

Again Paul Grimes nodded. "A bit," he said.

Hopkins got out of the cab in front of the Grand Hotel, over-paid the driver, looked around casually, and entered the lobby. He turned left toward the newsstand and purchased a day-old copy of the *Times* of London.

When he turned around, the plump woman in the green slacks and the orange sweater and the mouse-colored hair was just coming into the hotel. Hopkins turned toward the elevators and read the headlines as he crossed the lobby.

He came out of the elevator on the third floor and moved quickly down the corridor to room 318. The newspaper was now tucked under his left elbow. He reached into his right pants pocket, looked sharply left and right, took out a key, unlocked the door, and slipped inside.

The Libyan was standing in the center of the room. He was a tall man of about thirty with a prim, disapproving mouth and totally suspicious eyes. Hopkins wordlessly offered him the room key.

The Libyan took the key and in exchange handed over a thick ten-by-fourteen-inch manila envelope. Hopkins slipped it inside the *Times,* looked at his watch, then back at the Libyan.

"You speak English, mate?"

The Libyan shook his head no.

Hopkins pointed at his watch, then held up his right hand, all four fingers and the thumb widespread. The Libyan nodded. Hopkins looked around, found a chair, sat down, took out his cigarettes, and lit one. The Libyan moved to the dresser, folded his arms, and leaned against it.

After five silent minutes had passed, Hopkins ground out his cigarette, rose, and moved to the door. He turned and said, "Ciao," to the Libyan. "Ciao," said the Libyan as Hopkins opened the door and slipped out into the corridor, closing the door softly behind him.

Halfway down the corridor the mousey-haired woman in the green and orange outfit was slowly walking from door to door, a piece of paper in her hand, a frown on her face. She appeared to be looking for a room number. Hopkins put his right hand up to his face and started rubbing his eye. He averted his face slightly as he strode past the woman. She didn't bother to look at him.

Outside the hotel Hopkins found a taxi and showed the driver the address that Dunjee had spelled out over the phone. The driver nodded. Hopkins got into the back seat butt first. He noticed that the mousey-haired woman was just coming out of the hotel.

The mousey-haired woman watched Hopkins's taxi drive off. She turned and went back into the hotel. At one of the public telephones she made a call. It was answered on the second ring by a man's voice.

"Yes."

"He's on his way," the woman said. She spoke English with a slight Italian accent. "He was inside the room approximately five minutes and twenty-one seconds."

"That's long enough," the man's voice said.

"That's what I thought," the woman said and hung up.

It was Alex Reese who took the call from his mousey-haired CIA operative. But it was Jack Spiceman who was standing outside the villa's garage door when Hopkins's taxi pulled up.

Spiceman waited until Hopkins paid off the driver and got out of the taxi. Then he moved down the short drive. "You Hopkins?"

"I'm Hopkins. And who might you be?"

"Benedict," Spiceman said.

"Where's Dunjee?"

"Upstairs." Spiceman took out the small black box, aimed it at the garage door, and pressed the button. The overhead door went up.

"Magic," Hopkins said.

"Magic," Spiceman agreed.

Hopkins went first up the narrow wooden servants' stairs. When they ended, Spiceman moved around in front of Hopkins and led him down the hall and into the sunny corner room. Once inside, Hopkins looked slowly around. Leland Timble, seated, was wearing his silly happy-face smile again. Both Alex Reese and Franklin Keeling were standing. Dunjee sat in the chrome and leather chair, one hand still pressed against his stomach.

Hopkins's eyes settled on Dunjee. "Took in some partners, did we?"

Dunjee nodded. "A few. Did you get it?"

"I got it."

"Any trouble?"

Hopkins shook his head. "It went a treat."

"Give it to him," Dunjee said, nodding at Alex Reese. "The guy with no hair."

"He must mean you, mate," Hopkins said as he took the envelope from its newspaper wrapping and handed it to Reese.

It was a large map that Reese unfolded on a glass-topped table near the window. The map was almost five or six feet square and printed on extremely heavy paper. Timble was up now, the sheet of paper which designated the site of the farmhouse in his right hand. "It's an island," he said in a surprised tone as he stared at the map.

Reese nodded. "Comino."

"I never heard of it."

"It's the smallest Maltese island," Reese said, studying the map. "About a mile square. As I remember, the population at last count was nineteen. Maybe twenty."

"And our piece fits right in here—see the farmhouse," Timble said. Jack Spiceman and Franklin Keeling moved over to look. While the four men gathered around the map, Hopkins turned toward Dunjee.

"You know what?"

"What?" Dunjee said.

"We went right by it, we did, on the way over. Drove halfway around it, in fact."

"The Colosseum?"

"The Colosseum. Would've been a shame to come all the way and not see it. Looked a bit smallish, I thought, and kind of falling down, but it was a sight."

At the table, Timble said, "Would you get that ruler over there, please, Franklin?"

"Sure," Franklin Keeling said. He wiped one large hand across his mouth and moved across the room. He picked up a draftsman's ruler from a table and started back. When he reached the point just behind Harold Hopkins he paused.

"I'd've liked to've gone inside, you know," Hopkins was telling Dunjee. "I'd've liked to've seen where the lions ate the Christians. I used to read about that in school, I did. Seems a pity not to—"

He never finished his sentence. Keeling took the pistol out of his coat pocket in one smooth motion and placed its muzzle just behind Hopkins's left ear. It was a small pistol, an Italian-made automatic that used .22 longs. An assassin's pistol. Keeling pulled the trigger twice.

Hopkins stopped talking in mid-sentence. It may have been surprise that spread over his face. Or pain. It was difficult to tell. He managed to squeeze his eyes shut before he fell, slipping down sideways, a little bent at the waist, his arms limp and useless at his sides. He sprawled on the marble floor then, face down, two small reddish-black holes just below and behind his left ear. His right leg moved, kicked slightly, and after that he was still.

Dunjee was up quickly and then down on his knees beside Hopkins. Dunjee's right hand moved out, as if to touch Hopkins, possibly comfort him, but it hesitated, and hung there as if Dunjee was trying to decide how best to comfort the dead.

He denied it at first—to himself anyway. He denied the inescapable fact that Hopkins was dead. The evidence was plain, but Dunjee denied that, too, until the anger came. It was a hot anger, white hot almost, and directed not against Hopkins's killers, but against Hopkins himself. It's all your fault, you poor sod, Dunjee thought, unconsciously using an English expression to describe the dead Englishman. You should've stayed in London with your whore. You should've stuck to bits and pieces that fell off lorries. You shouldn't have been so greedy.

The anger didn't last long, because it quickly turned into rage instead—a rather fine, cold rage that made Dunjee's face go stiff until he remembered to smile. What he produced was a small set smile whose seemingly ineradicable permanence made it quite terrible.

With the awful smile still there, Dunjee turned to look up at Leland Timble. "That wasn't—" He broke off because he had wanted to say that wasn't right. But he knew they wouldn't understand that. So he said, "That wasn't—necessary."

Timble's expression was solemn. For some reason his eyes looked wise. "But it was necessary, Mr. Dunjee. For two reasons."

"I'm listening," Dunjee said pleasantly, wondering when his lips would start to ache.

"First, after your colleague completed his task, he became redundant, totally redundant. And secondly, we very much needed to get your full attention."

Dunjee looked down at the dead Harold Hopkins. Then he rose, his eyes fastened on Timble, his lips still smiling their terrible smile.

"My attention," he said.

Timble nodded. "Yes. Your attention. Your full attention."

Dunjee nodded back. "You've got it, laddy," he said. "All of it."

31

Using the full powers of his CIA position, it took Alex Reese only three phone calls to lay on everything—the plane tickets, the ground transportation, the boat—even the weapons, which would be waiting for them in Malta. Almost as an afterthought, Reese also arranged for the disposal of Harold Hopkins's body. That required the third call.

While Reese's deep bass rumbled into the telephone at one end of the still sunny room, Leland Timble carefully outlined the situation and options that Dunjee had open to him.

"According to what you've told us, the Libyans have removed Mr. McKay from the yacht, along with his female companion, and secured them in this old farmhouse on the island of Comino, correct?"

Dunjee nodded.

"Your Mr. Abedsaid also informed you that the two prisoners are now being guarded only by the three terrorists—two men and one woman, is that also correct?"

Again, Dunjee nodded.

"The two questions that we must now ask ourselves," Timble said slowly, "is why did the Libyans decide that the yacht was no longer suitable as a jail, and secondly, why did they choose this particular farmhouse and whom does it belong to?"

"That's three questions," Dunjee said.

"I stand corrected."

"First, the yacht was drawing too much attention, or so Abedsaid claimed. The farmhouse is isolated. It's really not much more than a stone shack. A year ago a rich Libyan tourist saw it, liked it, and leased it for twenty years with the idea of eventually turning it into a vacation home. Abedsaid claims that he ran out of money or interest or both. Abedsaid told me all this, but didn't tell me where the farmhouse was located. I had no idea it was on Comino."

Timble pursed his lips. "It does seem logical. I mean, the farmhouse would not only provide a suitable jail, but also sanctuary for our three terrorists. It's almost clever."

"What about me?" Dunjee said.

"You? Well, you, I'm afraid, Mr. Dunjee, have only two choices. You can either join your friend in the corner over there—" Timble gestured toward the body of Hopkins, which had been rolled up in the rug and tugged over to a corner. "Or you can join us."

"You already know my answer," Dunjee said. "What I don't understand is why. What've I got to offer?"

Timble chose his word carefully. "Credibility."

"You mean after Bingo McKay is rescued—providing he is."

"Exactly. It will then be made known to Washington that it was only with the help of me and my colleagues that the rescue was effected. Mr. Reese will also attest to this. Your testimonial will be the icing on the cake, so to speak. Of course, I do expect to compensate you. What would you say to $250,000?"

It was several seconds before Dunjee answered. When he did, the small awful smile was there. "I'd say yes."

"Good. That's settled."

"Tell me something," Dunjee said. "You expect to get a pardon out of this?"

"Certainly not. My crimes are too . . . enormous, let's say. But I think I can reasonably expect a light suspended sentence, don't you?"

"I have no idea. But why not just stay loose?"

"Because, Mr. Dunjee, I'm homesick."

The five men took the late afternoon Air Malta flight out of Rome's Fiumicino Airport. They flew tourist class. This time Dunjee found himself sandwiched in between Franklin Keeling and Jack Spiceman. In the seats just ahead, Alex Reese sat next to the window, Leland Timble next to him.

Timble had used a Canadian passport to slip through customs. He also wore a kind of disguise—a grayish-blond wig that covered his ears and hung a fringe of bangs down over his forehead almost to his eyes. After he put on a pair of dark glasses, he seemed to think he was invisible.

The flight to Valletta took not quite an hour. Because none of them was carrying any luggage, they breezed through customs. Outside the terminal building a thirtyish man with a drooping mustache and a John Deere billed cap on his head held up a scrawled sign that read, "Mr. Arnold."

"That's our taxi," Reese said and moved over to the man. Dunjee was again sandwiched in between Spiceman and Keeling in the rear seat. Timble sat next to the silent driver. Reese sat next to the window and sipped from a pint of brandy. Nobody had to tell the driver where to go.

The boat was docked on the quay at Marsaxlokk. The five men got out of the taxi and walked toward it. Nobody said anything to the driver. Nobody paid him any money. As soon as the five men got out of the taxi, it pulled away.

The boat was a twenty-one-foot cabin cruiser. It was painted a light blue with a darker blue trim. Its brightwork gleamed. Dunjee knew little about boats, but he thought it looked fairly new. The name painted on its stern was *Maria.*

"Who's the sailor?" Dunjee asked.

"Spiceman," Keeling said. "He used to have one a little smaller than this in Washington. Kept it docked over in Anacostia."

Spiceman was the first aboard. He went below and then came back up and turned toward the gauges. "The bilges are okay," he said. Nobody seemed to care. Spiceman started the boat's engines. They caught immediately.

Reese turned to Dunjee. "Let's you and me and Keeling go down and take a look at the goodies," he said. "Leland'll take care of the lines."

There were two bunks on the port side of the cabin and another one forward which could be pulled down. There was also a small galley and a head. On the bottom bunk were two large suitcases. Reese opened the first suitcase. Inside, resting on what seemed to be a thick bed of old bathrobes, were three M-16 rifles. There were also a stack of magazines and a roll of friction tape. Dunjee counted twenty magazines.

Reese looked at Dunjee. "You still know how to work one of these babies, don't you?"

"I think I remember."

Reese opened the second suitcase. It held another M-16, ten more magazines, a bullhorn, and six fragmentation grenades. Reese grunted. "They must've thought we were going to start a war."

He picked up a rifle and handed it to Dunjee. "Here," he said adding, "you'll need one of these, too," and handed him a magazine.

"I'll need two of them," Dunjee said, just as the boat began to pull away from the dock.

Reese handed him another magazine. "And some of that friction tape," Dunjee said.

Timble came down into the cabin just as Dunjee was taping the two magazines unevenly together. He clicked one of the magazines into the breech.

"Why do you have them taped together?" Timble asked.

262

"Because," Dunjee said, released the magazine, flipped it over, and slapped the fresh magazine into place.

"Oh," Timble said. "For when you run out of bullets."

"Dunjee was sort of a hero over in Vietnam," Reese said.

"Really?" said Timble, interested.

"Really," Dunjee said.

Spiceman ran the boat aground on the small, narrow rocky beach. Sharp rocks cut a jagged foot-long hole in the boat's bow. The five men jumped from the bow into less than two feet of water and waded ashore. Alex Reese was the last off the boat. He carried the loudhailer as well as an M-16. No one looked back at the boat as it began to fill with water. Again, no one seemed to care.

There was a full moon, fat and bright. Dunjee turned to Reese. "You lay on the moon, too?"

"No, but I fixed up the weather."

It was warm, somewhere in the low sixties. The five men were dressed much alike—in jackets and tieless shirts and slacks and ordinary street shoes. Two of the shirts were even white. Dunjee was grateful that his was blue.

They gathered around Franklin Keeling, who had folded the big map down into a thick one-foot square. "There should be some kind of steps leading up to the top of the bluff," Keeling said.

The bluff started where the rocky beach ended and went straight up for nearly forty feet. The bluff appeared to be smooth solid rock. If there were no steps, Dunjee didn't think they could climb it.

Keeling had a flashlight. He switched it on and moved its beam over the rock face. He found the first step a little to the left. It was nearly two feet high and very narrow, both in depth and width. The steps were worn smooth and seemed to have been chiseled and hacked out of the rock face a long time ago. "It's gonna take a goat to get up those," Keeling said.

"I think we should best start," Timble said.

Dunjee moved over to Timble. "Let me ask something."

"What?"

"When we get up on top, who's going to be in charge? There are three people up there behind stone walls who're probably going to be shooting at me pretty soon. So I'd kind of like to know who's going to be running things."

Timble nodded. "My experience in such matters is limited."

"I'm glad you appreciate that," Dunjee said.

"So Mr. Keeling here will be in charge."

"He gives the orders?"

Timble nodded. Dunjee turned to the big man with the rubbery face who sometimes liked to call himself Arnold. "You've done this kind of thing before?" Dunjee said.

"Once or twice," Keeling said.

"Just curious."

"I don't blame you." He turned to the others. "All right. I'll go up first. Then Dunjee, then Jack, then Leland. Reese, you bring up the rear."

Nobody argued. Keeling stepped up onto the first narrow ledge and then went smoothly on up to the top. Dunjee followed. It was easier than he had thought it would be. When he reached the final step, he stopped and slowly poked his head up over the lip of the cliff.

Keeling was almost flat on the ground. He turned his head back toward Dunjee. "See that?" he said.

Dunjee looked. There was a low stone wall some ten yards away. It was crumbling through age and neglect. In some places it was only a foot high; in others two feet; there was even one section which had managed to retain its original three-foot height. The wall ran for twenty feet on either side of Keeling and then seemed to give up. It simply dribbled away into small piles of stones.

"That's where we set up," Keeling said. "At the wall. Pass it back."

Dunjee passed it back to Spiceman and then began crawling

on his belly and knees and elbows toward the wall. He cradled the M-16 in his arms as he crawled.

When he reached the wall, Keeling was already peering over it. "Take a look," he said.

Dunjee smeared some dirt on his forehead before raising the top of his head slowly above the wall until he could see what lay on the other side. It was the farmhouse. It seemed to be some forty yards away. The house was a square flat-roofed one-story structure, simply built of round stones. There was a solid enough looking door, which was closed. On either side of the door were two windows. They were shuttered. Through the cracks in the shutters came some soft light. Dunjee looked for power lines, but could find none, and assumed that the light came from either oil- or battery-powered lamps. Or even candles.

"It's a fort," Dunjee said.

Keeling grunted. "If we can't get in, I guess we'll have to get them to come out."

Keeling turned and watched as the other three men crawled toward them. After each of them had taken a quick peek over the top of the wall, Keeling looked at Reese and said, "Remember that time I was telling you about in Luanda?"

Reese nodded. "Want me to try it?"

"Why not?"

Reese picked up the bullhorn. "I'm going to try to talk them out."

He put the bullhorn up to his lips. "You, inside the house!"

Reese's bass voice seemed to thunder out of the bullhorn. "This is the U.S. government. You are surrounded. If you throw out your arms and come out with your hands up, you will not be harmed. I repeat. Throw out your arms and come out with your hands up. You have three minutes."

Halfway through Reese's invitation the lights in the farmhouse went out. They were thick candles stuck into saucers and it was Ko Yoshikawa who blew them out. "Can you see anything?" he said.

Bernt Diringshoffen was already kneeling at a shuttered win-

265

dow, peering through the cracks. In his left hand was a Kalashnikov assault rifle. "Nothing," he said.

"I told you," Françoise Leget whispered fiercely into the dark. "I told you it was a trap. Now they're going to kill us. I dreamed it night before last. I told you then what was going to happen."

"Shut up, Françoise," Ko said wearily.

"They're not going to kill me," she said. "No. Not me. I'm not going to let them kill me like they killed Felix."

There was a thump. Ko looked around. There was no light. He used a disposable cigarette lighter to see what Francoise was doing.

The thump had come from the lid of the suitcase that she had thrown back against a wall. She was pawing through the suitcase, looking for something. Her rifle lay discarded on the floor beside her.

"What the hell are you doing, Françoise?" Ko said, the weariness in his tone overlaid by disgust.

"They're not going to kill me. I don't want to die. I can't die. I'm going out. Don't try to stop me. I'm going out and then I'll explain everything to them. They will understand."

"Let her go," Diringshoffen said from the window. "She's crazy."

"I'm not crazy. You're the crazies. You can stay here and get killed. I'm going to live. That's important—to live."

She stood up. Even in almost total darkness, Ko could see the white blouse she held in her hand. It was her flag of surrender.

"I will explain everything," she said. "They will understand."

"They'll kill you," Ko said.

"No. Not me. I will surrender and then explain everything and they will understand. And I will live."

She started toward the door. "So long, Françoise," Ko said.

Dunjee watched as the farmhouse door swung open. Something white was being waved.

Reese put the bullhorn back to his lips. "We see your white

flag. We will respect it. Just come out slowly with your hands high in the air."

Jack Spiceman put his M-16 up to his cheek and took careful aim at the doorway.

"You think it's a trick?" Dunjee said.

"Who knows?"

All five men watched as Françoise Leget stepped slowly through the farmhouse door, her arms straight up above her head. In her left hand was the white blouse.

She walked slowly toward the stone wall. When she was twenty yards away, Jack Spiceman shot her in the left knee. Francoise Leget crumpled to the ground. Then the screams began.

32

After Françoise Leget's screams had gone on without interruption for nearly five minutes, Dunjee asked Franklin Keeling, "Why don't you finish her off?"

"That's what you'd do, isn't it?" Keeling said.

"I don't know," Dunjee said.

"Well, the reason I don't have Spiceman finish her off is because in about two minutes, they're going to do something stupid."

"Like kill their hostages?"

Keeling shook his head as he peered over the top of the stone wall. Next to him Spiceman had removed one of the stones after working it loose. It afforded him a perfect loophole through which he aimed his rifle.

"Tell him, Jack," Keeling said.

Spiceman didn't take his eyes from the sights of his rifle, which were aimed at the farmhouse door. He barely moved his lips when he spoke. "They're not going to kill their hostages now. The hostages are their only way off this rock. But by shooting the woman, we shook 'em up. They're confused. And because they're confused, they'll probably do something stupid." Spiceman was silent for a moment until he added, "Of course, maybe they've already filled their stupidity quota for the day. Maybe they've already killed McKay and his girl friend. Before we got here."

Keeling shook his head. "No way. If they'd already killed 'em, they wouldn't still be here." He looked at his watch. "She's sure a screamer, isn't she?"

Inside the farmhouse, Bernt Diringshoffen looked through one of the shuttered windows. "If you could keep their heads down for five seconds, perhaps six, I could get her."

"No," Ko Yoshikawa said.

"Five seconds, no more."

"No."

"It would work," Diringshoffen insisted. "Two seconds out, three seconds back. I could drag her with my left arm, fire with my right. That'd help keep their heads down."

"No."

They listened to Françoise Leget scream. Diringshoffen turned to look at the dark shape of Ko kneeling by the other window. "It's over, isn't it?"

"Almost."

"I'm not going to let her die like that."

"You're crazy," Ko said. "You're as crazy as she is."

"I'm going," Diringshoffen said. "Will you help?"

Ko sighed. "All right."

"Two seconds out, three seconds back."

"Sure," Ko said.

Diringshoffen went out the farmhouse door fast. He was bent over low and firing as he ran. Everyone ducked down behind the stone wall as Ko Yoshikawa sprayed it with his own rifle. Everyone ducked but Jack Spiceman, who shot Diringshoffen nine times before he reached the screaming woman. There was a silence. Then Spiceman took careful aim and shot Françoise Leget twice through the head.

"She was getting on my nerves," he said.

Franklin Keeling turned to Reese. "Give him a little more razzmatazz on the bullhorn, Reese."

The bald-headed man put the bullhorn up to his lips, thought a moment, and said, "You in there. The last one left. You have one chance. Send out the hostages. I repeat, send out the hostages. It's your only chance."

Ko Yoshikawa listened as the bass voice rumbled out of the bullhorn. He thought almost indifferently for a moment about the hostages. He had grown to like Bingo McKay. He had liked his quick mind and his wit and his style. The one-eared man had had great style. But despite that, Bingo McKay had been the enemy. Not the real enemy, of course. The real enemy was out there in the dark behind the stone wall. But you could argue with Bingo McKay. And Ko had. Wonderful, wide-ranging arguments about politics and life and art and the future of mankind.

But it was useless to send out the hostages now. Completely useless. He wondered if those out there behind the wall realized that. It didn't matter. It was almost over. All of it. Ko slapped a fresh magazine into his rifle and used its muzzle to bang open the shutters. He rested the rifle's barrel on the sill and emptied the magazine at the stone wall. There was a silence.

Last words, Ko thought as he shoved a new magazine up into the rifle. Something memorable. No, not something memorable. Something their mentality can understand.

He cupped his left hand around his mouth and screamed at them, the American enemy. "Come and get me, copper!"

Behind the wall, Keeling turned to look at Dunjee. "What'd he say?"

"He said, 'Come and get me, copper,' I believe."

"Well, now. I guess that's what you're going to have to do, hero."

"Me?" Dunjee said.

"Sure. You."

"What a splendid idea," Timble said.

"We'll give you plenty of covering fire," Spiceman said. "He'll never know what hit him."

270

"No," Dunjee said.

Keeling sighed and moved his rifle so that it was aimed at Dunjee's chest. "You can either be a dead nobody here or a live hero inside the house. Which is it?"

"Well, shit," Dunjee said and turned to look over the wall. He ducked back down immediately as Ko again raked the wall with a full magazine. Dunjee lay against the wall, trying to think of a way to keep from being killed.

Ko began screaming again. It was the scream of his ancestors. Dunjee turned to listen.

"Banzai, you motherfuckers!" Ko screamed from the open window. "Babe Ruth eats shit!"

"Jesus," Reese said. "He's gone crackers."

Keeling turned to Dunjee. "All right, hero."

Dunjee checked his rifle carefully. He hadn't fired it yet. "I want you to keep him down behind that window," he said. "I don't want you to stop firing. I'm going in through the door. Just keep firing. Don't stop."

"When do we start?" Spiceman asked.

"I'll move straight toward the left corner of the house. That's five seconds, maybe four. Then I'll work my way to the door. When I start for the corner of the house, you start. And don't stop. If you stop, I get my head blown off."

"Good luck, Mr. Dunjee," Timble said.

"Fuck off," Dunjee said and started crawling toward the left end of the wall. He crouched there for a moment, taking deep breaths. He remembered the mechanics of what he had to do. Fast forward, down and roll. But that was the trouble, of course. He had to remember what once had been almost instinct.

"Well, hell," Dunjee whispered and started for the left corner of the stone farmhouse. He went fast and low—bent over almost double. He could hear them firing. At least they were doing that. He went into the roll six feet from the farmhouse and finished up lying pressed against the round stones. He found himself wanting to stay there—to hug the stone and not move.

He made himself move. He crawled. The door was a mile away, possibly two. It took him three hours to get there. It should all be coming back to you, he thought. It should be just chock full of déjà vu. But it isn't. It's just crawling along a wall in the dirt toward a door. It's the way you earn your living. It's your profession.

When he reached the door he didn't hesitate. He knew if he hesitated, he wouldn't go through it. Diringshoffen had left the door open almost a foot when he came out to die. Nobody had closed it.

Dunjee slammed the door back. He went through it in a leap, spinning in midair and firing at the space just below the windowsill where the dark shape should have been crouched, but wasn't.

Behind you, Dunjee thought. He's behind you at the other window. He whirled around. The shutters of the other window were now wide open. Ko had just emptied a magazine through the window at the stone wall. He was in the midst of changing magazines, his eyes wide and staring at Dunjee.

Full automatic, Dunjee thought. You had it on full automatic. Now it's empty. There was a time when he could have done it in less than a second. Release the taped-together magazines, reverse them, and ram them home.

He didn't think about how to do it now. He let his hands do it. They seemed to remember. He heard the magazine click into place just as Ko brought the muzzle of his own rifle up. Dunjee was surprised when Ko, kneeling, started to slump forward. There were red gobbets all over Ko's shirt, made by Dunjee's tumbling .223-caliber bullets. Ko's face was gone. He fell forward.

Dunjee looked down at the M-16 rifle. His forefinger was still wrapped tightly around the trigger. He couldn't remember firing. He couldn't remember the sound the shots had made. Dunjee started over toward the dead Ko but stopped at the sound of the bullhorn.

"Dunjee!" the bullhorn said. "Hey, Dunjee!"

Dunjee went to the door. "What?" he yelled.

"We're coming in," the bullhorn said. "Okay?"

"Okay," Dunjee yelled back.

The first thing they did when they came in was to take Dunjee's rifle away from him. Spiceman looked almost apologetic when he said, "It's sort of the end of the line. You understand?"

"Sure," Dunjee said, not understanding anything.

"Use the Jap's gun on him, Jack," Keeling said. "Make it all nice and tidy."

Spiceman was bending over the dead Ko Yoshikawa to pick up the rifle when the first two came through the far window. They were dressed all in black—black pants, black shirts, black stocking caps, black sneakers, and faces that had been smeared with black. They came through like wraiths, smoothly, silently. Two more came through the other window and one of them kicked Ko's rifle out of Spiceman's hands. It seemed to be a hard kick, well practiced, as if he had done it often before.

The final two flowed in through the door. All of them had submachineguns. The submachineguns, of Czech manufacture, were also black. The two who came in through the door seemed to be the leaders. One of them made a motion with his submachinegun. The message was clear. Keeling and Reese put their weapons down slowly on the floor. When they straightened up they raised their hands above their heads. A very frightened Leland Timble did the same thing. Timble's eyes were wide and staring and his mouth was a small round hole. Through it he kept saying, "Oooh, oooh, oooh," until Spiceman told him to shut up. Only Dunjee didn't raise his hands above his head.

One of the men with the submachineguns found the candles that Ko had blown out and lit them. Then he turned toward the door, as if waiting to be told what else to do.

He didn't have to wait long. Faraj Abedsaid strolled through the door, wearing a smart gray suit, with a rolled-up newspaper tucked under his arm something like a swagger stick.

"Well, Mr. Dunjee," Abedsaid murmured. "Everything went according to plan, I see."

Dunjee nodded. "Almost."

"Now, let's see, this one?" He pointed at Leland Timble.

Dunjee nodded.

"And this one?" This time the rolled-up newspaper was pointed at Franklin Keeling. Again, Dunjee nodded.

"What about this one?" Abedsaid asked, pointing at Jack Spiceman.

"Him, too."

"And this gentleman?"

"My name is Alex Reese and this is all part of a CIA operation. I suggest you—"

Abedsaid cut him off. "Mr. Dunjee?"

Before Dunjee could answer, Jack Spiceman said, "He's a fucking liar."

Abedsaid turned toward Spiceman and lifted an eyebrow. "Dissent—so soon?"

"My left lapel," Spiceman said. "Have somebody cut it open."

Abedsaid turned toward one of the men in black and said something in Arabic. The man produced a knife and slit open Spiceman's left lapel. He removed a narrow piece of folded-up paper, a little more than an inch or so wide and almost seven inches long. He handed it to Abedsaid, who unwrapped the paper carefully.

"Negatives, it would seem," Abedsaid said, "and contact prints." He moved over to one of the candles for a better look. "It would appear that the gentleman with the bald head is in the process of breaking some black gentleman's neck. What do you think?"

Abedsaid offered the contact prints to Dunjee, who examined them near the candle. They showed Alex Reese rising from the Central Park bench; putting his hands to Mapangou's neck and head; twisting the neck, and Dr. Mapangou falling to the ground.

"Dr. Mapangou," Dunjee said. "He was Gambia's representative to the UN."

"Really," Abesaid said. "Well, what do you say about our bald-headed friend then?"

"Sure," Dunjee said. "Him too."

Again, Abedsaid said something in Arabic. One of the black-clad men reached behind and brought out five pairs of handcuffs that had been taped together with masking tape to keep them from jingling. He stripped the masking tape off.

The first to be handcuffed was Leland Timble. "I demand to see the United States consul," Timble said. "I demand to speak to the—"

He stopped speaking when the man who had the handcuffs produced a roll of wide surgical tape, ripped off a piece, and slapped it across Timble's mouth.

"What'll he do with them?" Dunjee asked as he watched the last of the handcuffs being snapped into place.

"The Colonel? I'm not sure what he really does have in mind," Abedsaid said. "Something weird probably." He turned toward the four handcuffed men. "Anything you'd like to say to them before they depart, Mr. Dunjee?"

"No," Dunjee said. "Nothing."

Abedsaid snapped something else out in Arabic and the six black-clad men led Leland Timble, Alex Reese, Jack Spiceman, and Franklin Keeling out through the door of the stone farmhouse. Abedsaid watched them go with evident satisfaction.

"Well, now," he said, turning back to Dunjee. "I believe that does it, and very nicely done, too. The Colonel will be most pleased."

"It does it except for Bingo McKay and the girl."

"Oh, yes. Well, they should be down in the cellar—through that door over there. If they're still alive, of course."

"You think they might not be?"

"That's really not my concern, is it, Mr. Dunjee?"

Abedsaid turned to go, but then turned back. "Shall I give your regards to the Colonel?"

"Do that," Dunjee said.

It was a thick door that led down to the cellar and it was secured by a heavy padlock. Dunjee walked back and knelt down by the dead body of Ko Yoshikawa. He went through Ko's pockets and found the key in the second one he tried.

Dunjee rose and looked around for the flashlight that Keeling had carried. He found it on the table where the candles burned. After unlocking the door, he started down the stone steps that led to the cellar. Halfway down he paused to listen. He could hear nothing. He started to speak, but decided not to, afraid that there would be no answering voice.

At the next to the last step Dunjee paused and flashed his light over the small cellar. There was a pile of sacking that seemed to have served as a bed. Next to it was a bucket and a water jug. Dunjee continued to flash the light around the room. He found them in the farthermost corner.

The man had managed to rip a heavy piece of wood from somewhere. The woman crouched behind him. The man held the piece of wood like a club, his lips drawn back in a snarl.

Dunjee quickly reversed the flashlight and held it so that it shone up into his own face.

"It's me, Bingo," he said.

"Dunjee?" Bingo McKay's voice was a harsh croak.

"It's over. It's all over."

Bingo McKay let the club fall from his hands. He turned to the woman who cowered behind him. Eleanor Rhodes looked gray and dirty and disheveled. Her eyes seemed to be coated with a film. Nothing registered in them.

"You hear that, sugar?" Bingo McKay said gently. "It's all over."

Eleanor Rhodes continued to crouch in the corner, staring up at him, seeing nothing.

33

Two months later they held the reception for the new Ambassador in the Thomas Jefferson State Reception Room on the eighth floor of the U.S. Department of State Building. The room was a slight snub, almost imperceptible except to the most seasoned observers of such things in Washington. The seasoned observers were of the opinion that if the reception had been really first rate, it would have been held in the somewhat larger John Quincy Adams State Drawing Room, which contained the desk where Benjamin Franklin had signed the treaty of Paris in 1783 ending the revolution.

All the Thomas Jefferson room had were those awful blue walls, white woodwork, the famous chandelier, and that statue of Jefferson himself, plus all those Chippendale chairs, which nobody used during a reception anyway. The seasoned observers were to change their minds about the snub later on in the evening.

Chubb Dunjee and Paul Grimes stood on the far side of the room and watched the Nigerian Ambassador, Olufemi Dokubo, go through the line, chat with the Secretary of State, and then beam down on the new Ambassador from Libya. Dokubo was wearing his native robe getup of brilliant blue with intricate

277

white embroidery. On his head was perched a red round cap that looked something like a pillbox. The Libyan Ambassador wore a blue three-piece suit, white shirt, and dark tie. He might have been going to a funeral.

As they watched Dokubo and the new Ambassador chat briefly, Grimes said, "Cuts a hell of a figure in that robe, doesn't he?"

"Dokubo?"

"Yeah."

Dunjee nodded. "Is Bingo still on his honeymoon?"

"Still," Grimes said.

"Where'd they go?"

"Caracas."

"Caracas?" Dunjee said. "What's in Caracas?"

"Twenty-million dollars, Bingo thinks. It belongs to us, the Israelis, and the Libyans. Bingo thinks he might be able to get it back."

"How's his bride?"

"Better."

"Good." Dunjee looked at his watch. "He's late."

"He's always late," Grimes said.

He wasn't all that late though. Not more than ten minutes. First into the reception room slipped the four Secret Service men with the X-ray eyes to see if there were any bomb throwers present. After that came the President of the United States, Jerome McKay.

He moved down the reception line, the State Department spieler at his elbow to murmur the names of those he might not know. After shaking hands with the Secretary of State, whom he had last seen only three hours before, the President stopped before the Ambassador Extraordinary and Plenipotentiary of the Libyan Arab Republic, the Honorable Faraj Abedsaid.

"Mr. Ambassador," the President said.

"Mr. President."

"We'll have our talk next week when you present your credentials. A long one."

278

"I'm looking forward to it."

"So am I," the President said, his eyes already roaming the room to see whose hand he next should shake.

Not present and notable by their absence at the reception were the Ambassadors from Israel, the United Arab Republic, the Philippines, Chad, Niger, Algeria, and Tunisia, all of whom were still feuding with Libya about one thing or another. Also not present was the Ambassador from the Soviet Union, who was still grumpy over the resumption of relations between the U.S. and Libya.

The President worked the crowd skillfully, moving around the room in clockwise fashion until he reached four o'clock, where Dunjee, Grimes, and the rest of the nobodies were standing. "I don't think you know Chubb Dunjee, Mr. President," Grimes said.

The President grasped Dunjee's hand. "Dunjee," he said thoughtfully. "Dunjee. You were having a little tax problem, weren't you?"

"A misunderstanding," Dunjee said. "It's all been resolved."

The President nodded. "Good," he said. "Good." He gave Dunjee's hand a final pump and said, "Well, keep in touch—through Paul here."

"All right," Dunjee said.

Dunjee came out of the 21st Street entrance and climbed into the front seat of the rented car driven by Delft Csider.

"What'd he say?" she asked.

"He said keep in touch."

"Well, that's almost as good as thank you."

"Almost," Dunjee said.

When they were on the George Washington Memorial Parkway about halfway to Dulles airport, Dunjee said, "I wish you'd change your mind."

"What would I do in Portugal?" she said.

Dunjee thought about it. "Read, listen to music, run a few miles, do some shopping, hit a few bars—maybe screw a lot."

"And when the money ran out?"

"Well, I guess then we'd go out and get us some more."

"Just like that?"

"Just like that."

She turned to stare at him briefly. "You really are serious, aren't you?"

"Totally."

"I'll think about it."

Dunjee smiled his best smile—very white, very warm, very winning. It was his politician's smile.

"Do that," he said.

More About Penguins
and Pelicans

For further information about books available from
Penguins please write to Dept EP, Penguin Books Ltd,
Harmondsworth, Middlesex UB7 0DA.

In the U.S.A.: For a complete list of books available from
Penguins in the United States write to Dept CS, Penguin
Books, 625 Madison Avenue, New York, New York 10022.

In Canada: For a complete list of books available from
Penguins in Canada write to Penguin Books Canada Ltd,
2801 John Street, Markham, Ontario L3R 1B4.

In Australia: For a complete list of books available from
Penguins in Australia write to the Marketing Department,
Penguin Books Australia Ltd, P.O. Box 257, Ringwood,
Victoria 3134.

In New Zealand: For a complete list of books available from
Penguins in New Zealand write to the Marketing
Department, Penguin Books (N.Z.) Ltd, P.O. Box 4019,
Auckland 10.

WAYS OF ESCAPE
Graham Greene

The second part of Greene's acclaimed autobiography, which he began in *A Sort of Life*.

From Haiti under Papa Doc, Vietnam in the last days of the French. Kenya during the Mau Mau and Hollywood, to the making of *The Third Man* in Vienna and his time in the British Secret Service, Graham Greene writes exquisitely of people and places, of faith, doubt, fear and of the craft of writing, as he found himself repeatedly 'at the dangerous edge of things'.

'Marvellously rich' – William Trevor

THE MAGIC ARMY
Leslie Thomas

January 1940, and the people of South Devon watch as their sleepy villages turn into a theatre of war. Overpaid, over-sexed and over here – the Americans have arrived, sweeping a tide of protesting civilians from their homes in rehearsal for D-Day.

Leslie Thomas's brilliantly funny and achingly sad story magnificently recreates the hilarity and outrage of a community caught up in the greatest military adventure in history.

'It's bawdy, funny, sad and sometimes sorry and it brought those times vividly back' – *Daily Mail*

A KIND OF TREASON
Robert Elegant

A well-known syndicated columnist and bestselling author, Mallory was a success. Yet he was going stale – running out of ideas, of family and of friends.

Then *Quest* magazine came up with their *carte-blanche* offer: to find out what was really going on in Saigon. A free hand, a change of scene, a sensuous Vietnamese girlfriend, it was just what Mallory would have prescribed for himself – left to himself. But then there is a catch to everything, and the CIA wanted a job done. Very simple really, nothing dangerous – just a little spying on the side.

Winner of the Edgar Allan Poe Special Award

BLIND PILOT
Ambrose Clancy

Top terrorist, Joe Walsh, is sprung between prisons. The cost is eight lives and an uneasy truce.

For Special Branch this means that the two rival factions have negotiated a truce. A precarious, touchy alliance – but then both of them wanted the weapons on their way from Europe . . .

Ireland is the setting for this brilliant and unsparing new thriller. Its plot, an unbelievably tense story of terror and political violence; its theme, a country which cannot forget the past nor come to terms with the future.

'Compulsive' – *Daily Telegraph*

THE FALCON AND THE SNOWMAN

Robert Lindsey

'An absolutely smashing real-life spy story' – *The New York Times Book Review*

It will shock you. It will sadden you. It's a true story you'll never forget. The story of Daulton Lee and Chris Boyce – two decent Catholic boys growing up in happy, warm families in one of the most affluent suburbs in America living the American Dream and facing a bright future. Or so it seemed.

Little did anyone imagine that they were to become Soviet spies and perpetrate one of the most bizarre and damaging conspiracies against the United States since the war.

'Dynamite ... ranks with the best of Le Carré and Deighton – but it's all true' – Thomas Thompson, author of *Blood and Money*

SKYSHROUD

Tom Keene with Brian Haynes

The Soviet Union is perilously close to completing an infallible defence against nuclear weapons, whereby, safe from retaliation, Soviet global control would be absolute ... The weapon is Skyshroud, nurtured in fear, perfected by hate, the ultimate, ultimate deterrent.

Skyshroud is fiction created from fact – another five-star thriller from the bestselling authors of *Spyship*.

More bestselling Penguins

THE BLACK HOUSE
Patricia Highsmith

Brilliant ... disturbing ... menacing ... these eleven sinister stories reveal Patricia Highsmith's characters breaking the social laws (often unconsciously) and paying the price. They are victims trying to behave like protagonists – and the results are often fatal.

'Nothing is certain when we have crossed *this* frontier. It is not the world as we once believed we knew it, but it is frighteningly more real to us than the house next door' – Graham Greene

THE BLOOD OF AN ENGLISHMAN
James McClure

At first, it looked much like any other dead body – breathtaking in its own way, of course, but nothing special ... Then he saw that the arm bones had been fractured by a knot, a knot that must have been tightened by a giant – or a human gorilla.

The celebrated detective team of Lieutenant Kramer and Sergeant Zondi are on the track of what appears to be a gigantic killer possessed of hideous strength. A murderer so out of the ordinary should be easy enough to find, yet to Kramer's intense embarrassment, he proves remarkably elusive.

VANISHING LADIES

Ed McBain

A peaceful lake, a cabin in the country and each other ... It looked as though it was going to be an idyllic holiday for Phil Colby and his fiancée Anne. But then Anne disappears from her hotel room, and Phil finds a red-haired hooker in her place ...

In a town where everyone from the state trooper to the judge is on the take, Phil gets nowhere fast.

MIDNIGHT AT THE WELL OF SOULS

Jack L. Chalker

Volume One in his mind-blowing Well-World Saga

Entered by a thousand unsuspected gateways – built by a race lost in the clouds of time – Well World transforms creatures of any sort into a different form. So, spacefarer Nathan Brazil is not surprised to find himself accompanied by a batman, an amorous female centaur and a mermaid, as he sets out on his strange mission.

Yet Nathan Brazil's own metamorphosis is more terrifying than any of the others' – and with the gradual return of his memory comes the secret of the Well World.

'Excellent ... marvellously inventive' – *SF Review*

Volumes Two and Three are also published in Penguins

WHO'S ON FIRST
William F. Buckley, Jr.

TIME: The Cold War
PLACE: Paris, Budapest, Washington, DC, Stockholm, Moscow
SECRET AGENT: Young irresistible Blackford Oakes of the CIA
ASSIGNMENT: Win the satellite space race with the Soviets

Enter master agent Rufus, CIA Director Allen Dulles, former Secretary of State Dean Acheson, and Tamara, a beautiful Hungarian freedom fighter. Blacky's mission is complicated by the President, the US Navy, a KGB area chief, and the alluring Sally, who loves him, hates his work.

The Buckley tension, wit, ingenuity and high drama show why, in his class, he's first.

SHUTTLECOCK
Graham Swift

Prentis, senior clerk in the 'dead crimes' department of police archives, is becoming more and more paranoiac ... Alienated from his wife and children, and obsessed by his father, a wartime hero now the mute inmate of a mental hospital, Prentis feels increasingly unsettled as his enigmatic boss Mr Quinn turns his investigations towards himself – and his father ...

'An astonishing study of forms of guilt, laced with a thread of detection, and puckering now and then into outrageous humour' – *Sunday Times*